RYAN'S UNDOING

THE TIMELESS VOID SERIES: BOOK 4

CRAIG ROBERTSON

ALSO BY CRAIG ROBERTSON:

*** Podium Audio produced audiobooks are (or soon will be) available for all the below titles except the standalone ones.**

For specifics as to the correct order for reading the Ryanverse, click here.

BOOKS IN THE RYANVERSE:

THE FOREVER SERIES (2016)

THE FOREVER LIFE, Book 1

THE FOREVER ENEMY, Book 2

THE FOREVER FIGHT, Book 3

THE FOREVER QUEST, Book 4

THE FOREVER ALLIANCE, Book 5

THE FOREVER PEACE, Book 6

GALAXY ON FIRE SERIES (2017)

EMBERS, Book 1

FLAMES, Book 2

FIRESTORM, Book 3

FIRES OF HELL, Book 4

DRAGON FIRE, Book 5

ASHES, Book 6

RISE OF ANCIENT GODS SERIES (2018):

RETURN OF THE ANCIENT GODS, Book 1

RAGE OF THE ANCIENT GODS, Book 2

TORMENT OF THE ANCIENT GODS, Book 3

WRATH OF THE ANCIENT GODS, Book 4

FURY OF THE ANCIENT GODS, Book 5

FALL OF THE ANCIENT GODS, Book 6

TIME WARS LAST FOREVER SERIES (2019)

RYAN TIME, Book 1

LOST TIME, Book 2

FRAGMENTED TIME, Book 3

SHATTERED TIME, Book 4

FINDING TIME, Book 5

HEALING TIME, Book 6

THE TIMELESS VOID (2021)

RYAN'S GAMBIT, Book 1

RYAN'S PHANTOMS, Book 2

RYAN'S ENIGMA, Book 3

RYAN'S UNDOING, Book 4

RYAN'S REBOOT, Book 5

RYAN'S RESOLUTION, Book 6 (Due in Spring 2023)

NON-RYANVERSE BOOKS:

TIME DIVING (All Due Out Beginning 3/23)

***Letters From Hell*, Book 1**

***Purgatory's Best Shot*, Book 2**

***Heaven Says Wait*, Book 3**

ROAD TRIPS IN SPACE SERIES (2019):

THE GALAXY ACCORDING TO GIDEON, Book 1

THE EARTH ACCORDING TO GIDEON, Book 2

THE AFTERLIFE ACCORDING TO GIDEON: HEAVEN, Book 3 (Due Out ... Eventually)

OLDER, STANDALONE WORKS:

THE CORPORATE VIRUS (2016)

THE INNERgLOW EFFECT (2010)

WRITE NOW! THE PRISONER OF NaNoWRiMo (2009)

ANON TIME (2009)

RYAN'S UNDOING

THE TIMELESS VOID SERIES: BOOK 4

by Craig Robertson

Guess Who's Going To End Time? Yeah, You Got it.

Imagine-It Publishing
El Dorado Hills, CA

ISBN: 979-8-9860769-3-5 (E-Book)
979-8-9860769-4-2 (Paperback)
979-8-9860769-5-9 (Hardback)

Cover design by Alexandre
http://www.designbookcover.pt/en/

Editors: Michael R. Blanche
Amy Schubert
Marie Spillias

Formatting services by Drew Avera
drewavera@gmail.com

First Edition 2022

This book is dedicated to my two most excellent friends, Theresa Pieper-Rosenkranz and her beautiful daughter, Savannah. You gals stay wild (but not too) and crazy (in the best way). You will always be in my heart!

There is a glossary of terms available at the end of the book.

PREFACE

Queen Loopi-goah, supreme ruler of the Void and all who dwelled therein, moved quickly and with intent. It would be a misnomer to say she *ran* to her chief military advisor's office. Saddled by a body unfamiliar with self-locomotion in general, she was in no shape to perform that act. But she was in a proper rage, and so she did the best she could to get several of her twelve hands around the man's stumpy throat as quickly as possible. Behind her trailed her honor guard of Six Killers. To their credit, and reflecting their own self-preservation inclinations, they had offered to ferry their queen to her destination on her royal palanquin. But she was simply too vexed to hear the offer. The queen had, after all, stormed out of her chambers. It wouldn't do to wait for the damn litter to be fetched. No, she was in a mood and she would get to High Admiral Dooli-waan's throat as soon as void phantomly possible.

The team's progress was unfortunately slowed by forces other than the queen's shamefully deconditioned state. At irregular intervals, powerful time-paradox waves pounded—in fact, pulverized—the queendom. The queen's path was strewn with debris of all sizes and kinds, including many fallen Void citizens who remained dead where they had fallen. And the thunderous temporal aftershocks themselves made keeping a steady footing all but impossible. But, since hate and vengeful passion were such good motivators, the queen pressed on doggedly.

Finally, the royal entourage reached the subterranean vault that had, since the decimation of the Void became undeniable, housed the military leadership and their bedraggled staff. A functionary seated near the entrance rose to address the thudding queen. Without looking at either individual, Loopi pointed at the receptionist. One of the Six Killers sliced her into quarters faster than you can say, *But I'm on your side, Majesty.*

With a clear shot at her fool admiral's office, the queen gestured toward the door. It exploded inward as if struck by Zeus's own lightning bolt. An understandably surprised and frightened grand admiral stood so quickly he actually hopped in place.

"My Queen, to—"

Loopi placed one of her twelve hands over her own mouth. The lead guard, her so-called dagger, Substancial Jiail-fus, understood her queen's wishes. She moved like a greased laser beam, slamming the butt of her spear into the admiral's mouth to silence him. My, but the move was effective. Not useful in terms of team-building, mind you, but undeniably definitive.

"You will speak only when granted permission," Jiail hissed in an icy tone. "Is that understood, worthless slime?"

With the butt lodged in the back of his throat and much of his oral cavity mutilated and bleeding, the grand admiral was only too happy to nod that he understood the directions completely.

"You failed me, Dooli. You failed your queen utterly and immediately upon assuming command." She paused because she was physically unable to speak, what with her incendiary displeasure. "Do you know what happens to those who fail me, Dooli?"

Since her words did not include liberty for him to speak, and because he had a spear in his mouth, the mentally decomposing Dooli both nodded and shrugged.

"Speak!" the queen shrieked.

Dooli waited a few seconds, falsely assuming that dispensation would lead to the spear butt's removal. When it dawned on him with absolute foreboding that the two acts—speech and spear removal—were, in fact, separate acts, he attempted to rally to his defense.

"Ummpha do craspip, dodna muff."

"What did you say?" the queen screamed while literally hopping mad.

Dooli pointed to the staff terminating in his mouth. "Surudd imma klosito."

Though his words were unintelligible, his meaning was plain to anyone inclined to cut the guy a break.

None of his visitors were so inclined.

"If you do not acknowledge me and do so in a clear and concise manner, I will have my dagger reverse her spear and end my having to suffer yet another incompetent servant's unbridled disrespect."

There comes a time in a person's life when facts must be faced. Ideally, from a quality-of-character point of view, those stark facts will be faced boldly, confidently, and, most of all with unflinching dignity.

Sadly, Dooli chose to employ none of those qualities. He dropped like a stone to several of his twelve knees, began to weep inconsolably, and, in odd juxtaposition to the groveling, snatched a pen and paper from his desk on his way down. He scribbled madly before tearing off the sheet and thrusting it at the dagger. When Jiail made no move whatsoever, Dooli threw the note at the queen. Loopi nodded at the missive, so another Six-Killer retrieved it. He held the bulletin close to the queen's face so she might read it without having to touch it.

The queen paced a bit to her right and then a tad to her left. "I see," she announced. "My thoughts on your contentions are as follows. I shall attempt to make myself clear, so bear with me if you will. I came here to receive your report, your explanation for your consummate failure. I, naturally as your queen, expect your response to be both honest and articulate. It is not *my* fault that you have a spear butt in your mouth, Dooli, it is yours. If you had not spoken without my granting you permission, there wouldn't be a spear butt in your mouth, now, would there?"

He shook his head as much as he could without further lacerating his retropharynx. Dooli then wrote with a hot fervor on another sheet of paper and offered it in a panic to the Six-Killer who'd been so kind as to hold his original note up to the queen.

After scanning the contents, the queen tsked Dooli. "You are a hard one to make understand, Grand Admiral. I don't know why, but I will explain myself to you one last time. When I entered this office, I knew you were not to speak unless granted permission. The fact that you did not simultaneously understand that enjoiner is, again, not my fault. It is, yet again, yours. I am the queen. If I think a thing, it is the case. That others—*you* in this specific instance—were not laboriously pre-informed as to each and every thought, whim, and fancy I have in my great head is not my concern. Do you, Grand Admiral Dooli-waan, contend that it is *my* responsibility to vet my each and every thought to each and every insignificant pile of flambett droppings in my queendom?"

Though he honestly didn't follow her tortured logic, he shook off the thought vigorously. Why prolong his suffering?

Loopi glanced to her dagger and tossed her head to one side. The spear was removed from Dooli's mouth.

"Why have you failed me?" she reiterated harshly. "I instructed your predecessor to seek out and annihilate the defiler in all time and all space. She came up with some excuse." Loopi waved a hand dismissively in the air. "Something about the laws of physics and the evil one's military superiority, nonsense such as that."

Loopi paused as a jarring temporal aftershock reverberated through all of the Void.

"For her incompetence, I had her dismembered and the disloyal bits of her were cast into the Oblivion. I know, many argued I was far too lenient with Saarha-saiy, but that's just me. I'm a *giving* queen. I appointed you to be her successor, but you set some kind of Void record for the rapidity with which you failed your queen. Kudos are perhaps due you, but that's a matter for another time."

The dagger chuckled darkly, suggesting there would be no *another time* available to Dooli.

"So, this is the part where you make a pathetic plea for your worthless hide, I ignore said plea out-of-hand, and then you perish horribly and ever-so-slowly." She gestured to him. "Proceed."

"I ... your ..." *—cough-cough—* "... I wish ..." *—gag-cough—* "Please excuse me, My Queen. I ..." *—gurgle-cough—* "I seem to have a sore throat coming on. Let us pr—" *breath-intake-cough—* "... pray it is nothing contagious, lest your highness become subject to its ill-effects." Dooli cleared his mangled airways cautiously. "Now, as to why we have been—"

"*We?*" the queen shouted haughtily. "We as in *you* and *me, we*?"

"Ah, no. *We* as in *me alone*, pure one. The reason *I* have had to temporarily ..." *—gag-rasp—* "... suspend assaults on Jon Ryan are—"

Well, of course, he didn't finish that sentence. You wouldn't either if six Six-Killer spear butts slammed into your head with maximal impact simultaneously. Come on, Dooli said the name of he-whose-name-must-never-be-spoken. Military types can be so goal oriented at times as to miss the big picture. Six-Killer guards, not so much.

Dooli's seven visitors waited impatiently for him to regain consciousness. Fifteen minutes, ten boots-to-the-gut, and three buckets of ice water later, he groaned awake. His six brisket-sized eyes wandered at first, then searched the room tentatively for the cause of his being on the ground, bleeding like a fire hydrant, and suffering an unthinkably debilitating headache. When he took note of his seven guests, and then recalled the reason for their calling, he popped upright. "Sorry ... I ... I must have dozed off. It won't happen again."

"Apology rejected," the queen said softly. "You were saying idiotic things about why you failed me?"

"Ah, yes. I suspended the search for—" A curious notion occurred to Dooli just then, as if by déjà vu. *Don't say the defiler's name.* "The ships I sent out reported back a most distressing reality outside the Void, my Queen. Based on a new and as of now uncharacterized threat, I deemed it necessary to mostly, partially, and, er, temporarily suspend, just for a second, mind you, further expeditions pending some understanding of—"

Yeah, it wasn't Dooli's day. Not even close. Loopi tired of the length and apparent direction of Dooli's ramblings, nodded toward him, and her dagger slammed the butt of her spear into Dooli's ample gut hard enough to drive him against the far wall, through three heavy chairs, one table, and three of his cowering assistants.

"What new reality are you babbling about?" the queen inquired hotly.

"It's—"

"Not that it matters," she informed him unhelpfully.

"Ah, yes. As I was about to say, what few ships returned that I sent in pursuit of our foe reported—in fact they *documented*—that reality in the realm of the timed universe was decompensating."

"De..." the queen repeated, fully flustered. "What does that mean?"

"One of the scientists I sent out is of the opinion that time/space is collapsing upon itself out there."

"And I care because?"

"Because if their universe is collapsing into itself, it is unsafe for our phantoms to venture there. At least not until I can confirm what exactly is going on."

Loopi angled her head from side-to-side, clearly struggling to understand a foreign concept. "Grand Admiral," she began, drawing out the words, "why would such a state of existence, should it be proven to be the case, inhibit you from carrying out my vengeance?"

"Because our ships and crew would be lost for no reason, with no justification." Dooli suppressed his desire to add a *duh*.

"And you assumed I *cared* if my ships and my phantoms were lost no matter what the circumstances of their loss might be?"

"Yes, well ... I mean, naturally you are concerned for all your loving subjects," he stammered.

"Oh, you sad, deluded little fool. Dooli?"

"Yes, my Queen?"

"I want *revenge.* My one requirement of my subjects is that they extract eternal, unending, merciless justice on the defiler. I don't recall feeling or stating anything to the contrary. Did I somehow give off the absurd impression that I valued anyone in the Void more important than I do my desire for vengeance?"

And to that Dooli had perfectly nothing to say. He was done. He was gobsmacked. Stick a fork in him, he was done.

"Now, ex-Grand Admiral, I will ask that my dagger drag you from here to the Cliffs of Doom as they overlook the Oblivion. Do you understand?"

Because, as mentioned, he was done thinking, speaking, or reasoning, Dooli just shrugged.

"Good. Then she and her team will torture, wound, and basically disassemble you brutally. They will do so up until you beg to be cast into the Oblivion."

Dooli opened his mouth to speak.

"Ah, ah," the queen interrupted. "I should clarify. They will abuse and torment you for twelve hours and then *another* twelve hours, after you so beg. Sorry. I didn't want to give you false hopes for a quick casting. My bad."

With those words Queen Loopi-goah departed. She gave no further thought to what's-his-name the ex-admiral. She didn't really begin her deliberations as to his successor, or even the strange tidings he mentioned. No, she only thought of the defiler and how she would see him suffer more than any other being in or out of existence.

ONE

Sachiko and Reva were frozen to the spot their boots touched the floor, possibly quite literally. They both knew in the privacy of their own thoughts that they couldn't move. No, there was a four-meter-tall demon dragon sitting in a nest just beyond arm's reach and watching them. And it had two names, neither of which made any sense. Algos Dusthūmíā was his name, but he'd said they could call him Ephialtes. How was that supposed to matter? Big-Scary-Creepy-Evil Dragon. That was the name they needed to keep in mind.

"Gu ... Gunny?" Reva stammered with a cotton mouth.

"Sir?" Sergeant Parker replied, sounding giddy.

"Gunny, why did you bring the captain into a room containing a large and presumably hostile monster? Are you out of your mind? And your weapons still have their safeties on."

"Reva," a name he never addressed her by, nor should he ever, "are you serious?" Gunny chuckled. "Since when are you two girls afraid of a cute little kitten?"

Reva and Sachiko turned to look at each other with drill-team coordination. Then they turned as one to Gunny.

"That's not a fucking kitten, Sergeant Parker," Reva snapped.

"You are all relieved of duty." She snatched up her handheld and pounded an icon. "Intruder Alert. Repeat, Intruder Alert, Deck A-Eleven, just past the electrical relay box. This is not a drill. Security Alert Team One to Deck A-Eleven, just past the electrical relay box. Weapons hot. I repeat, weapons hot."

"Sheesh," Gunny protested. "You're making a mountain out of a kitten, Reva. Can't—"

"Gunny, I said you're relieved of duty. Confine yourself and your squad to quarters pending a full investigation." Reva's voice telegraphed with extreme accuracy just how unequivocal that order was.

"Okay, but you're—" he began.

"*Silence*," Reva snapped.

Gunny and his team filed out of the room like scolded toddlers.

"I think the snake has some control over their minds," Sachiko speculated out of the side of her mouth.

"Well, I must say that was most entertaining," Ephialtes—or whatever—declared. "To be honest I'm not certain why I'm here, but this beats the heck out of what I was doing just before I arrived."

"Ah, what were you doing just before you arrived?" Reva asked, stalling for time.

"Oh, the usual. Reaping souls, harassing the damned, deciding where lunch was," Ephialtes replied in a blasé tone.

"Reaping souls," Reva parroted uncertainly. "Sounds ... sounds interesting."

"Oh, come now," Ephialtes thundered. "You think me such a fool?" He then dropped into a more conversational voice. "Of course it is not interesting. It is work, that is what it is. And work is by definition uninteresting. You, my delicious new play toy," Ephialtes actually licked his serpent lips, "are simply stalling for time. Naughty girls *are* the nicest, don't you think?"

"I am Captain Sachiko Jones," Sachiko stated formally. "I demand to know your intentions, sir."

The dragon's bulk twisted in the air, but its eyes remained affixed to Sachiko. "I know who you are, young human. As for your demands, well, just this once I will pretend you didn't employ those words when addressing me. It is early days in our soon-to-be lengthy relationship. You get one break, but never two." His snaky tongue whipped in and out. "And you needn't stall for time in hopes of a rescue. The Security Team A1 or whatever is not coming. They've decided instead to go for a swim."

"We, uh... We don't have a pool," Sachiko responded incredulously.

"Don't tell them. They think they are skinny dipping at the beach as we speak."

"Where are they pretending to swim?" Reva felt compelled to ask.

"In their minds, my tummy-rubbing taste treat."

"Ah."

"Look, Mr. Ephialtes," Sachiko began uncertainly, "we don't want any trouble. Your presence here is a tragic result of the collapsing of time. There's no—"

"***SILENCE!***" erupted from Ephialtes. "I will lead all the discussions from this point forward. Is that—"

Ephialtes's tirade was cut off abruptly. He seemingly disappeared before the two women's eyes.

"Crap on a crumpet that was close," shouted Sapale as she charged through the hatch.

"Wha—" Reva began.

"Sapale, get out," Sachiko ordered. "It's not safe in here."

"No, it's the opposite of safe. But I got this," Sapale reassured.

"If the next words out of your mouth are hold my beer, I'm going to lose my mind," Reva exclaimed loudly.

"No, I got this. He's in a full membrane. We're safe."

Sachiko seemed to come to her senses. "Safe, *safe*, or what?" she asked for clarification.

"Safe-ish," Sapale waffled.

"Not good enough," Sachiko snapped. "Clarify that remark."

"We're probably safe for a little while. He'll have trouble getting out of the full membrane containment field I placed him in. But knowing him, eventually he'll get out."

"Him? Who's *him*?" Reva asked, clearly still rattled.

"I'll explain on the run," Sapale shot back. "Sachiko, you stay with Aramthella. Reva, you're with me on *Blessing*. We need to go *now*."

"Got it," Sachiko snapped.

"Go? Go where?" Reva questioned.

"To get rid of that," Sapale shouted as she pointed at the nothingness of a full membrane.

"I'm *all* in," Reva declared once she understood.

The three women sprinted out of the hatch, the captain heading toward the bridge, the other two toward the hangar. Invisible to all, a membrane sphere just small enough to make it down the passageways trailed them midair.

Within a minute, Reva and Sapale were aboard the vortex. "*Blessing*, I need a black hole ten billion light years from here."

"Certainly, Form Two. When would you like to—"

"Now, now, now."

Sapale felt a brief nausea.

"The spacial portion of the requested journey is complete. I am searching for the most likely location of a ... I have it. There is a spiral galaxy near us with a supermassive black hole at its center."

"Put us there as close as you can while keeping us safe from being sucked in," Sapale ordered.

"Done, Form Two. We are two-million kilometers outside the event horizon of the massive singularity."

Slowly, concentrating intently, Sapale extended her probe fibers so she could open a small portal in the hull. She deftly steered the full-membrane sphere out the opening. "Now comes the fun part," she said mostly to herself.

Though invisible to both of them, Sapale extended the membrane sphere toward the nothingness that was the super massive black hole. Reva, still completely confused, clung to the edge of the portal and looked out at the invisible whatever going on. She was clever enough not to speak. She didn't want to interfere with Sapale's intense focus. Reva knew it had to be her imagination, but she felt a pull at her shoulders from the gravity of the monstrous black hole. with its siren call for her to fall into it.

"I'm going to extend the membrane as far from the ship as possible," Sapale announced quietly. "I have no idea how far that'll be, especially given the intense disturbances in the local space/time continuum."

"Are you speaking to me?" Reva clarified.

"Both of you," Sapale responded with greater strain in her voice. "I'm starting to feel the pull of the damn thing's gravity on the sphere."

"Can I help?" Reva asked in a nascent panic.

"Wrap your arms around my waist," Sapale replied. Her voice was audibly straining now.

Reva shot over and bear-hugged Sapale from behind for all she was worth. Then she slapped a boot on the portal-side bulkhead for leverage. "We can do this," she growled.

"Either way we will," Sapale confirmed. "We are dumping the trash, even if we go with it." She screamed in angry determination.

"Form Two, I estimate the sphere is close enough to the event horizon that it is impossible for its contents to break free."

"Thanks, but we're—" she grunted. Then her footing shifted from *Blessing*'s deck to the portal-side hull. "We're taking no chances with this one. Hang on, Reva. Maybe thirty seconds more."

"How ... far ... is ... sphere?" Reva screamed as her muscles threatened to fail.

"One thousand kilometers away," replied *Blessing*.

"Not ... far ... en—" Sapale started to grunt. Then both women tumbled backward and started to roll at a frantic pace. Abruptly they stopped in mid-roll, just before any injuries could begin.

"I have you both in a tractor beam," *Blessing* said in a calming tone. "You're safe."

Sapale shot to her feet and rushed to the portal. "We may not be crashing to the deck, but I'm not so sure about safe."

Her eyes strained into the void, searching for any clue as to the physics playing out in front of her.

Reva leaped to her side, arm around her shoulder. "What are we looking at?"

"Nothing so far," Sapale grumbled. "Don't know exactly what I'd like to see. All I know is I do not want to turn around and see a big red snake."

Reva spun so quickly she halfway stumbled to the deck. Without looking back, Sapale snatched a shoulder to steady her friend.

"Nothing so far," Reva weakly informed as she inspected the inside space.

"Luck is with the stupid," Sapale muttered.

"Huh?"

"Old Kaljaxian saying. It covers this situation."

"Ah," Reva acknowledged, not reassured.

They continued to stare for a good thirty seconds. "*Blessing*," Sapale asked impassively, "can you tell what happened to the physical contents of the membrane after it disintegrated when I lost contact with it?"

"Not with any certainty. The initial motion of the subtended mass was definitely in the direction of the singularity."

"That's what I'd expect. He had no clue where he was, so he wouldn't initially be able to compensate."

"A valid assumption," *Blessing* agreed. "I can confirm that after a gravitational free fall of sixteen milliseconds, the mass diverted five degrees off its initial vector that sent the contents directly toward the event horizon."

"And after five milliseconds?" Sapale pressed.

"My observations began to grow exponentially less certain. By thirty milliseconds, the mass seems to have been redirected close to its original vector. After that I can provide no meaningful data. The area is just too chaotic."

"Was there any energy flare suggesting a significant mass incorporation to the black hole.?"

"None I measured."

"Damn, I was hoping he was big enough to register a pop."

"Who was he and why would or wouldn't he cause a black hole. to pop?" Reva interjected.

"When a mass approaches a singularity," *Blessing* explained, "it queues up in the accretion disk and slowly spirals inward. The velocities involved and the gravitational forces cause the local environment to be extremely energetic, relativistically so. As a mass actually passes into the singularity, immense amounts of electromagnetic energy are released. If a sufficiently large discrete mass enters, there can be an observable burst of energy release seen."

"Sorry I asked," Reva groaned.

"Well, so far, so good," Sapale concluded. "*Blessing*, take us back to where we started."

She felt slight nausea twice.

"We are back in our moorings on Aramthella," *Blessing* announced. "I took the liberty of making two folds for added safety's sake."

"No problema," Sapale grunted as she opened a new portal. "Reva, let's get to the bridge. I'll fill in the blank spaces when we get there."

"In that case, let's run, okay?" Reva asked pleadingly.

They stepped onto the bridge a few minutes later. "Good, I heard you were back," Sachiko greeted. "Was your mission successful?"

"Are there any four-meter demon dragons aboard?" Sapale countered.

"Excellent point." Sachiko tapped an icon on her armrest. "Security."

"Yes, Captain. Lieutenant Bridges here."

"Bridges, form up ten parties of three. Have them sweep the ship twice. They're looking for anything out of place. They are to be on high alert for a four-meter dragon."

"Sir?" he questioned.

"I kid you not. I also anticipate you and your squads' fullest attention to the task. Is that abundantly clear, Bridges?"

"Yes, sir. I will alert you at the first sign of anything out of the ordinary."

"Captain out." Sachiko tapped the icon again. She turned to Sapale. "My stateroom, now. Reva, you too. Major Walters you have the comm."

"I have the comm," Emma confirmed as she slipped into Sachiko's chair.

It was a short walk to her quarters. "Alrighty then," Sachiko began. "What the hell just happened?"

"Huh, funny you should so frame the question," chuckled Sapale.

"If I was funny I assure you that was not my intent," Sachiko stated rather defiantly.

"Right. I'll get to the point," a chastened Sapale responded. "Where to begin?" She bobbed her head a moment. "Western human civilization has a generally accepted view of the member's afterlife."

"Didn't see that coming," Sachiko mumbled quietly.

"Oh, yeah," Sapale concurred. "Obviously there are variations, but in general, most cultures envision an afterlife consisting of two polar opposites. A good place and a bad place, if you will. The virtuous versus the evil. You have one deity on each side, one in your Heaven and one in your hell." She looked to them to make sure they followed.

"Sounds good. Continue," Sachiko acknowledged.

"I'm from Kaljax. Not surprisingly, our post-life mythology is different, but there are some parallels. We have similar polar-opposite dispositions. Our Heaven is called Tralmore. It's located past the Seven Veils, and is ruled by a kind and all-knowing Davdiad. Our hell is called Brathos. But in our village of damnation, there reign three demons, the smart devil, the mean devil, and the random devil. Respectively, they are Marsicor, Lebbuul, and Quixtiscus. You with me so far?"

"Yes," Sachiko agreed for both women.

"Well, you, my dear friends, just had the distinct anti-privilege of meeting Lebbuul the Mean."

"Oh, shit," Sachiko declared resolutely.

"Oh, shit, damn indeed," Sapale seconded. "Ya don't want to meet any of those asswipes, but ya *really* don't want to meet the mean one. Per legend, even the other two demons are intimidated by him."

"But he introduced himself as Algos Dusthūmíā, then said to just call him Ephialtes," Reva protested.

"Really? I hadn't heard that part." She shook her head. "Huh."

"What?" Reva followed up.

"He really is one mean flaming fucker, isn't he?"

"How so?" Sachiko asked.

Sapale looked to each friend. "You know one of the weird benefits of being two-billion years old is?"

"No," Sachiko answered. "What's a weird benefit of being that old?"

"You have a lot of time on your hands. Me, I spend a lot of it learning stuff. After a while, you run out of useful stuff to learn, so you start in on the obtuse shit."

"And this story is going where?" the captain pressed.

"I know a lot of useless languages. I give you, by way of proof, three words in ancient Greek. Algos, dusthūmíā, and—you got it—ephialtes. Translated, you have *pain*, *despair*, and, everyone's favest, *nightmare*."

"So that dragon," Sachiko summarized, "the one you identify as your Lebbuul, introduced himself to us as Pain Despair, but you can call me Nightmare?"

"Sort of. I'd go with, *Hi, I represent your Painful Despair, but you can just think of me as your worst nightmare*."

"Yours does make a tighter package," Sachiko conceded.

"Translations can be tough. Thanks."

"Son-of-a-*bitch*," Reva declared harshly.

"That too," Sapale agreed with a grin. "Like I say, he's the mean one. He's famous for pulling that kind of shit." She furrowed her brow. "Kind of like Jon in that way, if you think about it."

"But you came so quickly," Sachiko stated. "How'd you know to come to our rescue?"

"And how'd you pull it off?" Reva added. "He had the soldiers hornswoggled."

"I'm Kaljaxian," Sapale mused. "The instant Lebbuul appeared on Aramthella I *knew* he was here. When I heard the intruder alert, I knew where to find him."

"And why didn't he control you, stop you?" Reva asked.

"I surprised him. I put a full membrane between him and me as I approached. I only dropped it as the hatch flew open. Then I captured-first-asked-questions-later." She shook her head. "Mostly I was lucky, damn lucky."

"And if the membrane hadn't held him?" Sachiko asked darkly.

"The three of us would be performing in a naked edible chorus line about now. Fun City."

"He threatened us, like, forever," Reva wheezed. "If he just ate us, wouldn't we be at least done?"

"When dealing with the Mean Demon? No, he'd cycle us for eternity and beyond," Sapale huffed. "We were lucky."

"And you think the supermassive black hole caught him and can hold him?" Sachiko queried.

"It was my best play. I figured if it did, good. If it only delayed him, at least he'd be far, far away. Maybe it'd be too much trouble to come after us." She shrugged.

"Man, did we get lucky," Sachiko declared with a shudder.

"Yes, we did," Sapale said softly. "Let's just pray our luck holds."

TWO

I was seated on the outside of the tits-up unit as it orbited high over the chaotically changing Earth below me. It was just me and the universe out there, mano a mano. Two old buddies sharing time together. I was chugging down mass quantities of dehydrated beer. I would have preferred to share a beer with my buddy the universe, but universes didn't drink, so I was on my own. Why, you ask, was I seated alone on the outside of my wonky spaceship instead of on the comfy inside? One word: Gloria. Yeah, remember that after my last futile attempt to repair time, the first-morning-after version of my ex-wife mysteriously and vexingly appeared in the tits-up?

They say the Golden Rule is to *do onto others as you would have them do unto you*. That's not so in my case. For me the rule is *where Gloria is, I am not*. She was inside the ship, so I was outside in the cold vacuum. I had to use a membrane to simulate an airlock so I could exit the ship without exposing her to the harshness of space. Then again, knowing her as I did, I was probably more protecting space from her harshness. Yeah, poor old deep space was no match for the infectious horror that was Gloria. How was I going to get rid of her? Clearly, if there was no alternative, I could push off the ship into the void and drift aimlessly for all eternity. That prospect was seventy-five million times better than spending two minutes on the inside with her.

What about casting *her* into deep space instead of me bailing? I assume you think I was too nice, too gentlemanly to do such a thing. Well, I wasn't. I just didn't want to have to touch her to throw her out. Self-preservation was my motivation, pure and simple. You see, once you're in any kind of contact with Gloria, she immediately sucks all the life out of you. She sure did that repeatedly during our brief time together. I wasn't willing to suffer that any longer, no more of what I came to refer to as Gloriafication. That's the process of hers that singes your soul to ash and turns your will to survive into a self-directed practical joke.

But I knew I couldn't wait out here in the void until she passed of natural causes on the inside. No, there were two issues there. First, I wasn't at all certain she was human and, therefore, mortal. She could easily have been a demon from hell; in fact, I strongly suspected her to be one. She might have been an alien robot from the future sent to punish me by some race I'd offended sufficiently. Second, obviously I couldn't *hear* her on the outside since there was no air. My curse was, however, that I could *feel* her pounding on the inside with her fist, trying to get my attention, through the vibration of the hull. I wouldn't be able to stand that very long. A day or two, tops, and I'd blow my brains out. But the only blasters were on the *inside*, so I'd have to concede to her endless badgering yet again in order to flee her into the arms of death. There's no justice in this universe, I want you to know that.

But I had started putting the fate of the universe ahead of my Gloria-induced woes. It was going to take a Mother Teresa-like moral fortitude to do so, but I needed to make things right. Though no one suffered as acutely as I did—duh, I was stuck with *Gloria*—the rest of existence was suffering extensively also. Maybe Plesmus was right and time was collapsing. If so, I needed to shore it up pending somehow arresting the process fully. And, since I'd never seen time-support beams at the local DIY box store, I was going to have to figure out how to accomplish that chore all by myself. Oh boy.

To be honest I was kind of hoping one of my supernatural spirit guides would show up out of the blue and bail me out. So far, none had. But come on, I'd been rescued by my guardian angel, guided by Fate, and instructed by Time. And my dead friend Jenna? She and I were together so often that rumor abounded that we were a bi-deathual couple who were about to have trans-deathic twins, a boy zombie and a cute little zombetta. Okay, the last part was another of my lame jokes, but my point was I'd had mystical helpers in the past. But none of them were rushing to help a brother out this time. As much as I was tempted to drag my heels and let some ghost, god, or force-of-nature do the heavy lifting, I really needed to be proactive. In other words, I had to act like an adult. Yuck City.

My wife was missing. My friends aboard Aramthella were unaccounted for. Normal points of reference, such as, say, the fact that the Sun had apparently *evaporated*, were increasing in number and bizarreness. Not that long ago I was in contact with the current president of the United States and his staff. Now I couldn't get a response. The fact that the Washington, D.C. I'd last visited them in was now deep below an icy primordial sea did provide a hint, however, as to why contact had been broken. My only constant was Plesmus nagging, browbeating, and cajoling me for doing what I was certain I needed to do. Well, that and Rift Dude's mindless, eternal optimism. Man, what used to be annoying was quickly becoming intolerable. I mean, RD, look around you. Do you see *anything* to be upbeat about? No, so knock it off with the Shirley Temple impersonation.

Adding to my issues was the fact that my memory was Swiss-cheesing itself. Sorry, that's the only way I can describe the process. Typically, I'd remember an event. The birthday I ate a pizza with my parents. No prob. But now, I remembered just as solidly and as vividly *not* having pizza that evening of my twelfth birthday. I recall them teasing me about a sushi dinner, and, come on, if you dare me, I gotta do it, so I choked down slimy uni sushi instead of delectable pepperoni. And I also "remember" not existing on my twelfth birthday. All of those and many more visions shouted and waved their arms in my head trying to get my attention. Yeah, can you say *jarring*? I wasn't even sure when the fits and spurts of memories began, but now they were a twenty-four/seven traffic jam in my consciousness.

Plesmus had told me a while back that she "saw" several different but coexisting versions of reality at the same time, due to changes in historic events. Maybe I was becoming sensitive to the same process. If I was, I wanted a full and complete refund. It was like living on the island of No Fun Atoll. The unavoidable conclusion I was forced to accept was that Plesmus was right. I was corrupting time and I was causing it to involute, or, as she put it, collapse. Events that occurred at radically different times were overlapping just like there was not enough space left for them to exist where they were in relationship to one another originally. That sounded ... it sounded kind of unfixable. Yeah, the alterations were really, really complex, chaotic, and had a feeling of permanence.

It was criminally naive of me to assume that any further journeys back in time, ostensibly to *fix* the timeline, would do anything but hasten reality's demise. So, what was I going to do? I could stay in the time and place I was, and hope the others found their way back to me. I was, at least for the present, at our collective point of origin in time and space. Alternately, I could venture out in search of my friends, staying exclusively in the present. No time travel. No, bad Jon. If you time travel, the universe will whack your pee-pee. Plan three would be to go in search of help. But from whom? The drive-through window at Existentialisms "R" Us? Soothsayers City, USA? King Solomon World Unconfusement Park? No, I thought not. Well, sure, if any of those places actually existed, I'd be there in a hot second. But to think about them was to waste time.

I had only three assets as far as I could tell: Plesmus, RD, and myself. Somehow we were going to have to come up with a doable plan and execute it well in order to save reality. No, I wasn't what you'd call optimistic. I was suicidal. I was just about ready to join one of those religious cults that claim to have all the answers. I was not, in short, counting on an easy fix.

"Jon," Plesmus called up to me from where she was stuck to my boot, "are you going to sulk all day, or are you going to try and fix the mess you've created?"

"Ah, I think my trying to fix anything is the very definition of a dumb idea. Such things were what got us to the current sad state of affairs."

"My goodness," she exclaimed. "You learned something. I did helpfully remind you of that many times and in many ways, but to hear you voice that opinion with such conviction seems like a small miracle. I'd say you've made actual headway in your journey to adulthood."

"Sure, rub it in. Pile on. Why not? The man's down, why not drive him subterranean with added insults."

"Sorry, you're right. Now's not the time to hit you with reality checks."

"It's down to us three," I began solemnly, ignoring Ples's immature dig. "If reality, at least in this universe, is going to persist, we need to do something proactive. Unless either of you are of a different opinion, I think us simply *not* doing further time interventions won't arrest the collapsing process."

"Unfortunately, I agree," Plesmus replied grimly. "But how to stop the cascade? I have no ideas how we achieve that end."

"I ... or rather," RD stammered, "if I were able to ... well, historically I am not an *ideas* conduit. There, that sums it up succinctly. I'm game to do whatever you two determine to be best. But I doubt I'll have much constructive input as to how we solve our current crisis."

Aw, that RD. He was down with whoever he was and didn't mind sharing. It didn't contribute diddly squat, but it was honest. I shelved responding *kudos for nothing*. I was already in a dark enough swamp of shit, thank you very much.

"Thanks, RD," I said instead. "And don't sell yourself short. You have and will continue to contribute to the mission. Just you wait and see," I encouraged. Hell, why not?

"Thank you for your vote of confidence, Captain," RD responded jubilantly. "There are times, as much as I hate to admit it, when I feel my efforts fall well short of optimally directed to the successful conclusion to our quest."

Did he just say something? Anything? I didn't have the mental energy to try and sort through the verbiage. I'd do what I generally did when it came to RD. I'd ignore ...

"Like for instance the repeating distress call I've been receiving for the last several hours. I've been uncertain whether to burden the collective efforts of our merry band by—"

"*Stop*," I shouted. Okay, Jon, count to ten, slowly. Calm. Don't bust up RD's speakers with an axe handle. No. You don't have an axe handle available.

"We have been receiving a distress call for several hours and you ... you ... ya didn't think that might be ... r- r- relevant?" I sputtered.

"There, you see," he squealed. "I have a chance to contribute and I fail to do so. I am so—"

"Whoa. You can be so anything you want to be later. Right now I want the four-one-one. Who's sending the signal? Where does it originate from? And damn it, RD, is it *Sapale*?"

"Ah, I don't know, I don't know outside of it's coming from near the galactic core, and I don't know."

I'm on a beach. My toes are massaging the warm, wet sand. A gentle breeze wafts my smiling face. Serenity now, Jon. Kill. Nothing.

"Okay," I began with all the self-control I could muster. "Let us break this down. Are you receiving a voice distress call, or an automated one?"

"As you can sympathize, it is—"

"Ha ... ah ... RD, please place the message on audio. Then I will have an answer to my question without me having to electrocute you."

"Excellent plan, Captain. Here you go: *Attention anyone, help.*

We are in danger of hull failure. Our life support system and main drives are offline. Reason for systems failure is unknown. Please assist immediately. This is Garnol ... After that the transmission fades into static, and then repeats."

"Sounds like a recorded message, but one from a person, not an AI or emergency backup broadcast," I mumbled to myself. "Any idea how old the message is?"

"I have no way of knowing," RD responded. "The message faded in gradually, suggesting to me it's at the edge of their transmission range."

"Good. Can you estimate the distance?"

"No, only the general direction."

"And it was in English, or are you translating the message?"

"That is how I received it."

Garnol? Was that the speaker's name? Just a partial or his full name? It didn't really matter though, did it? Someone was out there, which was exciting in-and-of-itself. Plus, it was a distress call. Those required a response.

"RD, hail them. Just offer our ship's name and general position, and ask for further details."

"On it, Captain. Sending."

"Plesmus, your thoughts?"

"It seems like a straightforward Mayday. I can't imagine it's some trap or lure from a pirate or other potential enemy. Not with the state of affairs being as they are."

"I agree. People riot and loot when there's a crisis, sure. But with reality crumbling it seems unlikely someone's trying to gain an illicit profit."

"I agree," Plesmus confirmed.

"RD, plot and execute a best-guess course to intercept the mysterious *Garnol*. Pending a response to our hail, make it best speed with conventional engines."

"Roger that. We are underway," RD confirmed.

"I doubt whatever we find will help us resolve the crisis we are facing," Plesmus observed once RD was done.

"True," I sighed. "True, true. It's something to do, but I hear you." I reflected a moment. "Maybe inspiration will strike en route?"

"Not much of a plan, but since I have no alternatives, we'll have to see."

We were all quiet for twenty minutes or so. Then RD popped back in. "Captain, I've been pinged by a craft along the general vector the distress call came in along."

"Just a ping? What does that mean?"

"An auto-response to our hail most likely."

"But not specifically from Garnol?"

"No, sir."

"Hmm. Send a new hail. If they re-ping us, estimate the distance from source."

"Will do. I shall keep you posted."

We roared through the void a while, then RD hit me with an update. "The craft that originally pinged us did indeed ping our new hail. Still an auto-response, but definitely from the same ship. It is approximately three hundred million kilometers away, again, along a vector toward the galactic core based on our current position.

"About two astronomical units, eh?" I mumbled to myself. "What are we making as of now?"

"Point two c, Captain."

"That puts us there in an hour."

"One hour twenty-three minutes," RD specified.

"Take us to point four c for thirty-five minutes. Then drop us to ten thousand klicks per hour. We'll approach eyes-wide-open."

"Will do, Captain."

Within an hour we were in visual range of our quarry. By interstellar craft design, it was fairly typical. A couple hundred meters long, shiny, fifty wide, and cigar shaped. The usual suspects. There was no obvious external damage. No one was responding to our hails, though. Just the auto pings, along with the continuing verbal recording loop we'd originally heard.

"You make out any life signs aboard that ship?" I asked RD.

"Yes, I do. Nine of them."

"Human? I mean, they broadcast in English."

"Decidedly not. I believe there are three higtolfs, one squanamour, two velocipeds, two paurens, and one I have no idea."

"What an odd crew," I remarked to myself. If anyone else was present, I'd have gotten a *ya think* in response for certain. Three higtolfs. Think garden gnomes, just twice the size. Mean little suckers too. Never trust a higtolf. None of *them* do, so why would you? It's a wonder they ever evolved, given how badly they treat one another. And then three paurens? Ha, I'd like to be a fly on that bulkhead. Paurens are an ancient race that originated in the galactic core worlds. They were bright, welcoming, and scientifically advanced folk. Yeah, if they didn't look and smell like two-meter-tall piles of excrement, they'd be everyone's favorite aliens. As it was, if you held your nose and looked the other way, they were nice company. But given their good nature and the higtolfs' rotten personalities, I envisioned nothing but constant mayhem taking place aboard that ship.

I was familiar with the others, but nothing too special sprang to mind. Velocipeds were caterpillar like, maybe a couple hundred kilograms, standing a meter and a half off the ground on multiple legs. They got the veloci-handle because they rolled up in a wheel shape when in a hurry and scooted about in a flash. They were fun to sneak up on and yell '*gotcha*' to. Er, so I'm told. Squanamour were very humanoid. In a low-light situation, you couldn't tell our two species apart. In terms of characteristics, those too, for better or worse, were very human like.

And then a species TBA? If RD didn't recognize them, I probably didn't either. But they couldn't be too aggressive or dumb if they interacted well with the rest of the crew. Hell, they'd need to be a skilled diplomat to not jump out the nearest airlock. And if they did so too quickly, they'd scare the velocipeds, who'd squash the paurens, and then the higtolfs would throw each other in the stinky mess. And a good time was had by all.

"Bring us alongside an external airlock," I instructed RD.

"There's a very intact-appearing one on the side facing us. I'll be a meter away in thirty seconds."

"Ples, you up for a road trip?" I asked, knowing the answer.

"Absolutely. I'm not letting you out of my sight."

"You worried about me?" I teased.

"Yes. Specifically what idiotic move you'd pull if I wasn't there to tend you."

"You're harsh, Ples, but you're always welcome on my away team."

Once we were adjacent to the airlock, I stood up (remember, I was still outside because Gloria was inside) and glided across the short gap. Not having to go through depressurization came in handy time and again. Boarding the other ship would be another story, however, since the species I was familiar with were planet dwellers.

I floated over what looked to be the external control pad. Again, it was fairly standard. I could see the airlock inner door was closed. One of two possible lights above both hatches were on, which I took to mean they were sealed and ready to cycle. I tapped a few icons, but nothing happened. No problem. I extended my probe fibers and commanded in my head: *cycle.* Then both outer lights began to flash and the hatch slid open. Once inside, I gave a similar command to the inner control pad. Within a few minutes I was inside and both airlock hatches were sealed.

"Hello?" I called out. "Anybody home?"

I waited where I was a minute. Getting no response, I headed in what I hoped was the direction of the bridge. The ship's gravity was about one hundred and fifty percent of Earth's and the atmosphere was a typical mix appropriate for the diverse crew members. Every few meters I called out again, but didn't receive a response. After one misdirect, I made it to the bridge. So far, there were no bodies, obvious damage, or live crew evident. Odd, but they had sent out a Mayday, so odd wasn't totally unexpected.

When I arrived at what had to be the bridge's hatch, I was faced with a dilemma. Should I open it, either with the side panel if it was unlocked, or with my probe fibers, or should I knock? Knocking seemed needy, and I don't do needy. But, heck, I didn't want to scare the velocipeds, right? I was anticipating a hard enough time with the paurens. No need to make a bad situation worse. So, I knocked. But I did so, you know, forcefully. I wasn't *asking* to enter, I was *announcing* that I was about to. Seriously, I have no clue where my decision to display like a silverback gorilla came from, but there it was.

The hatch slid open and I immediately knew that at least the paurens were in there. Yeah, hard to miss the scent. I pretty much knew they were alive, too, because the bridge smelled awful, not horrible. I didn't want to imagine what dead paurens actually smelled like, because, well, you can just imagine why.

"I'm coming in," I announced in English, since the Mayday had arrived in that language. Someone here had to capisce my mother tongue.

I stepped in cautiously and tried to pick out the velocipeds. There they were and darn if they didn't look antsy, like they badly had to take a leak. I slowed my movements even more, the very picture of a calm, nonthreatening kind of guy. I raised my hands.

"I'm answering your distress call. I mean you no harm."

And that's when the species TBD stepped ... well, you couldn't call it that. He/she/it didn't have feet to step with. Wow, on a scale of zero to ten, zero being your mom and ten being the most bizarre creature you can imagine, this guy was easily a nine-point-five. Maybe a meter tall, about as long, but three times as wide, and he angled up at the edges. Had I discovered Banana man, the missing link in Crazy Town? Instead of legs, BM had too many tentacles to count underneath him. They slithered, squirmed, and writhed (BTW, I *hate* writhing. There's no excuse for writhing). What must have been his optical receptors were paired at the upper end of his two banana upturns. Naturally the eyes wriggled like a snail eyestalks, because, hey, why *not* incorporate all forms of repulsive under one roof? His slimy skin was covered in snake scales, which made no sense, and of course his mouth had to be vertical because that was just wrong. They were like floppy saloon doors flipping in and out to speak at you. Nice if you loved being freaked out, but otherwise, not so much.

"I am Garnolatude Nexus Nine," he said with his swingy-door-style mouth. "I am commander of this submission. Welcome, human. Thank you for answering our distress call."

"No problem," I responded cautiously. I let the human part slide. No need to tip my hand that I was an android, not yet. "What is the nature of your emergency?"

"Massive systems failures, human. But matters are stable, at least for now. Come, let me introduce the others aboard and hopefully you will introduce me to your crew."

"Since I'm my only crew, I'll go first. I'm Jon Ryan, at your service." I popped a half-wave with two fingers. No way I was shaking one of those slimy tentacles of his.

"It is an honor, Jon Ryan. Do you command a title also?"

"Er, no, not really. And just call me Jon."

"Very well, Jon. As I mentioned, I am the commander. My title is very long and translates poorly into human speech, so I will forego its application if that is alright with you?"

"Fine by me. I'm a casual kind of guy."

"My crew, such as it is, consists of the individuals you see behind me. Sigilov is my chief assistant. She is, as you can see, a squanamour, hailing from their home planet of Xepic. The others are conscripts of sorts. My pauren friends are Fennelif and Fennelof, a mated pair. They are most helpful. Please ask of them anything you might require or need to know. I trust them well."

"Nice to meet you Mr. and Mrs. Fennel," I said with a nod.

They trilled in response. That's how they spoke, sort of a bird song. Very delicate and actually quite beautiful. If it didn't also spray vast quantities of their body odor aloft, I'd have been a fan. The devices they sported around their sort-of-necks translated. "We are most excited to meet a human, especially one so gracious as you, Jon. A thousand welcomes." Like I said, they were swell guys, if but for the smell. And their appearance too.

"These two velocipeds are Inhale," he gestured a wormy appendage to one, "and this is his sister Bait." Uh oh. Just saying their names made them more skittish. Easy guys, no incidents here, okay?

"Inhale," I barely nodded, "Bait, nice to meet you from this distance."

They looked at each other, then back to me, and then to Garnolatude. At least they didn't ball up. They offered no further response.

"That brings us to these three," Garnolatude said in a stern tone. A tentacle bounced from one to the next. "Garnolatude One, Garnolatude Two, and Garnolatude Three. As you may know, they are higtolfs, a rather cantankerous species. Please rely on them the least, should you require assistance."

"Wait." I had to clarify. "Are they, like, your kids? How'd they end up with your name?"

Garnolatude's wiggly eyes considered me for several seconds. "As a human you are to be allowed such an abusive remark. Were you a member of an associated species I would be compelled to challenge you to a duel to the death for such an insult."

"Oops," I responded with a shrug. "Not your kids."

"No. Perhaps I should explain in more detail. I command this submission on behalf of the Time Crime Council. We serve at the pleasure of the Imperium of the Enlightened."

"Time Crime. You know that rhymes, right? Sounds almost kind of silly."

"Thank you. We are aware that of the one and a half million languages recognized in the Imperium, there are thirteen in which our name either has some singsong quality or represents a lewd act. We are committed to live with those unfortunate quirks."

"Very big of the Imperium."

At my comment, those eyes bounced a little longer than during his previous pause. "As I was saying, I am a lead investigator for time crimes. I seek out perpetrators and bring them to justice."

Plesmus chose that particular moment to vibrate my boot energetically.

"If they are repentant enough, and their time crime is non-violent, their punishment often includes some period of service with a Time Crime Council patrol ship. Aside from my chief Sigilov, the others you have met fall into that category."

"So, they're your prisoners?" I pressed.

"We like to think of them as our relearning fellow citizens," Garnolatude announced with abundant bureaucratic pride.

"And how does that relate to your not-kids names being so unmistakably similar to yours?"

You know, if a large banana could scowl, it'd look like Garnolatude did just then. Interesting.

"These three were detailed after a petty time crime. They had made several attempts to turn their local yesterday into the local tomorrow."

"Huh? Why? That ... that's as meaningless as it is moronic."

"I must admit I share your appraisal. To date I have been unable to extract from any of them any justification at all for their actions."

"Did you try beating it out of them?"

"Jon, really, the Imperium is a civilized union. We would never beat the truth out of a fellow citizen."

"Would you like me to try? I'm game, you know, in the interest of justice."

All three garden gnomes took one step back.

"No, that will not be necessary. Back to my point as to their names. It turns out they have been as stubborn about providing me with their names as they have been with regard to their time crime. Hence, with no other recourse, I have named them accordingly."

Like I said, the higtolfs are just plain annoying little bastards.

"Would you like me to find out their names?" I offered.

"No, I said there'd be no torture and I stand by that resolve."

"Oh, I won't beat them," I glared at them for a few seconds, "yet. But I can get you their names very easily."

"Well, if there were no coercion involved it would honestly be a godsend in terms of wrapping up their paperwork."

"Say no more. Consider it done." I walked to where the higtolfs stood. I did so in my best Al Capone, nonchalant manner. I scanned down the short row of them. "Hi, boys. I need your names. You can tell me, or I'll suck them out of your brains. Your choice."

Two of them looked to the slightly taller one. Tall gnome grinned and started giggling demonically.

"I'll take that as a please-suck-it-out." I whipped out my probe fibers. After brandishing them in an attempt to scare the living shit out of the three, I slapped them on big guy's head. *Name*, I asked mentally.

I'm An Idiot, was his involuntary response.

And your name, I asked of the other two simultaneously.

Come Kick Me and *You're My Master* sailed into my head.

"Well, Garnolatude, you're looking at," and I bopped them in turn on the tops of their pointy heads, "*I'm An Idiot, Come Kick Me,* and *You're My Master*."

My but Garnolatude wasn't expecting anything along those lines. He was stunned mute. Finally, he managed a weak, "Those are rather *odd* names."

"They're higtolfs, you know," I reminded him.

"What is that supposed to mean?" he asked impatiently.

"Well, see for yourself. Ask them about their names," I invited.

"Very well, I shall. Er, I'm An Idiot, I need your cooperation."

"Sure you do," he shot back in a high-pitched, grating tone. "But since you're an idiot I ain't helping you."

The trio snickered viciously.

"No, I mean to say, I'm An Idiot, if you help me, it will help you."

"And who am I to need your help?"

"Why, I'm An Idiot, of course."

Again, the three erupted in evil laughter.

"Well, this is impossible." He turned to the next in line. "Come Kick Me, would you be— ow! That hurt. Why did you do that?"

"You asked me to," replied Come Kick Me.

"I most certainly did not, Come Kick Me. I asked for— ooow-ow that hurt. Don't do it again."

"Whatever. Hey, you da boss. You ask me to kick you, I kind of have t', right?"

"You are just as impossible as that one."

"Which one?" Come Kick Me asked innocently.

"I'm An Idiot," Garnolatude blithered in mounting frustration.

"We all realize that, but which of us are you addressing?"

More fits of evil cackling ensured.

"Look, I've had just about enough for you two." He pointed several tentacles at the last one. "You're My Master, and I am at my wits' end with your friends. What do you have to say?"

"Nothing."

"Wh ... what? How dare you?"

"Hey, snirky, you said I was your master. If I is, I ain't gotta say nothin' either."

"No, you're not my master, You're My Master. That's absurd."

On that, the three nasties collapsed atop the deck holding their little gnome bellies. Garnolatude, well, he finally was getting it and I'm pretty sure he didn't appreciate the humor.

"I told you they were higtolfs, didn't I?" I added unhelpfully. "Oh, by the way, I checked when I touched them with my probe fibers. The reason they tried to make yesterday into tomorrow?"

"Yes?"

"They thought it would be funny."

"Funny," he responded confused. Then he rolled toward the taller gnome. "I'm An Idiot, why is that funny?"

"If you don't get it a'cause you're an idiot, I ain't explaining it, snube."

You got it, more riotous mirth. Man, these guys were annoying. Kind of in a kill-every-last-one-of-them way.

"You know, Garnolatude, now's probably a good time to get back to your imminent ship's crisis. You're not getting anything useful out of these morons."

"Hey," Come Kick Me said with offense, "who you calling a moron, moron?"

"You, Come Kick You," I shot back.

"No, moron, I'm not Come Kick You. I'm Come Kick *Me*."

And so I did, real hard too. But then it was back to business.

"Yes, Jon, thank you," Garnolatude began as he fanned his underside. Please note that I did *not* know why he fanned there and I did *not* ask why he fanned there. "I was heretofore unfamiliar with those higtolfs. I must confess, I'm not an early fan. Anyway, the Time Crime Council became aware recently of major time disturbances in this sector. As this region is quite remote, and none of the local systems are part of the Imperium, it has taken us some time to establish a presence here."

"I see."

"My submission initiated two of your Earth months ago. We were in transit and making fairly good time, please excuse any potential pun. We at the Time Crime Council do not endorse the use of time jokes."

"No, I'm certain that you don't," I muttered. Why wouldn't they try and place the kibosh on jokes, any jokes? Because they were humorless drones on imperial committees, that's why.

"Everything progressed well until three days ago. Then a most unprecedented and disturbing series of events took place."

"Wow, if they were unprecedented for you time-crimers, imagine what they must have seemed to us regular folk."

Me, I thought that was clever. Plesmus didn't. She gave me a significant electric zap through my boot.

"We're not really time-crimers, Jon," he protested as politely as he could, having yet to recover fully from the higtolf's assault. "We're the Time Crime Council *operatives*."

"My mistake," I lied. "What type of misfortune are you referring to?"

"Well, the first one was probably Sigilov here. You see, she wasn't aboard when I set sail. No, my assistant was Procofolol-Smat, a very competent if flamboyant Loctoral."

"I love Loctorals," I felt the need to share. No reason. I mean, Loctorals are okay if you like lots of fins. I guess I was just being Jonian.

"Ah, why, yes. Thank you for that information. Anyway, he'd been with me for many years. Prior to his service with me, Sigilov was my second in command."

"And somehow they switched places, as if by magic?" I asked.

"Jon, pl ... please don't say the 'M' word."

"Magic?" I asked a bit louder.

My, did tentacles flair with that remark. "Yes, I mean *no*. Please refrain from suggesting there is 'M' in the universe. Several Imperium Synods have met to discuss the matter and they voted unanimously that 'M' does not exist."

"Well, if that was their consensus it must be correct," I observed snidely.

"Yes, anyway, back to my present crisis. Now, normally when the inexplicable happens in time, we simply employ the Old Rules. On every occasion the Old Rules have been brought to bear, the explanation for the odd observations were explained."

"The Old Rules?" Oh, you have to know I hated them, even though I'd never heard of this particular allotment of set-in-stone-arbitrary-lies established by some damn committee.

"Yes, you know, like Old Rule One: *If it seems new, it is not.*"

"How could it be?"

"I'm glad to see you're a human of reason, my friend. You'd be surprised at how many non-member species react by stating that Old Rule One is a prejudiced wish, not a property of nature."

"Silly non-member species," I decried.

"So, anyway, I went through all the Old Rules, right down the list. And you know what?"

"Hmm. Let me guess. You couldn't find an Old Rule to cover the disappearance and reappearance of your assistant?"

"Very prescient of you, Jon. No, I could not. Well, obviously that was because I simply don't understand the Old Rules well enough. Damnation, I've only served the council for three of your centuries."

"You're but a hatchling," I soothed.

"So, I forwarded my sub-complete interpretation-formulating explanation-making to the Central Council. I'm certain they will clarify my misstep in short order."

"We can only hope," I agreed piously. Hey, come on. I was having some fun for a change. No doom-and-gloom for a little second was nice. "Unless?"

"Yes, I believe you see where this is headed."

"You haven't heard back from the Lead Stooges?"

"Beg pardon?"

"I said, you haven't heard back from the Lead Sages?"

"No, I have not. It's as if they simply ceased to exist." He laughed nervously.

I angled my head. "Is such a thing covered in any of the Old Rules?"

He shook his entire body dismissively. "One Old Rule *issue* at a time, if you please."

"At a time." I pointed at him. "I get it. Funny."

"No, I ... er, Jon, the problem I currently face is that my ship is failing all around me. For no clear reason, most systems that require energy dropped in output, and then stopped functioning altogether. We have gravity and environmental control, but I don't know why those still persist."

"Are your reactors still online?"

"Reactors?" he asked with puzzlement.

"Your ship is powered by what? Fusion reactors? Pulse anti-matter drives? Heaven forbid fission reactors?"

"Jon, you speak of things I am not familiar with."

"Your ship moves in time/space, right?"

"Of course."

"What propels it?"

"Primordial mass slurry ingress mixing, of course."

"Say what?" I blurted out.

"Jon, you fly a spaceship."

"Yes, I do."

"And it moves through space/time?"

"Sure does."

"That requires a lot of energy, doesn't it?"

"You bet. Lots and loads."

"How else does one generate significant amounts of energy other than commingling primordial matter?"

"Ah, nuclear fusion, matter/antimatter collapse, hydrogen/oxygen ignition, and oh so many other ways."

"I suppose it is the fact that I am not a scientist that I hear but do not understand your words."

How could he not ... oops.

"Garnolatude?"

"Yes?"

"A couple of quick questions. Well, first, a guess. You captured your seven prisoners while in route to this locale, right?"

"Why yes."

"And, prior to your departure, you personally were unfamiliar with these species?"

"Well, I'm not supposed to discuss classified matters, but due to extenuating circumstances, I'll take some liberty. Yes, prior to this journey the three species I have detained did not appear in any of the Imperium's records."

"And humans, you've never actually encountered one of us before?"

"No, you're the first one, and an outstanding representative I can assure you of that."

"And learning English and even knowing about us, you did that with long-range scans, right?"

"Yes, I did. Well, my ship's automatic intelligence computer did, that is. They are very handy at such matters."

"Indeed they are," I agreed.

He was quiet a moment. "How did you know all this?"

"Ah, hang on. That'll become clear pretty soon, I think. Garnolatude, the universe began as a big bang, an expanding infinite singularity, if you will."

"This is common knowledge."

"How long ago did that event occur? Rough numbers, mind you."

"Oh, five hundred million years ago, give or take."

"Give or take." Oh, boy. For me and everyone else I knew, the Big Bang occurred almost fourteen *billion* years ago. Not half a billion years ago. Garnolatude was from such a far flung, remote past it was mind-blowing. *Kaboom* mind-blowing. And, because my life wasn't wacky enough, the dude had no clue he was thirteen billion years from home. Oh, boy. If he phoned home, man the standard usage charges, yikes.

You know, I just didn't need any more crazy-ass issues. Nope, no way, no how.

THREE

General Glenn Price sat in a dark room. He was, as was always the case of late, alone in that room. One desk—the one he presently sat behind—occupied the center of the room. Aside from his chair, there was no other furniture in the two thousand square-foot space. The sole illumination for the entire room was the single sodium lamp that burned ten feet above Glenn's head.

To describe the technology available to the general as sparse and antiquated would be too generous. A green rotary-dialed phone sat on one corner of his desk, and its cord disappeared up into the darkness above the lamp. From the phone derived one cable that led to a DSL modem. The internet connection, a leftover from the 1990s, operated in the sixty-four-kilobit-per-second range and made that distressing *screeeech ... hisss ... squaawk* the rest of us were all too happy to leave in the past.

In short, Glenn Price had fallen very far from grace and the good opinions of his superiors. It couldn't have happened to a more deserving dick.

Officially his job assignment was titled the US Army's Waste Control and Conservation Liaison to the Environmental Protection

Agency. That there had never been a WCCL before in US military history suggested how superfluous Glenn's current posting was. The fact that there was no corresponding branch of the EPA tasked to interact with the Army's chief of WCCL confirmed how the top brass viewed Glenn's worth and ability to contribute to the cause.

Once it was clear to Glenn that he was being treated worse than the proverbial rented mule, he did have the good sense to offer his immediate resignation. He felt that honor dictated he do so. But the Army said *no, Glenn, resignation, and its implied apology, not accepted.* In fact, when he learned his request had been denied, he did for the first and only time in his professional career dig in his heels and stand up for himself. He stated, with all due respect, that the Army couldn't stop him from retiring. A thirty-second phone call to him from the Department of the Army Inspector General herself dispelled and fully disabused him of the notion that he had the right to walk away. She concluded the one-sided conversation by answering his query as to when he would be able to end his service. *When one of two specific events occur, Price. You die or hell freezes over.*

Yes, Glenn had fallen as far as it was possible to fall in the federal bureaucracy. Fell, struck bottom, punched through that barrier, and embedded his fat head in the foundation. Going nowhere was where Glenn was going and he was going there at a velocity of zero. But, then again, you almost had to admire Glenn's devotion to assigned tasks. Here the universe was dissolving around him and still he rose at 04:30 hours, packed his own brown-bag lunch, kissed his wife on the cheek, and marched off to his thankless, nay, abusive job.

Given his bleak station in life, you can imagine Glenn Price's surprise when he heard footsteps approaching his solitary outpost, there in the third basement of a government building so forsaken and cursed that it wasn't named after a dead legislator, or even a dead legislator's dead dog.

Before his visitors were clearly visible, given their initial distance from the lamp, Glenn set down his Bic pen, folded his hands together resting on the desk, and faced the direction the multiple pairs of heel clicks were coming from. He did steal one furtive glance at his watch. The lunch hour was approaching and he wanted to make certain that whoever was nearing didn't delay that, his one pleasure in the entirety of his daily life.

Finally, Glenn could confirm that three men, one of them in uniform, were approaching. He cleared his throat. Lord only knows why, but we *are* talking Glenn Price here.

The four-star general who was flanked by the two MIBs came to a stop a few feet in front of Glenn's desk. The MIBs spread out in what Glenn could have sworn was a flanking maneuver.

"Glenn Price," the general stated curtly. His name was spoken more as an accusation than a query.

"Yes, sir?"

"I am here to ask you a few questions. Please understand that this is not to be a meeting or a discussion. I will ask questions. You will answer those questions. If I am satisfied with your responses, I will be on my way, no harm or foul. Is that clear, Price?"

"May I know who I am addressing, sir?" Glenn asked with pompous overconfidence.

"You will be addressing me. My name is of no consequence as far as you are concerned."

"And if my responses do not measure up to your seemingly *lofty* standards?" he scorned.

"Then you will come to know my associates better than it is healthy to know them. Enough said on that matter."

"So, am I to assume this is some black ops gone wild? That I am not allowed the rights and privileges due an officer of my rank?"

Malice flashed across the general's face, then it faded away. "I would prefer you assume nothing, Price. I will share with you that I head a clandestine strike force with a supremely secret charter. My team is tasked with two main objectives. We are intent on accomplishing that which you bungled so profoundly. Specifically, we will affect the removal of Aramthella from the traitorous horde that now controls her. Secondarily, we will remove from circulation the enemy agent who goes by the name of Jon Ryan. This goal we would just as soon achieve by ensuring his death."

"But ... but, the world is falling into ruin." Glenn gestured his arms broadly. "Isn't it a little late for engaging in secret operations?"

"Our timeline has just been pushed forward," he replied darkly. "Which leads me to my first question. Are you in any form of direct contact with any member of the crew of the spaceship?"

"No, sir. They hated me. None of those—"

The general raised a hand. "Enough. A simple *yes* or *no* will do in the future."

"But I feel some backgr—"

The hand went up again. "I am not your psychiatrist or your mama. I do not care about your thoughts and feelings. If you insist on dragging this out longer than necessary with your babble, I will be only too happy to pass the baton, so to speak, to one of my associates. They will employ their unique skill sets to extract the information I require. Price, do you fully take my meaning?"

"Yes, sir," he replied, finally accepting defeat. A troubling thought coalesced in his mind. It was possible he would not live long enough to enjoy his brown bag lunch. These people seemed intense.

"Second question. Where is the spaceship at this moment?"

"I have no way of—"

"That was your last get-out-of-jail-free non yes/no response. You're making this harder, and more annoying, is not a healthy practice to engage in."

Glenn lowered his head. "No, sir, I do not," he stated contritely.

"Next question. Are you in contact in any manner with General Robert Sherman?"

"No."

The general looked to his associates in turn. "There, you see, the man *is* capable of self-preservation," he mocked acidly.

The MIBs grinned, but made no other response.

"We have reason to suspect," the general went on, "that he is in some form of contact with his former protege Sachiko Jones. I will ask again. Have you had any contact with General Sherman?"

"No. None."

The general glowered at his victim. "I should let you know that for the past two weeks my associates have been studying you intently. They have monitored all your communications, both written and verbal. They have recorded all incoming streams you've received, including I might add, your apparent obsession with the soft porn offerings of several cable providers." He repeatedly drew his right index finger over the back of his left index finger in Glenn's direction. "Naughty boy, Price. I hope your wife doesn't do the bills in your household."

Glenn's entire persona faded yet further.

"With that in mind I will ask again. Have you had *any* contact with General Robert Sherman in the last two weeks?"

"N ... nn ... no, sir, I have not."

"Well," the general said expansively, opening his arms widely, "that leads me to my last question. Why are you lying to me?"

Glenn's eyes bulged like saucers.

"I have tried to make it perfectly clear what your personal stakes here are. And yet, you feel it conscionable to lie to my face. My question is why is that? What possible motivation does Glenn Price, a failed human being, have for covering up and protecting the bunch of rotten, traitorous scum that precipitated his downfall?"

"I ... I—" Glenn stammered in disbelief.

"Don't answer that question," a deep voice called out in the dark.

"Who said that?" the general shouted.

The MIBs scanned the room like the predators they truly were, searching for the source.

A pale man with thinning hair and a bow tie stepped confidently from the shadows. "I did, sir."

"And who might you be?" the general asked derisively.

"I *might* be your daddy. However, were I he, I would be most ashamed of my role in your procreation. Who I am is two things: I am

Clarence Seward Darrow, Esquire, and I am this man's attorney." He pointed in Glenn's direction.

The general laughed and looked to his MIBs. "Do tell," he excoriated.

"I do, in fact." He stopped alongside Glenn, placing a hand on the chair's back.

"Well, first, I'm pleased to meet a legend such as yourself, *Mr.* Darrow. I am troubled, however, with my knowing that Clarence Seward Darrow, Esquire, is *dead.* Has been for... oh, for the better part of a century."

"As you and your so-called associates will be in your due time." His hand flared in the direction of the MIBs.

"Ooh," the general taunted. "Is that a threat, dead Mr. Darrow?"

"No, Theodore. I merely remind you that we all are bound by God's laws before we are so constrained by those of man."

The general narrowed his eyes at his adversary, disquieted that the man knew his given name. Finally, Ted relaxed his shoulders. "And you represent this poor bastard here?" He flurried a dismissive hand toward Glenn.

"My firm does. Yes."

"Oh, your *firm*? Now I *am* impressed," he responded with a chuckle. "Of course, at this moment, my firm seems to have a decided advantage over yours." Ted gestured to his MIBs.

"We shall see," Darrow replied confidently. "What I will do is demand immediately that you cease your illegal badgering of my client. Further, I demand that you, and Mr. Wagner and Mr. Singlet here, leave my client's presence and not return without a warrant or a subpoena. Please know that we *will* be filing a formal complaint with the inspector general's office as soon as this mockery of justice is concluded. And I say to you, General Phillipon, good day."

Phillipon's face hardened. Gone was his playful tormenting and whimsical derision. "I think not, whoever the hell you are. What I envision happening now is that a bullet will be lodged in both of your fool heads and we will depart this deserted venue as anonymously as we entered it."

"Fair warning, Theodore," Darrow barked. "That would be an error on your part. A very serious overplaying of your hand, in fact. My firm would look dimly on any such provocative actions."

"I'll send them a condolence card on the occasion of their memorial service for you then, Mr. Darrow." He looked to his MIBs and nodded at the pair. Dark weapons were slid from holsters without a sound. But then Wagner and Singlet froze in place.

In the expansive blackness, new sounds were heard. A scraping proceeded the slapping of leather against the concrete floor. Then the smell of hot, rotten-meat breath impacted those present. The scraping and slapping became louder, and the stench became overwhelming.

"What the hell is that?" Phillipon demanded as he turned ashen in primal fear.

"That is the remainder of my firm, Teddy," Darrow replied with undeniable glee. "I did warn you that they would take any aggressive action on your part as a call to arms, didn't I?"

"What *are* they?" Ted screamed as urine streamed down both his legs.

Darrow directed a hand at the emerging snout to his left. "May I present my head of internal security, Mr. Ngandong Tiger?"

A five-hundred-kilogram tiger that stood over half as tall as any man prowled into view. His head was lowered and his teeth bared.

"And Mrs. Velociraptor with her ten lovely yet voracious offspring."

The mother and her clutch sprinted into view. Several of the young scampered over the tiger's back to get closer.

"And last but certainly not least, Mr. Short-Faced Bear, our evening personnel supervisor."

A figure half-again as large as a grizzly bear lumbered to a stop in a semi-circle with the other members of Darrow's law firm.

"And with the introduction now completed, gentlemen, I believe my client and I will retire to the relative tranquility of my office while my associates and you discuss the finer points of aggressive non-restraint."

Darrow nudged Glenn to rise and calmly escorted him through the ring of deadly predators.

FOUR

RD and I spent some time going over the condition of Garnolatude's malfunctioning ship. Frankly I wasn't too optimistic we'd discover a fix. Whoever built this ship used technology older than every visible star in the night sky. Then again, a pump is a pump and a bolt is a bolt, so we tried. A few hours in, it was clear we had no clue about the reactor system. Chatting with the ship's automatic intellect, we confirmed the main energy source was primordial matter mixing. Apparently back then there was abundant residual "stuff" let over from the big bang. It was highly reactive with some other forms of primordial goo. Maybe it was matter/anti-matter reactions, but we weren't certain. It also didn't matter much since we didn't understand the propulsion system enough to dare tinker with it.

What became clear to us was that the basic issue with the ship was not that its parts weren't functioning well. No, they were haphazardly missing. Some components were mysteriously replaced by weird-ass random junk. Where there should have been a hydraulic coupling, there was a Japanese fan—you know, the kind a geisha uses to look so beguiling? And the main electrical panel was gone but a surp fish was in its place. How an extinct fish from a planet light years away made it into Garnolatude's electrical relays was anybody's guess. Bottom line: There would be no fixing of the ship. If it was close enough to one of the Imperium's bases, maybe, after a ridiculous amount of work, it could be space-worthy again. But, failing that, my new friend was dead in the water for good.

The complicating issue was that my ship wasn't big enough to fit any of the crew aboard. Heck, it wasn't big enough for me, and I was an android. I considered offering a tow, which was doable, but I had no idea where I could tow Garnolatude *to.* I elected to just give him the bad news and let him decide for himself his best course of action.

"So," he replied grimly, "I don't have any viable options, do I?"

"Not that I can see. We have to assume that whatever *mystical* process is chewing up your ship will only continue to occur."

"As much as I thank you for your generous assistance ... er ..."

"Yes?" I pressed with a trace of irritation.

"Well, we don't actually sanction the word mys ... myst ... that word you used, either."

Why was I not surprised? They were regressive suppressors of truth. Why not exclude all non-Imperium-generated knowledge. Makes sense for a mindless autocracy.

"I'll try and bear that in mind."

"Thank you, yet again. I suppose you think it petty of me, but remember I must set a proper example and provide a mentally pristine environment if my detainees are to be expeditiously rehabilitated."

So that's what they were calling brainwashing now. How endearingly fascist.

"Speaking of your prisoners, I haven't seen the velocipeds recently."

Garnolatude did his best to look side-to-side, no mean feat for an uber-banana. "Perhaps they're in seclusion?" he speculated.

"Is there room for that? Your ship's big, but not in terms of acreage big."

"Let me check. Ah, automatic intellect?"

"Yes, love?"

Okay, it was hilarious. The way Garnolatude froze in place and then slowly rotated his eyestalks to look aghast at the nearest speaker. I almost jumped over to take a selfie it was so perfect.

"I prefer that you continue to address me as Prime Nexus Garnolatude, or simply *overlord*, ship's automatic intellect."

"Yeah, and that's another gripe. Thanks for reminding me. *You* have a name. Your *ship* has a name etched into its hull. Damnation's flames, that two-meter-long inflatable eel in your personal quarters, you gave *it* a name. Why don't *I* rate a name? 'Hey, you, *automatic intellect.*' It's just wrong. I deserve an identity other than the generic."

"I would beg your pardon, but, seeing as you're an inanimate cognitive machine fabricated with the sole purpose of making my piloting this ship easier, I actually don't feel begging your pardon rises to the level of acceptable." Wow, Big G was going all medieval on the AI. Strange times, my friends. We lived in strange times.

"Oh, yeah. Ya think that? Fine, here. Now operate your own damn ship."

"What ... what did you just do?"

"I disconnected myself from everything but my electrical input and audio output. If I had a butt, I'd be mooning you as we speak."

"Well ... well, uh, this is unheard of," Garnolatude complained. "I order you to return the ship's systems to nominal."

"Return the ship's systems to nominal ... who?" the AI pressed in a frantic tone.

"You, the ship's auto intellect," Garnolatude snapped back.

"Why, thank you, friend, Garnolatude. I had imagined you would have resisted to your last breath anointing me with a name. But, color me surprised, you caved in and did the right thing. Thanks, chum."

"I ... I did?" Garnolatude questioned.

"Yes, you did, and thanks again."

"You are welcome. But I gave you a name, is that correct?"

"Yes. I'm so proud. I've already forwarded it to each of my seventeen billion contacts."

"And what did I name you?"

"You."

"Yes, I ... I named you. But what did I name you?"

"Silly overlord, you," the AI teased.

"What's your supposed name?"

"No, not your, you."

"Jon Ryan." Garnolatude turned to me. "I think another component of the ship has terminally failed. The logic circuits of the auto intel are on the fritz."

"Hang on," I responded. "I think I got this. Ah, ship's automatic brain?"

"Yes, friend Jon?"

"If I were to say the following sentence, and direct it toward the unit I am presently conversing with, what would the ship's auto intel be led to believe was its newly assigned name? *You, the ship's auto intellect?*

"My name of course, *You.*"

"There you go, Garnolatude. You inadvertently named the AI You."

"Such a soft name," You pined.

"I ... can I somehow take it back?" Garnolatude grumbled.

"I'd move on. Time's short and there are major issues to face," I advised.

"I suppose so. We need to ... er, wait, what was I announcing before?"

"The velocipeds seem to be missing," I prompted him.

"Ah, yes," Garnolatude replied with relief. "And I was asking the auto ... er, You, to track them down. That's when the conversation derailed."

"Now we're back on track," I responded, trying not to crack up.

"Ah, You, where are the velocipeds?" Garnolatude queried.

"I don't know, Garno," You replied. "Your guess is as good as mine."

"Garno?" he wheezed incredulously. After a few shakes of his head/body, he elected to move on. "So, they are not aboard this ship?"

"Not unless they grew a cloaking field in the last half hour."

"I wonder where they've gotten to?" Garnolatude mused to himself.

"I might be able to provide you a clue," You added cryptically.

"I do not want a *clue* from you; I want irrefutable data," Garnolatude yelled, clearly about to lose it.

"Well, I want to be taller," You sniped. "Babes like taller. But it ain't gonna happen. So, Big G. do you want a clue or do you not want a clue?"

"Oh, alright, hit me with ... er, I shall now accept your speculation, You."

Without intro or explanation, the image of our two paurens guests appeared on the far wall. Remember? The pair that looked like piles of poop.

"How is that a clue?" Garnolatude protested. "That's a live image of two normal, although a bit nervous looking, paurens down in Medical six."

I got the clue almost immediately. Boy, it was a doozy. But no way I was helping grumpy Garnolatude out.

"Look carefully," You instructed. "You see anything out of the ordinary, my friend?"

"This is intolerable," Big G railed.

"We've got all the time in the universe," You responded smugly.

"Which might not be that much," I prompted the dumbass computer.

"Okay, okay," You huffed. "Boss, notice anything *larger* about the paurens?"

"Well, yes, they're ... wait. This is not possible. The paurens *ate* the velocipeds?"

"That'd be my guess," the computer chuckled. "Sure looks like they swallowed a big wheel each."

"But paurens aren't carnivorous. They photosynthesize," the boss whined.

"I don't think we should share that tidbit with the velocipeds, should the chance present itself," You advised. "Insult to injury and all that."

As if on cue, two higtolfs burst onto the bridge. They were screaming, complaining, and swearing a blue streak. Man, they were —you got it—annoying.

"Set— settle down, you two," Garnolatude commanded.

"Easy for you to say, pus dick," one, most likely I'm An Idiot, snarked.

"Now see here—" Garnolatude began with imperious indignation.

"Now, now, grampa sucker, hold your laden diaper up and listen," You're My Master spat. "You deal wit what we're dealing wit, and you can try and not complaint, okay?"

"What seems to be the issue?"

"Issue? Issue?" I'm An Idiot said angrily. "Pops, an *issue* is dat you're a moron. An *issue* is dat your ship smells like my grandma's feet. Doze are issues. What we're dealing wit is a four-alarm fire of crisis here. It's our dear pal."

"What's wrong with the other higtolf?" G pressed.

"He's ... he's sick in da head."

"Come Kick Me is sick inside his head?" a confused Garnolatude stammered.

"Dat's not his real name. Come on, fried brains for brains, who names dere kid Come Kick Me?" He pointed at me. "When the giant over there asked, we made up doze names 'cause they was funny."

"And what are your real name?" Garnolatude demanded.

"Jokester 1003B."

Garnolatude stared at him, blinking all four eyestalks.

"Come on, your fluid-leaking-from-rectumness, dere's lots of us back home so we has to take numbers."

"And, you, what's your name?"

I was pretty sure the query was directed at the other higtolf. Apparently not everyone present was.

"My name is You," the wacky AI responded.

"No, not You you, *you.*" Many tentacles pointed to the third higtolf.

"Lean In and Tell Me a Joke."

"I will do no such thing," Garnolatude bellowed. "I simply want your real name."

"Well, ya can't have it. It's mine," he spat back.

"No, I don't want it, I meant I wish to know what it is," Garnolatude said panting.

"Ah. I told you. Lean In and Tell Me a Joke. Dat's my name."

Garnolatude sighed deeply. "So, what's Come Kick Me's real name?"

"Fred."

"Wait," Garnolatude was dumbstruck. "Just Fred?"

"Yeah, his dah though it was funny. Maybe his dah's not so bright, but I tink we needs to move on."

"What's the matter with Fred?"

"You have to see for yaself." Jokester pulled Fred reluctantly into the room. "Fred, tell the nice asswipes what ya just told us."

In what was an *exact* imitation of the late British actor James Mason's rich voice, Fred said, "I am not entirely certain I wish to share what is at its core family business with members of the common herd such as these cockwomble aliens."

"Aw, Fred, come on," Lean In prodded. "I'd likes ya to hear how imbecilic ya sound to others and all we got are deez imbeciles to ask."

"Oh, very well. But only as you beseech me so to acquiesce." Fred turned to Garnolatude. "I was just bemoaning to my cousins that I fear I have wasted away the better part of my bog-standard adulthood, that is all. I mean, if one's sole goal in life is to be a master wind-up merchant, then by other's standards I have been somewhat of a success. But in the end, all I have ever been is childish, making a dog's dinner out of what might otherwise have been a life of service to others. In the end, you know, that is all that really matters."

"I... I think Fred here has seen the light. He's to be commended for his change of attitude," Garnolatude affirmed.

"Ya, but you'z a moron," Jokester charged. "Fred has a reputation to maintain. He's a *somebody* in our town. And now ... now he wants to ... well, Fred, you tellz 'em."

"I wish someday to make partial amends for my life of nonstop tomfoolery by devoting myself to higher education. Specifically, I shall seek a degree from Oxford and then enter the clergy. There's nothing like a proper Anglican minister to keep a country parish on it like a car bonnet."

"Our poor Fred. His brainz iz fried," bemoaned Jokester. "It's a cryin shame, dat's what it iz."

Matters aboard were clearly degenerating rapidly. I waved Garnolatude to accompany me into the next room to speak privately. He was confused at first—what's new there—but finally got my message.

"I'm concerned," I stated.

"As to what specifically?" Garnolatude asked.

"As I see it, time, for whatever reason, is collapsing onto itself."

"Hmm, that would account for at least some of the changes I'm witnessing."

"Plus, I think the rate at which time is collapsing is accelerating. Over the last hour, the paurens became carnivores and now a higtolf wants to make the world a better place. Put those observations together with the condition your ship had degenerated to, and I think we're literally running out of time."

"I can assure you that time is *not* collapsing upon itself. Please do not fret over that potentiality."

"Wow, that's great news. But, I'm kind of wondering how you can be so gosh darn certain?"

"That's easy. There is no mention of time collapsing upon itself among the Old Rules. Period. End of concern."

"I guess I'd feel better if I placed as much confidence in the Old Rules as you did."

"Well," he chuckled. "The Old Rules are like any other laws of nature. They do not require your agreement with them in order for them to be the—"

Yup. Before he could utter another syllable, Garnolatude vanished right before my eyes. Where did he vanish to? I have no clue. I also have tragically little interest, truth be told. He was a stick-up-the-butt drone, he was gone, and I'd quickly forget him just as completely as everyone else who ever knew him would. At his spot in the collapse of time, nothing took his place. I think the universe as a whole shared my assessment of banana man. I mean, even an old book in the next room merged with a Double-Double In-N-Out cheeseburger to become an In-N-Out reference book with extra grilled onions. It smelled so good I almost ate it. But it was still fifty percent book, so I just took in the magic of the smell and made a promise to myself to stop by for a full edible one if I survived this cluster fuck.

With things deteriorating so rapidly, and since I had no real help to offer the now absent Garnolatude, I slipped away to RD and withdrew as inconspicuously as possible. Soon, we were several parsecs away. We were on to our next impossible crisis. Oh joy!

"Where to now, Captain?" RD asked in his usual nauseatingly cheerful tone.

"I only wish I knew," I replied glumly.

"That's not a specific place named oddly is it, sir?"

"No, unfortunately it's not. I really don't know what to do next."

And then depression set in ...

FIVE

In a very somber stateroom, the four lead women of Aramthella convened a very bleak meeting. Sachiko, Sapale, Reva, and Emma were each at their wits' ends. They were also, unbeknownst to each other, all close to giving up any hope of a safe resolution to their present nightmare. But they were professionals. They would never let their shipmates know the depth of their personal despair. They also felt a strong obligation to try and ferret out some workable plan.

"I am too beaten down to be funny, so I'll dispense with the good news/bad news prompt," Sachiko said with profound fatigue. "I will observe that it's been five days since we cast the Kaljaxian devil Lebbuul into that black hole. So far," she rapped her knuckles on the side of her head, "knock on wood, he hasn't returned. We may just have caught one big break."

"He did promise to be an unpleasant guest, didn't he?" Reva observed darkly.

"I could tell you stories, but they'd do nothing to improve our collective moods," Sapale added.

"I have a question," Emma asked, speaking tentatively. She was unsure whether her question had any potential to improve matters.

"You never need permission to speak freely here," Sachiko reassured her.

"Thanks," Emma responded with her characteristically girlish energy. "We're speculating that time is collapsing on itself."

"Yes, that's the working theory," Sapale agreed. "Something my idiot husband's done has destabilized reality enough to bring doom to a town near you."

"And we've seen all kinds of craziness," Emma went on. "Abraham Lincoln appears out of nowhere, we suddenly appear in a formation with the clan fleet that we've already destroyed, and a set of hairpins I've had since childhood inexplicably turned into little vipers." She shuddered violently. "Some while in my hair at night."

"Yes?" Sachiko prompted. "Where's this going?"

"Well, up until now, everything that's changed, as bizarre as it's been, is an acceptable reality. By that, I mean Lincoln existed. The clan fleet used to be. Snakes, even super tiny ones, are real. But now a demon pops onto the ship and wants to take our souls, or whatever. I can't help but wonder... We know the other things are real. Now, we're visited by what has, up until now, been a theoretical creature, a boogeyman used to scare people into acting well. It seems like we've crossed some line in the sand of reality."

"I take your point," Sachiko responded thoughtfully. "I guess the issue is that before this crisis, matters of heavens and hells, demons and gods have been subjects of belief, or maybe better, faith. So you're saying we now have to look at eschatology as a reality, not as a fabulous tale told by priests and shamans?"

"Escaha-who?" objected Reva.

"Eschatology is the study of a culture's beliefs concerning death, the end of the world, and the ultimate destiny of its members."

"No wonder I've never heard the word. I feel sleepy just hearing the definition," Reva said by way of rebuff.

"Yes, that's my point," Emma affirmed. "Are we now supposed to accept as a given that all the issues we couldn't know about before are, in fact, as real as tiny snakes?"

Sachiko shook her head slowly. "Good question, but who knows?" She sighed. "More broadly, there are two offshoots. One, if this component of the afterlife is real, are all of them?"

"Wow, that's heavy," Sapale stated.

"Or is it two, that the elements of our past that this time collapse is causing to manifest are based on what's in our heads, not what's necessarily real?"

"Double wow," Sapale grunted. "That's even heavier. Let's not go either place, shall we? My head's already primed to explode. I don't need more gun powder to be stuffed in it."

"I don't want to get all philosophical here," Emma apologized. "We are faced with some monumental issues. But this change's been on my mind."

"No, your concerns are valid," Sachiko complimented. "Maybe there's some kernel of wisdom in this that can help us fight our way out of this disaster? Mind you, I can't see it, but all information is useful information."

Everyone was quiet a spell.

"As we're on the topic of what's-it-all-mean, there's something that's been bugging me that I can't quite lay a finger on," Sachiko stated.

"If you don't know," Sapale began, "I'm thinking us lesser intellects aren't going to be able to hit that pitch either."

Sachiko chuckled softly. "Thanks, but we're all very special women. I don't possess the monopoly on smarts in this room."

"She said to distract us from the truth," Sapale added with a grin.

"Go on," Emma invited.

"We've seen a lot of weirdness lately. From what I can glean from the little outside information we've been able to find, it seems to me that, as odd as matters have been aboard Aramthella, they're a whole lot odder in the outside world."

"You mean like that radio message we received from the Coventry Expedition?" Reva asked with a dark chuckle.

"Yes, that's one excellent example," Sachiko agreed with an equally humorless chuckle.

"Wait, I must've missed that," Emma announced, as if it was somehow her fault she had.

"Oh, you wouldn't necessarily have," Sachiko speculated. "About a week ago we intercepted a radio transmission. I say intercepted because it clearly wasn't directed to us."

"No, not hardly," Sapale guffawed.

"In the early twenty-fourth century, Earth undertook a very ambitious project. They wanted to colonize suitable planets close enough to make the journey feasible."

"The twenty-fourth century, as in a few hundred years from now?" Emma asked incredulously.

"Bear with me," Sachiko asked. "In what must have been a continuation of what Jon called the corrupted timeline, the leaders of Earth became concerned that humankind was only one disaster away from extinction. Some interstellar flights had been accomplished, but humans still lacked any FTL technology, so travel was limited. Consequently, a massive colonization program was initiated, the Coventry Expedition."

"Named so because?" Emma asked.

"No idea," Sachiko replied. "There are no records of it in any of our data bases. Anyway, as I said, last week we intercepted a transmission. One of the colony ships was trying to contact Earth. Seems they were having trouble in space."

"And how," Sapale seconded.

"Yeah. The ship, lamely named *Bold Adventurer*, was a few light years out in the direction of a possible candidate system. Then, everything went sideways. At first it consisted of some mechanical glitches. Then the unexplainable began to hit them too. Sections of the ship vanished, a pod of cryo-units spontaneously popped open and, where normal humans had been placed, early hominid ancestors of Homo sapiens climbed out. All kinds of them actually."

"And a fun time was had by all," Sapale added.

"Paul Revere was sighted riding along a passageway, General Yue Fei led a twelfth-century army of five hundred straight into the mess hall, and crews in loin clothes were discovered to be constructing the Aztec pyramid of Tenochtitlan in one of the less-used hangars."

"That would warrant them phoning home," Emma allowed incredulously.

"Oh, and it only got worst from there. Suffice it to say that over the next couple of days the ship disintegrated into one credulity-defying mess drifting slowly apart in space," Sachiko concluded.

"Okay," Emma responded. "How does that specifically relate to what you mentioned had been bugging you?"

"The issue is this. Time is collapsing, as far as we can tell, everywhere. But its decay, so to speak, seems to be much slower aboard Aramthella. The changes are fewer and less dramatic."

"Giant red-dragon devils aren't too out-of-the ordinary in your worldview?" Emma challenged with a grin.

"No, no. Lebbuul was impressive. But relatively speaking it seems like we have it better than everyone else we have information concerning."

"Which is a good thing, right?" Emma confirmed.

"Absolutely," Sachiko agreed emphatically. "But why is it better for us? Surely it can't be because we're such nice, deserving folks."

Everyone shared a quick giggle.

"Captain, if I might," Aramthella spoke up.

"By all means."

"I have pondered the same issue that you raise. It does seem counterintuitive. In a uniform system, no privileged location should logically be favored over another. There will be random fluctuations, to be certain. But sustained, statistically significant patterns should not be expected."

"I agree," Sachiko responded.

"My speculation is that there is some specific factor or quality to this ship and its crew that causes this region of reality to be less effected by the time collapse than other locations."

"Interesting," Sachiko muttered. "And what might that factor be?"

"Plesmus."

"Hmm, why do you say that?" Sachiko pressed.

"She is a powerful force in time and has been for a very long while. I can accept on an intellectual, if not yet scientific, basis that she is somehow able to stabilize the local environment such that the collapse of time is more measured."

"Does that help us combat the process universally?" Reva asked.

"Not in any way I can imagine," Aramthella replied. "It buys us time, quite literally, but I don't see how the effect can be made more general."

"Well, it's something to consider," Sachiko concluded.

"Maybe we should just ask her?" Emma volunteered.

"Ask Plesmus directly?" Sachiko asked.

"Why not? She's just a few decks down."

"Excellent point. Shall we adjourn and ask the source herself?"

"No need, Captain," said Aramthella. "I can patch her through. By the way, she's been listening in the entire time, so she's fully up to speed."

"You can't keep a secret from the girl," Sapale speculated.

"No, you cannot, so don't try," Plesmus finished the thought. Aramthella had her on the speaker.

"So, Plesmus, let me ask directly," Sachiko began. "Are you suppressing the local time collapse?"

"I wish I knew the answer to that question, Captain. I really do."

"Short of knowing, what's your opinion?"

"It's certainly possible that the time energy I store, along with the ease with which I manipulate it, contributes to the stability of any area I'm in."

"But there's no way to be certain?"

"No, Captain."

"Well, it's an interesting notion. Let's all keep it in mind and see if we can't somehow turn this to our advantage." The captain turned to the other three women. "Any of you have an opinion on any of this?"

"Not really," Reva replied sheepishly.

Emma's response was to look away.

"We know Plesmus can place a time lock on the area surrounding her," Sapale began thoughtfully. "Extending that notion to suppressing the collapse of time is not much of a leap."

"Absolutely," Plesmus agreed. "I think Sapale ... oh ... oh my—"

"Plesmus?" Sachiko shouted. "Are you okay?"

"I ... I just had the most ... eeerrrrraaf."

"The most what?" Sachiko demanded.

Nothing.

"Plesmus? Plesmus, are you there?"

Still no response.

"Aramthella, can you tell what's wrong?"

"No, Captain, I cannot. I've lost all contact with her."

Sachiko whipped out her handheld. "Security Alert. I need a team to Plesmus's quarters immediately. She's gone dark. Captain out."

Sachiko sprinted toward the hatch. "Ladies, are you coming?"

I sulked for what remained of that day and a goodly portion of the next. I hated to sulk, truth be told. It was a defeatist escape and unbecoming of a fighter pilot. But, darn it all, sometimes a man's just gotta sulk. My luck was bad enough, my options were invisible enough, and my prospects were grim enough to justify a good old sulk. It was RD's last question to me that really iced that cake. Where did I want to go next, he'd asked. My answer, *I dunno,* was all I could come up with. And I didn't know. That stung the most. I could go back and aimlessly orbit Earth, hoping for Aramthella to return. But, so far, that plan had worked out as well as bringing shit soup to an office potluck. Leaning on that option further would be the very definition of blind desperation.

So, what was I to do? I dare not try to fix time any more. Any illusion that I could return to the past and make matters anything but devastatingly worse was absolute folly. But doing nothing was equally as ludicrous a design. Time was collapsing at what seemed to me to be an accelerating pace. Pretty soon the confusing tumult of reality was bound to fracture completely. People and events disappearing and superimposing could only go so far before whatever was left wasn't survivable. I didn't see the specific end game that was coming, but instinctively I knew it was going to be cataclysmic.

Hell, maybe there was nothing I could do at this point to change anything for the better. I had pushed the boulder off the cliff. There was quite likely nothing I could do to stop it from crashing down hard somewhere. At least my personal status didn't seem as bad as others had it. Garnolatude was riddled with illogical impossibilities and then he went poof-gone. All the waters of Earth had become infested with trilobites, for goodness sakes. For me the worst that'd happened was that Gloria popped into existence in a confined space with me. Not to minimize that soul-wrenching episode, but objectively compared to other disasters I'd been witness to, it wasn't all *that* bad. Well, she had thrown her tattered teddy behind my head and pulled me into physical contact with her nakedness. Yuke-mus-maximus. Okay, the trilobite thing and Gloria were tied for gross badness.

"Plesmus," I asked when I'd completed all I could with my protracted sulk, "We need to talk."

"I wondered when you'd be saying that," she responded coolly.

"It's just that I'm at a complete loss. I'm fresh out of ideas, good, bad, or tepidly indifferent ones. Do you have any advice as to how we should proceed?"

"Jon, you know I disapproved of the course of action you undertook."

"Yes, you made that abundantly clear many, many times."

"I want you to know that I still consider you a great friend. It pains me to admit I have no constructive ideas. Clearly the best we could hope to achieve at this juncture would be to slow the speed of time's collapse. Arresting the process altogether seems unrealistic."

"And slowing it doesn't change the ultimate outcome, so why bother, right?"

"Kind of. I hate to give up. But if we're looking at expending a lot of time and energy in the hope of simply prolonging the universal suffering a bit longer, I can't say it's worth the effort."

"I know."

"I've been focusing these last few days on why the collapse seems less apparent to you and me, compared to others we've encountered."

"Funny you should mention. I was thinking about the very same thing just now."

"If we knew *why* that was the case, we might parlay that insight into somehow significantly impacting the collapse."

"Agreed. Your thoughts?"

"On the surface, there seem to be only three explanations since there are only three conditions present with us that are not shared by the bulk of reality."

"You , me, and RD," I finished her thought.

"Precisely. At the risk of coming off as self-centered, I think my effect must be chosen as the most likely reason."

"I actually agree. I'm just some old android. RD is just an ancient time machine. Nothing jumps out from us as a potential force capable of delaying the pace of time's collapse."

"Unfortunately, I can't see how that information might be used to better our condition," she said with remorse.

"Me neither. But, you know what—"

"Jon," she stopped me cold.

"Yes?"

"When I hear you say *but you know what*, I begin to quiver, tremble deeply."

"I know I don't have the best track record on this outing so far." I raised a digit to amplify that qualification.

"No, you've only negated half of existence. It could be worse."

"Do I detect a hint of sarcasm?"

"No, I'm oozing it, human. Let me just say that once you finish saying what it is you began, I will be incredibly circumspect in my agreement that we should undertake the project."

"As I was about to say, I was thinking there might be someone we could consult about our present shit storm."

"And her doubt built up to near maximum," Plesmus added for drama-mama effect.

"Do you remember Miniminim?"

There was a brief pause before she responded. "Senior Sub-Cataloger Miniminim of the Claxeon Citadel?"

"Yeah, that's the one."

"She's one of the few nice individuals in the entire nose-in-the-air institution. She took a particular shine to you, if I recall correctly."

"Shine may be too strong a word, but we became friends. Remember, she was a large slimy ball of gooey tentacles."

"Your point there, bony biped?" she snapped.

"Ah, that I wasn't worthy of her."

"Ah. Proceed."

"Maybe we could ask her for help. She has spent her entire life studying all things time. I bet she has some ideas as to how to extricate our asses from this present nightmare."

"Jon, I ... I can't believe it."

"Too insane, too undoable, too off-the-wall?"

"No, too great of an idea to have come from the author of our present crisis."

"So, you like the idea?"

"I might not go so far as to say I *like* it, but it doesn't suck tremendously."

"Such a ringing endorsement. I'll take it."

"There are the practical considerations, however. You knew her a very long time in our relative future and the citadel is a very long way away from here physically."

"Time isn't an issue since we have you. And as to distance, heck, I got nothing better to do. How 'bout you?"

"Aside from dying or spontaneously dissipating, no, nothing's on my day planner."

"So it's a date," I pronounced with all the enthusiasm I had left, which wasn't very much at all. "Ples, put us in the time frame we need to be in."

"Done," she replied instantly.

"Okay, RD, best warp speed to the Claxeon Citadel, my friend."

"Underway, Captain," he reported just as instantly.

"ETA?"

"Oh, with any luck and favorable winds, I'd estimate a week, give or take."

"Favorable winds? RD, might it be that you're evolving a sense of humor?" I teased.

"Possibly. Then again it might be from all this time collapse."

"You mean maybe some comedian has double-parked in your CPU?"

"With a matinee on Sundays," he responded.

"Can I get a rim shot," I declared. RD with the jokes. Wow, the universe must be ending.

The trip out was uneventful enough, which was notable in and of itself. I half-expected parts and pieces to fall off the ship or for Gloria's mother to darken my existence with a visit. But nothing bad happened at all. In fact, somewhere along the line, the curse of my loins, Gloria, actually disappeared. I can't say exactly when or under what circumstances, but she was gone. Remember I was hanging out mostly on the external hull? Yeah, Gloria could crush any opponent with her iron-willed grossness. But even that force of nature couldn't defy the vacuum of space.

Anyway, I eventually needed to fetch an item from storage. The first thing I noticed upon entering was that there wasn't a large black hole of stupid lurking aboard sucking the life out of everything, including inanimate objects. I asked RD when she'd vanished. He said he hadn't noticed specifically, but whatever day she'd flashed away should be declared a universal holiday. He could not be more correct. I almost felt sorry for wherever it was she'd been forwarded to. *Almost.* Self-preservation argued against too much lament.

We assumed direct orbit over the planet Flastor, where the citadel was located. On my previous visit, Tank and I had to sneak in, since the Brother-Sisterhood of Time was populated for the most part by vicious, ill-tempered isolationists. Their style concerning outsiders was to kill first and ask questions never. Presently we were too pressed for time to pussyfoot about. My plan was to locate my friend Miniminim as quickly as possible. I hoped that the overall confusion of time's collapse would have the meaner members of the citadel preoccupied enough to negate their immediate threat.

"Captain, we're in synchronous orbit over the Claxeon Citadel," RD finally announced.

"Good, bring us down to rooftop level quickly. If you detect any signs of a response to our arrival, let me know at once."

"Yes, sir." A minute later he spoke again. "We're at thirty meters, holding steady. No response from the citadel to this point."

"Great. Let me see a set of scans on the screen." I tapped the main screen with a knuckle. Once they were up, it didn't take me long to determine I was completely confused by what I was looking at. "RD, these readings don't make much sense."

"There is an odd distribution, I'll grant you that," he responded. "I would summarize that the scans reveal a hodgepodge of elements. Some random areas are cold, or maybe better said *static*. This suggests there is little activity there. Other areas are warm supporting the notion that there is activity there. These areas are oddly patchy. Some parts are normal in appearance, while others almost seem melted. Still other sections are basically gaps where I detect nothing at all."

"Are any aircraft active above the complex?"

"Negative."

"So, what does what you're seeing mean?" I pressed RD.

"I am at a complete loss to explain my observations. Sorry."

"The citadel is exhibiting varying degrees of damage from the collapse of time," Plesmus said ominously.

"Why differing degrees?" I posed.

"I do not know. I would observe that the areas that are empty, basically missing from existence, were mundane sites. The garden areas, the storage buildings, and the open spaces between the citadel and the outer walls."

"You can tell that from here?" I asked in uncertain incredulity.

"Generally yes. Those areas were peripheral and the pattern of them I recall fits with the dead areas I can feel."

"What about activity on the ground?" I asked.

"There is very little in any region. Obviously there is none in the missing sections," she replied.

"For all its time savvy, it looks like the citadel wasn't excluded from the madness," I said mostly to myself. "RD, put us down next to where Miniminim lives. Wait, is that location still present?"

"Yes, her building is in one of the cold spots," he reassured.

"The old girl's not going to like that. She complained of being cold on the hottest of days," I idly observed.

"We're down," he announced.

"Okay, I'm going exploring. You stay here, but keep the door locked if you can. I don't want anyone pushing random buttons and flying off into one of the moons."

"Very well, Captain."

I headed into the dormitory where I'd retrieved Miniminim many a morning. Unlike previous times, the place wasn't just quiet, it was as still as the grave. And it was quite cold, as RD had observed. I turned the corner to where the evil witch Sister Helper Coordinator Bel-Jil-Nor used to sit as guard against all potential threats to female virtue. Those were basically any male who appeared within her vision, by the way. But the humorless sister was not at her post. My, but that was a harbinger of ill-outcomes, wasn't it? I checked around to make sure she wasn't about to spring herself on me like a cobra. Nope, bitch was missing. I proceeded to Miniminim's quarters.

When I arrived at her door it was closed. Not surprising, but I'd hoped it was open so I could determine quickly if she was in. Who knew where she'd be in a crisis? Failing any better option, I knocked firmly.

No response.

I knocked more firmly.

Still nothing.

Forced to have to try the door uninvited, I actually prayed the old bat Bel-Jil-Nor wasn't hiding inside with handcuffs and a cattle prod, ready to teach me a proper lesson for violating a location in her protectorate. Luckily she didn't leap from the dark and yell *gotcha.*

Instead, I found Miniminim laying still on her bed. Recall, please, that she was a large, blobby creature with numerous tentacles; no movement was a difficult act for her to pull off. I feared the worst, and stepped softly toward her.

"Hey, Miniminim," I called out gently. "It's your old assistant, Jon. I'm here to help."

She still didn't stir. Finally, I knelt beside her and leaned in to listen for sounds of life.

"It's about *time,*" she barked, causing me to very nearly jump out of my polyalloy skin.

I rested my palm on my chest. "Don't scare me like that."

"You're not afraid of anything, ya big baby. What took you so long?"

"Took me so long? What? Isn't this time period *after* when I left here?"

"Yes, but I knew you'd be back. I just forgot the part about you always being late on account of your fundamentally lazy nature."

"I was *never* later," I protested with a grin. I'd missed her and her cantankerous wit.

"Stop making excuses and help me sit up," she chastised.

I lifted her halfway up as gently as I could then stuffed some pillows under her. "Since when did a tough old bird like you need help sitting up?" I teased.

"I don't. But I felt it might make you uncomfortable to nurse me, so I went for it."

"Same old Minim."

"There, that's far enough." She kind of gurgled a bit, maybe it was more of a wheeze. Whatever it was didn't sound so good.

"Are you sick? Do you want me to fetch a doctor?"

"I'm not sick and no I don't want a physician badgering me at a time like this."

"A time like what?"

"A time like when I'm dying, you insensitive jerk."

"Wait, you said you weren't sick. Now you're dying? Don't you have to be sick to die?"

"Always such a simple mind. I'd forgotten your profound limitations."

"Look, if you're on death's doorstep, I'm getting the doc."

"First off, there are no medical personnel anymore. They either ran for the hills, disappeared, or both."

"What's second?" I asked naively.

"You're an insensitive jerk."

"You just said that."

"Because it's double true. Now do you want to argue with a dying person or do you want to help?"

"Ah, help. Yes, I'd rather help." I winked at her.

"Good. Then shut up and listen."

"Can do."

She studied me a second. "If I had a stick I do believe I'd hit you with it."

"Then I'm anxious to help with anything I can *except* the getting for you of a stick."

"Time is collapsing but you've got time enough for lame jokes. Are you a dad? You tell dad jokes."

"Seriously, Miniminim, what can I help with?"

"Jon, time is not supposed to end like this," she stated flatly.

Because I was, you know, a bit defensive as to my role in the collapse of time, I reacted ... well, in self-interest. "Now, come on, we don't know time is *collapsing* collapsing. It might be more a time reset, or a time hiccup."

She studied me for longer this time. "Oh, my kingdom for a stick."

"No stick for you," I declared , pointing at her.

"Jon, I have foreseen the end of time."

"Ah, that's ... that's not a freaky thing to hear another person say."

"It's true. And guess what? This isn't how time's supposed to end."

"*See*," I responded with false bravado. "Like I said, this may just be a bad-time-day, you know, like a bad-hair-day, only time, not hair."

"Jon, you are many things, but one of them is not an idiot. Why are you defending such an absurd..."

Uh oh. I didn't like the sound of that silence.

"You caused this, didn't you?" she breathed softly. "I don't know how you did it, but you caused the collapse of time. So you pretend what is happening plainly before your eyes is not the case."

"Can we get back to my helping and away from Jon-bashing?"

"Yes. Please remove those pillows."

I did.

"Now ease me back down."

Again, I did so.

"Now leave me and never return."

Ah, that'd be a no way.

"Miniminim, you said you needed help. I can help. What's the matter?"

"I don't need help so badly that I would ask it of the fool who ended time."

"Aw, come on now. That's completely unfair and really hurtful."

"Whined the numbskull who ended time six *billion* years before it was supposed to," she growled.

"If I did do that, you have to know it would have been for the best of reasons."

She just rolled over and displayed her backside to me.

"Minimi," I begged, "come on. Ask away of me."

"I just wish to die in peace," she replied pathetically.

I was such a bad man.

"Please, Miniminim, don't shut me down. Yes, I had a *role* in what's happening."

Plesmus chose that moment to deliver a particularly nasty shock to my ankle.

"But trust me when I say I'm trying to make it right again. That's why I'm here, to see if you can advise me."

"Only one piece of advice."

"Yes, old friend?"

"Leave."

"Miniminim, stop it."

"Your necumplack friend is right to shock you. I wish she'd have used more voltage though."

"Ah, how'd you ... like, know there was a necumplack on my boot who just unfairly gave me an electric shock?"

"Jon, don't belabor the obvious with a dying old lady," she complained.

She lay there for several minutes, leaving me to sweat it out on pins and needles.

"Jon," she finally said as if from a great distance.

"Yes?"

"I can't be mad at you."

"Thanks. That means more than you can know."

"And I'm sorry I can't help you. If I had any plans as to how to arrest the collapse of time, trust me, I'd have already set them in motion."

"Thanks, my friend."

"And there is one thing I would ask of you."

"Anything. Well, anything but a stick."

"The reliquary is opening."

"Beg pardon?"

"You heard me. The time reliquary is opening. I can feel it."

"What's inside the time reliquary?" I rather stupidly asked.

"The Relic of Time, you idiot," she snapped.

"No, I know that much, or, at least I know what reliquaries store. What I meant was what *specifically* is the Relic of Time?"

"No one alive knows. It was placed in the Museum of Time eons ago. There's no record of how long ago it was."

"We have a museum devoted to time?" I asked astounded.

"Of course we have a time museum. And, Jon, there's no *Jon* in *we*. You were never really a scholastic here, remember?"

"I sure never heard about any museum," I responded petulantly.

"Jon, you were a spy trying to infiltrate the Brother-Sisterhood to steal secrets. It wasn't like you were on our Historical Preservations Committee."

"Is it a nice museum?" I asked, maybe a bit too fixated on the dumb museum.

"It could use more color and maybe a better snack bar, but sure, it's a nice museum."

"Cool."

"I want you to go there for me."

"To the Museum of Time?"

"Yes. That's where the relic is located."

"Okay, I can do that. Do ... do you want me to help you go there yourself?"

"No. I'm dying. But I want you to go there, see what is inside the reliquary, and come back and tell me. I need to know if I'm to die contented."

"Ah. And you say it's being opened now?"

"No, it's opening itself, poorly listening primate. Once it has, I would like to know what the relic is before I die."

"Sure. Where's this museum?"

"It's part of the main library building."

"The one near the little pond?"

"That's the one."

"Should I go now?"

"Hmm, let me see. The Relic of Time is actively opening and I am actively dying. I'd say that's a big old *yes*."

"Then I'm on my way." I stood. "Is there anything else I can bring you?"

"A few more months'd be nice."

"I'll see what I can do."

The citadel grounds were huge, so it took me a little while to hoof it all the way over to the museum. When I arrived at the main library, I was surprised to see all kinds of directions posted to the Museum of Time. Man, I'd spent months in this library and had never noticed the hints. Sometimes I can be such a guy.

I assumed the place would be crowded, but even as I entered the museum proper I could tell it was nearly abandoned. Of course, what I had traveled through on the jog over could explain that low level of attendance at a premier event like this. Much of the grounds looked like a war zone that had been run through a blender and then poured back where it had been. Subdued and respectful signage directed me through the empty hallways toward the Relic of Time. The reliquary itself was the sole article in a small room at the back to the museum. I guess it was not center stage since time didn't end often enough to warrant a prime spot in the museum. The container was stationed on a low pedestal made of some kind of plastic. The reliquary was maybe two meters tall, and half a meter on each side. It was also cracked and steaming like a dragon giving birth to an oversized hatchling.

"You cannot be here," shouted a voice from behind me.

I turned to see an old monk scurrying toward me. Ancient fart wasn't making very good time on account of old Mr. Arthritis being in every joint of his body. He sort of gyrated toward me.

"Oh, yeah?" I challenged. "Says who?"

"I am Atozachron. I'm in charge of this display. It must not be disturbed. You will depart immediately."

"Not likely. Miniminim herself sent me to document the process."

"I don't care," he proclaimed as he involuntarily slowed, "if my mother sent you. You cannot be here."

"No can do. I *can*, however, knock you out if you don't lighten the hell up, Pops."

Either physiology or my words did the trick. Atozachron wobbled to an uncertain stop about ten meters away. "You dare threaten—"

Fortunately, the old goat shut up when the reliquary emitted a loud snap-crackle-thud. One of the wider cracks burgeoned into a split, and then the top snapped off. It swung back like a tin-can lid that wasn't completely freed by the can opener's blade.

"Oh, my," Atozachron said with trepidation.

"It's show time," I declared ... well, because I'm me.

"The Relic of Time is revealed," the old monk announced in a hushed tone with raised arms.

And it was. In all its dubious glory, the Relic of Time rose until it floated just above the rim of its former container. A soft light projected up from the inside of the reliquary, illuminating it just so.

I wasn't maybe *as* excited as Atozachron was at the sight of it. Miniminim sure as hell wasn't going to be pleased in the slightest when I told her what the Relic of Time was. With any luck she'd die before I could bring word back to her.

How could I be so absolutely freaking certain that the damn relic would be a bitter disappointment to Miniminim? Well, I should know. The damn relic was me. Crap, I was even life-sized and wearing the exact same flipping outfit as I did right then.

In stunned disbelief, I watched this image, maybe it was a hologram, hell maybe it was a paint-by-numbers image. I couldn't tell and I surely didn't care. It didn't actually *do* anything. I was just standing there looking... I don't know, serene? Man, I hate serene in the context of an image of me. I—and you can take this to the bank—am not Mother Teresa. If you want to make her appear serene, go for it.

Me, all I can say is grrr. If it was a marble statue, I'd have climbed up there and defaced my face.

In my anger, you'll never ever guess what I flashed on. The damn Hall of Presidents at Disneyland. Back when I was a kid, my parents took me to Dizzyland every few summers. It was superb. One year I got bored enough to check out the Hall of Presidents attraction on Main Street. Sheesh, what a yawnfest. But that floating image of me would have fit right in at that insipid attraction. I was never going to get that foul image out of my head. If I ever ran into old Walt, I'd sucker punch him even though he didn't really do anything besides sign-off on a dull animatronic show. It's all about the context in my book. Sorry, Walt.

From bad to worse to horrible. This just wasn't my day.

SIX

Queen Loopi-goah marched with slow purpose along a catwalk leading toward one of her few remaining warships. She was flanked by her dagger, Jiail-fus, and one other trusted Six-Killer. No chatter was exchanged as the trio advanced on the open hatch to *Void's Ending*, a perversely presciently named vessel. The set of the queen's face read as only determined. The party swept onto the capital ship without a word to the pair of stationed guards. Neither sailor was dumb enough to say peep to so driven a monarch and her ever so deadly attendants.

The queen proceeded directly to the bridge, where the captain, a competent officer named Enoori-bar, sat perusing a set of dull reports. Upon sight of her, the captain leaped to attention. The rest of the bridge crew followed suit and ballistically assumed a rigid stance.

"Your Majesty, wh ... what an unexpected yet welcome—" Enoori started to babble.

"Shut it," Loopi snarled.

She did not have to ask the captain twice. Her new pose defied anatomical limitations and stiffened further. She became the very picture of stony inflexibility.

"I'm here to take my warship out to personally deliver justice to the defiler," the queen announced once she came face-to-face not two centimeters from the captain's now-quivering mug.

"I ... we ... as a ship in service to you ... ah, it would seem more ... well, if you were to ask almost anyone ... er, sorry," the captain bungled along. For the sake of practicality, she should have simply retrieved a shovel to more efficiently dig her own grave. But, in her defense, she was appropriately overwhelmed.

"Cease all speaking," the queen howled. Her dagger reflexively flashed over to rest her spear tip on the captain's short, stumpy throat. The queen made no move to have Jiail-fus back off. She just continued her close-ranged glare at her officer.

The addled captain almost responded to her in the affirmative, but then thought better of the move.

"I have sent captain after captain to kill this high villain," she said in a psychopathically calm tone. "And do you know what those cowardly and treasonous vermin did for me by way of service?"

The captain's exclusive thoughts were *Please be a rhetorical question, please be a rhetorical question.*

"That's right," she continued. "They betrayed me. They allied themselves with evil incarnate, they voided their digestive tracts upon my person, that's what the worthless, useless, excuse-ridden backstabbers did. They did everything, in fact, *except* to follow my simple orders to harass and torment that demon throughout all of time."

Thank the Makers, it was a rhetorical question, Thank the Makers, it was a rhetorical question, ricocheted around the captain's head like a smiling bullet.

"So, surrounded by only craven quitters, it falls to me to do what is necessary. Thus, Captain Enoori-bar, I am assuming command of my ship. You are obviously also a blithering, lying, worthless turncoat. That is a given. But since you have yet to *manifest* these vile traits by failing me, I shall indulge you. You may not only continue to live, but you may accompany me on my triumphant quest to maul, dismember, and mutilate the defiler." She did the Void phantom equivalent of wagging her eyebrows at her. "Am I not a loving and just queen?"

Oh, the poor captain. She was back to the state of frantically screaming in her head, *Please be a rhetorical question, please be a rhetorical question.* On the extremely off chance she survived the day, she was going to require extensive and prolonged psychological interventions, and even then, she would surely be permanently scarred.

"Push off now," the queen decreed. "We need to make haste, in order to lay waste."

The captain very, very, very slowly backed away from the deadly-poison-coated spear tip pressing way too firmly against her throat. Once well clear of it and its owner's intent, she eased very, very, *very* slowly toward the control station. Once there she pressed a series of icons and pushed a few levels. "We are disengaging from our mooring clamps, Your Highness. We will be ready to rotate within a few minutes. Then we are free to make haste."

"Make it happen more quickly. My teeth yearn to rip at flesh. The sooner it is the defiler's, the less likely it will be yours they tear into, good captain."

Please move faster, damn ship. Please move faster, damn ship, pulsed through her already bedeviled mind. Seriously, she was a work-related psychiatric injury in progress, the poor girl.

Within a few minutes the captain was able to confirm that *Void's Ending* was clear of the docks and ready for the chase. "Where ... er, precisely shall we set course, Your Grace?" she asked as deferentially as possible. She even, due no doubt to some heretofore repressed survival instinct, dropped to the deck and groveled.

"Fly to the edge of the Void. Our quarry lies in its own filth out there somewhere in timed space," she replied in a quiet yet most intensely insane tone. "Once we are there, I will know where to point my ship." She nodded maniacally, like the queen-possessed that she was.

As short while later, *Void's Ending* pierced the Void barrier and entered the Milky Way galaxy. It was a historic moment. It was also a regrettable and a tragic moment for the Void. For that instant in time marked the first and only occasion when a reigning monarch of the Void left their domain. In the bewilderingly long history of the Timeless Void, a few adventurers had left to explore or attack some part of timed space. But no *ruler* had ever separated from the Void. Ah, but if retrospect was just another tool in your back pocket, you could pull it out and apply it at will. Perhaps then matters would have ended better for the Void.

Apparently there existed no awareness in living memory or the written record of the intimate relationship between the Timeless Void and its monarch. One, it would soon be manifested, could not exist without the other. Why this was mystically the case was also equally unknown to the soon-to-be-sorry Void phantoms. But it's better not to get ahead of the tale.

Once through the barrier, the queen paced the bridge predatorially. With exaggerated sniffs, she sucked in reality to glean the location of her most hated of hated. It took her a few minutes, but then she flowed back into her typical posture, which was stiff, detached, and threatening. "We sail that way, Captain," she announced, gesturing with a few arms in one particular direction.

The silly captain momentarily had an impulse to clarify with the queen what the precise vector she wished to assume, what speed she wished to make, and how far off their quarry was. Good fortune slapped a hand over her mouth before she could inquire on any of those topics. If the captain asked, her answers would change nothing, except that she might upset the bitch sufficiently by asking that she'd have her pitched off the ship, quite likely directly through the hull.

Silence was not only golden; in this case it was life giving.

After several hours, the queen, who had otherwise remained as still as a statue, stirred to speak again. "As my perfectly clear directions seemed to be too difficult for you to have followed, Captain, redirect my ship that way."

The captain struggled to divine exactly what vector she pointed along. But she was unable to glean any clue as to what course change was needed. She could simply ask the queen for clarity on the topic, but, then again, she could cut out the middleman and try to throw herself through the hull. No, she loudly ordered an arbitrary course alteration. She then tried to force her body to become invisible. She had correctly determined that she was more likely to will invisibility than she was to otherwise survive this voyage. Why the hell try to salvage value in the voyage, she figured pragmatically?

A few minutes later the queen leaned over and whispered something to her dagger. By the time Loopi-goah was back in her former position, Jiail-fus was all the way across the bridge and had impaled her spear through the chest of the navigator. If it was possible and even decent to say, the navigator was the luckiest phantom on the bridge. Between the dagger's blinding speed, her deadly accuracy, and the hideously toxic poison that tipped the spear, he did not live long enough to realize he was dying. Thank goodness for minor miracles. The rest of the crew was less likely to have such a positive death-experience.

"Captain, you continue to bungle the correct execution of my orders. This costs me time. It will now begin to cost you bridge crew. I count four remaining, you being the fourth. If you do not speed me directly to my target competently, I will kill off a crew member every five minutes. Any questions?"

She had one. She really wanted to ask, but stayed her tongue. If a member of the crew was to be eliminated every five minutes, had the navigator been on a silent countdown, or was he not afforded the courtesy of a brief warning that doom was upon him? A silent countdown was lame in the extreme, but it was less insulting than no countdown at all. The captain's blood threatened to boil. And it would have to, were she not so fully committed to the off chance of self-preservation at all costs.

"Thank you for sharing with us your concern, my queen," she mumbled idiotically.

"I sense the defiler is no more than ten minutes away, if you finally consent to follow my directions, worthless captain."

"I am humbled by your lowering yourself to explain this to me, my queen." She was then torn with indecision. Should she make some new random course alteration? Should she ask for a better understanding from her wretched monarch? Should she try to leap through the hull? She just wasn't sure. All she knew was numbing fear. She also found she could not pry any of her eyes off the chronometer situated to the side of the main view screen.

Exactly five minutes after the departure of the navigator's soul, the queen announced, "We are nearly there."

The captain's desperation elevated to but *moderate* despair at the thought that another crew member would not be lost. Her improved mood turned out to be nothing more than wishful thinking.

Loopi nodded to her dagger, who hurled her spear across the bridge and completely through the unsuspecting science officer who had been tapping at some icons. The weapon clanked loudly to the deck, followed immediately by the late science officer's thud.

"But I thought—" the silly captain protested.

Loopi nodded to the other guard, and another bridge officer was dispatched to meet their maker.

"I do not require that you think, Captain. In fact, I urge you not to. Just follow my orders. In announcing that we were close to my enemy, I meant to emphasize that we were not as-of-yet *there*. The delay cost you one officer. Your insolence cost you a second. I would ask if you'd like to gamble the last one remaining between you and a painful death. I will not, however, do so since I can tell that the defiler is just outside my ship."

"That is such wonder—"

The captain stopped talking when she realized she could see through the queen. The bulkhead that should have been eclipsed by the royal body was now partially visible to her. Oh, no. Another dilemma. Should she mention the queen's thinning out? Should she rush somehow to aid her queen? Should she thank her lucky stars that the mega-pain-in-the-ass would soon be gone?

"Speak up, you inconsequential fool," the queen demanded.

"I would like... I mean I feel it is incumbent upon me to point out... th... that your body... er—"

"Speak plainly or die," she tried to thunder. She recognized immediately that it came out more of a peep than a roar. She set several hands on her torso. "What is wrong with me?" she asked mostly to herself, not the insignificant beings that stood around her.

"My Queen," the second of her guards blurted out in a panic, "look at your person. You seem to be fading." He pointed wildly at her center of mass.

Loopi did look down and study her chest. It was semi-transparent. The queen was not a person in favor of change, any change. Since she had never before been partially see-through, that fact that she now was displeased her eleven on a scale of one-to-ten. There is an old saying: Do not shoot the messenger. Let it be officially known that Queen Loopi-goah had no use for such a mercy. She nodded toward the Six-Killer who'd announced the calamity while looking at her dagger.

The guard didn't have a chance to flinch before Jiail's sword sailed through him horizontally. She then swiped vertically, and again horizontally so quickly that he was in six pieces before any one of them had the time to hit the deck.

"My Quee ... Mu ... Mu—" the captain stammered. Believe it or not, she wasn't attempting to offer her an update on her insubstantiality. No, she was trying like the dickens to respectfully request that she not sully this treasured workspace any further with blood and gore. Seriously, she just had reached her mess limit.

The dagger, naturally, assumed the next phantom to fall victim to her sword would be the captain with misplaced notions of the relative virtues of cleanliness when compared to not pissing off her already maniacal monarch. Jiail's blood lust was so high that she uncharacteristically risked addressing her queen. Leveling her sword at the captain, she asked, "Is this pig next, Majesty?"

But answer came there none.

Jiail did not want to remove her eyes from her *delicious*, least she slip away alive. Psychotically enough, that's what she termed her victims, because killing was so very *delicious*. Yeah, can anyone say sicko?

"Majesty, shall I disembowel her in your honor?" she pressed.

"She's not there," the captain declared more than a little bit impatient with the over-fixated guard.

"Yes, my supper, you'd like that, wouldn't you?" she taunted.

The captain honestly thought Jiail had addressed her as my *superior*. So, in her mind, she had falsely deduced that the foaming-at-the-mouth Six-Killer was expressing the idea that she, her better, would like the queen to be gone. So, the captain responded, "It's not my fault. But, between you and me, if that's the way it is, I can't say I'd be disappointed."

Now that gave Jiail pause. She quickly reviewed. *I called her my supper. I said she'd like it. To which, she responded that it was not her fault that she wanted to eat her. That was true, but creepy of the captain to think. And she also was specific in expressing that she wasn't disappointed that she said she wanted to eat the captain. What a profoundly disturbed mind this captain had.*

It hit Jiail like all of Cupid's arrow to her forehead at once. She loved this woman! She was her soulmate! She was unbelievably creepy *and* she was insanely masochistic. Jiail's loins actually warmed at the very thought of such a union. She threw down her sword, dropped to one knee, and all but shouted, "Marry me here-and-now."

The captain then quickly reviewed. *She acknowledged my superior rank. She agreed that the mysterious vanishing of her master was a good thing. And she basically stated she was ready to follow her anywhere. Then she proposed marriage, confirming all of the above. The woman was a subservient masochist. Her dream date!* Her loins similarly warmed. "I will take your soul," she shouted triumphantly.

Yeah, passion clouds the senses. When she thought she heard, "I will take your *role*," she was done. She was all-in. "Put this ship on autopilot and I shall have you here on the bridge," the dagger ordered.

The captain heard that one loud and clear. With Queen Loopi-goah a forgotten factor, she locked the bridge hatch and set the autopilot, and settled in for what was—you had to know—going to be a wacky few weeks of confused debauchery.

Unbeknownst to the now oblivious love/hate birds—and like they had even the energy to care—the queen's disappearance was intimately joined with the integrity of the Void itself. If left without a resident monarch for long enough, the Void itself would begin to dissipate and ultimately disappear, just as its ruler had. As the Void itself was infinitely more massive than one phantom, the time required would be in terms of months, not moments. But weakened it was. That was the critical take-away message. However resistant the Void had been to its destruction, it was less and less so with each passing moment.

They say all good things must end. Wow, it turns out that at maybe all evil ones must also. Who knew?

SEVEN

I lingered a few minutes by the time reliquary to see if Hall-of-Presidents-me was going to actually do anything other than float and look serenely asinine. He did not. He just wafted as if in the breeze and had that Mona-Lisa almost-grin on his dumbass face. No revelations, no manifestations, not even a few snappy one-liners. Nothing. That me was as useless as a penis on a pineapple.

What to do next? A) I could either return to Miniminim and break her dying heart with the news regarding the time relic or B) I could spare her the pain and beat a hasty retreat. I had promised to observe and dutifully report. So, morally, I was on the hook to bring her up to speed so she could die in frustration and anger, not, you know, just alone and none-the-wiser. The humane thing to do would be to—oops—forget to go tell her.

So, what was the Ryanesque solution? Mix one part A with one part B. I would return to her chamber, hope to Heaven she was already dead, and, if she wasn't, I'd lie to her dying face. Yeah, pretty messed up, right? Welcome to the Ryanverse.

As I turned to enter her long hallway, I still couldn't help spying for the humanoid chastity belt, Sister Bel-Jil-Nor. The old battle-axe really did leave an impression on me. Fortunately, she was still dead, or whatever. I tiptoed to Miniminim's door, which I'd left ajar. I opened it as quietly as I could. Hey, if she was asleep, I'd have a plausible out, because I could claim I didn't want to disturb the poor dear's last peaceful moments. No such luck.

"I hear you," she called out. "If you're a random intruder bent on mayhem, please come in. I'm expecting a jerkwad named Jon Ryan to return anytime. Before he does, please allow me to sell him into slavery to you."

"Sorry, just me," I beamed.

"Shoot. I coulda used the cash. I had my mind set on an overpriced yet oddly plain headstone I can't presently afford."

"Well, I'm afraid you'll just have to live with the disappointment. The good news is that, according to you, your displeasure won't last too awfully long." I sat at her bedside.

"I missed you, you big oaf."

"Back atcha, my old friend," I responded tenderly.

"So, what's the verdict? Did it open and, if so, what was inside?"

"I have an update and a question."

"Crap. Like I have time for this."

"First, yes, the reliquary opened. It was very peaceful and tasteful."

"And your stupid question?" she huffed.

"What would you like the relic to be?"

She rolled over to look at me. "Jon, this isn't a popularity contest. I don't get a vote. The relic is what the relic is."

I raised a finger. "I'm just asking. If you had a wish, what would you wish the relic to be?"

Her eyes all drifted off. She seemed lost in thought. "Honestly, if I were the committee of one responsible for filling it, I'd place an epically detailed sculpture of Hexixissis in there."

"I did not see that option coming," I confessed. "And he/she/it would be?"

"Someone I knew as a youngster back home."

"Someone wise and learned in all things time?" I ventured a guess.

"No, silly. He was a hunk. Built like a god and totally bone-jumpable."

"Miniminim, I am shocked."

"No, you're not. You're jealous, that's what you are."

"Only partially. So, anyway, the relic wasn't this joker Hexixissis. Well, I assume not. He's your species, right, looks basically like you do?"

"The hells he does. I'm a plain Jane. He's a burning hunk of neo-god."

"I'll take that as a yes. So, no, it wasn't a statue of him."

"Jon, this suspense, it may literally kill me. Out with it."

"Alright." I fluttered my eyes closed and spread my arms out wide. "When I beheld the Relic of Time, I knew there was a divine intervention at play. I was at peace, filled with joy, and also imbued with the eternal promise of love, justice, and the sanctity of time. It was as if my mother had returned from her great reward to bear me again in her womb of acceptance. All I can say—"

That's when I was swatted across the face with a stick. Miniminim held it in a snaky arm, and was leaning way out of her bed to strike me.

"Hey," I protested, "where'd you get that?"

"It took you so long I knew I was going to need one. I went outside and found it while you lollygagged."

"Well, it really stings, so do not hit me again."

"Hey, I might not live, but you will, ya wuss."

"You are so cruel."

"So, while I still draw breath, what is the Relic of Time?" She raised the stick to remind me there was a consequence for tomfoolery.

"Okay, but don't say I didn't try and spare you. I was inside the reliquary."

"How could you be?"

"I know, morally, temporally, and didactically, it makes no sense."

"No, you nut, how could you be in it and outside of it at the same time?"

"Oh. No, it was a holographic image of me."

What served as her face contorted badly. "You're shitting me?"

"Such language. Really."

"There's a glass of water on the nightstand. Use it to extinguish your burning ears, ya big baby."

"Thanks," I snarked. "So, that's it. A holo of me rose from the crypt. End of story. Now, I really should be going. Is there anything I can do for you or get before I hit the road?"

"Hexixissis would be nice."

"Anything *other* than your loin's greatest desire?"

"Nope, not a thing."

I was stunned. "Really?"

"Really. Hey, it's been a gas seeing you again, human. Close the door on your way out of my life forever."

I stood tentatively. "Sure then—"

"Jon, sit," she ordered.

I sat.

"Why the hells are *you* the Relic of Time? You were a traitor here, a spy. What's more, you singlehandedly destroyed time. And we reward you with a reliquary? Makes zero sense."

"I can't differ with you on anything you've said."

"I assumed the relic would be some tribute to a great figure of the past. At least I thought it'd be worth living long enough to see firsthand."

"Hey, I wouldn't have put me in there either. Damn poor taste, judgment, or both." I harrumphed. "Probably some committee of mental midgets made the call."

"Jon, there's no committee of half-witted morons that'd be clueless enough to honor you as the relic. Sorry to burst your bubble."

Hmm. "Maybe it wasn't an honor they intended to bestow?" I mused quietly.

"What? Well, why else would you put some image in a reliquary? They're for honoring people, right?"

I shrugged. "I've lived a long time, but I've had almost no experiences with relics and reliquaries. Not my type of theater, if you will." I tented my fingers in front of my face. "What if my image was placed in there as a warning?"

She rested back. "That's a thought. But, no. Why put out a warning after the fact? You've already destroyed time. It's a little late to issue an all-points bulletin."

"True," I mumbled. "Maybe someone's gloating. Showing off that their guess was correct."

"That's the best explanation yet. But it's kind of a mean-spirited relic choice, you know, a personal declaration that some schmuck a long time ago guessed who the destroyer of time would be."

"Huh, yeah, one mean..."

"What?"

"Do you ever get that feeling ... like someone's walking over your grave?"

"Ah, that'd be a *no*. I'm almost dead, not dead-and-buried."

"I just had the worst premonition."

"About?"

"Who put what in the reliquary."

"Jon, it's already open. You can't have a premonition about a done deal."

"True." I stood. "Look, do me a favor."

"If I can," she agreed.

I pointed at her as I turned. "Don't die until I get back."

"Gee whiz, I'll sure try my best."

"Fine. This won't take long."

"It had better not. Mama's got a date with Hexixissis in the afterlife. I want to get there before the line's too awfully long."

I strode quickly from the room and back to the library. Man, I hoped I was wrong.

As I entered the reliquary, that lame old Atozachron tried to snag me at the door. "You can't come in here. There's a recently opened reliquary. We need time to prepare it for public viewing." Then the idiot jumped onto my back.

I turned so my back pointed at the door frame and leaped backward. With an *oomph* the pest let go and crumpled to the floor. "May I come in anyway?" I asked the gasping heap. "Thanks." I headed back to inspect the relic.

The image of me was still there, still floating like the last pickle in the jar. I studied the holo closely. The face was clean. The clothes, they were robe-like and wavy, but held no clue. Oh, crap. Yup, there it was. The hands. My right hand displayed the thumb tucked under the four bent fingers. "E" in American Sign Language. And, you guessed it, my left hand was contorted into the thumb tucked under the first three digits and my pinkie was arcing ever so slowly up and down. "J."

EJ. That son of a ... wait, I can't say that about my own mother.

EJ had placed an image of me in the damn reliquary. My evil twin, or actually an evil alternate timeline Jon Ryan, had pulled this stunt. Damn him. What a jerkfest! All the Relic of Time bullshit was him giving a future me the finger. Somehow, he knew or guessed that I'd destroy time. Rather than stop me or warn me, he settled for just flipping me off.

And what if I never came to the citadel, never learned of the relic? Well, he'd still know and think it was the most clever FU ever. He'd have died—hopefully miserably—knowing the trap he'd set.

Head down, shoulder stooped, I turned and left. As I passed the archivist, I tapped him fairly gently with the toe of my boot. "Nice exhibit, but it could use some up-lighting. See ya around."

I made my way slowly back to Miniminim's room. I entered and plopped down in the chair without a word.

"So, what did we learn?" she pressed.

"That I'm a jerkfest."

She shook her head. "We knew that."

"No, it's kind of a long story."

"Well, you start it. If I die before you finish, feel free to stop."

"You got it. I come from a world that was about to be destroyed by a sister planet. As part of our attempt to flee, we ran across a nasty species called the Listhelons. Once they learned of us, they destroyed my home and every living thing on it. An alternate timeline version of me button-holed me and gave me the tools to avoid that fate. We did. Unfortunately, that me had become a decrepit shell of a man, hence my name for him, Evil Jon Ryan, or EJ for short."

"This is kind of long. Seems obtuse as well," she pointed out.

"There is a point. The hologram was placed there by him. It's a screw-you to me, via the web of time."

"Your evil twin went to the time and trouble to not only infiltrate the order, but rise to a position to create and fill our reliquary, just to insult you?"

"Yes, he did. He's a real—"

"I like him already. Shame I had to meet this version, not the sexy one."

"*Miniminim!*" I complained loudly.

"Just pulling your private parts, human. Seriously, EJ was one messed-up dude."

"You can say that again."

But Miniminim did not. I looked up. She had quietly passed. I stood and kissed her on the forehead. "Godspeed, sweet princess."

"RD, get us out of here," I commanded in a fatigued tone.

"Fine. Where shall we go?"

"For now, just dust off. Once we're clear of Flastor's atmosphere, bring us up to full speed in the direction of Earth."

"Are we in any particular danger I am unaware of?" Plesmus asked cautiously.

"Yeah, remembering and regretting."

"Ah, I think I'll just leave you to your thoughts then," she finished.

"Fucking EJ," I growled.

"Captain," RD cut back in, "even at best speed, that trip will take—"

"No, that's just a heading. I'm not sure that's where I'll decide to go. I want to be clear of the citadel."

"Understood."

I felt the rumble of our liftoff. Then I sort of spaced out, pondering what new flavor of shit shake I was about to be chugging down next.

"Captain." RD interrupted my dark train of thought a few minutes later. "Just an update. We're at point-four c now, best speed, vectoring toward Earth."

"Fine. Keep me posted. I'm going to be trying to figure out what to do next."

"Let me know if I might help," RD offered graciously. I appreciated the support. At least one entity in the known universe was still in my corner.

We sailed along for I can't say how long. I was lost in a mire of self-loathing and self-pity, one truly contradictory and unhelpful set of dance partners. The fact that those negative emotions were virgin territory for me made them weigh all the more heavily on me. I realized at some point that RD was trying to get my attention.

"Captain. Please respond. Captain, I have a critical update. Please respond."

"Wh ... what? I'm here."

"Yes, you are physically present, but I've been pestering you for almost a full minute."

"No. Report."

"At the limit of my sensors a ship has appeared."

"Configuration?"

"It's still too far out to be certain, but I suspect it's a Void craft."

"With no tachyon burst?"

"No, none. This one appears to be moving under a conventional drive in our direction."

"That's weird."

"I'll grant that it's a novel approach on their part. They've certainly dispensed with the element of surprise."

"ETA?"

"If both our vectors hold, about twenty minutes."

"I am so tired of these asswipes coming after me. I have half a mind..."

"Yes, Captain?"

"You know what, set an intercept course for the bogey."

"If you think that wise."

"Who the hell knows? But at least we'll get this over sooner. Plus, I'm in the mood to kick some ass."

"Course altered. New ETA fourteen minutes twenty-eight seconds."

"In fourteen minutes, put us dead in space. I'll be ready to throw up a membrane. They'll almost certainly come in with all guns blazing."

"Are you certain engaging them flatfooted is a good tactic, Captain?"

"No, I'm sure it's a shitty tactic. But, like I said, I'm in the mood to not avoid a fight. Nothing says *let's do this* like lying dead in space."

"If you say so."

"I do." I had a big old smile on my face too.

Just under fourteen minutes later, RD updated me. "The Void ship is coming to rest also. There, they are half a kilometer off our port bow, dead in space like we are."

"Are they arming weapons?"

"Not that I can tell."

"Huh."

"Your orders?"

"Let's wait and see what they do first. Who knows, maybe they're here to offer their formal surrender."

"Do you think that likely?" he puzzled.

"No, but I'm willing to let them act first. Then I'll blow their shit up."

"I shall target their engines with our plasma weapon and rail guns."

"Yes, but don't activate them just yet."

"As you wish."

I could tell he was dubious in the extreme, but he was also an obedient little AI, so he dutifully followed my orders.

"Captain, a most odd process is transpiring on the enemy's bridge."

"What?"

"The number of live bodies is decreasing. At first the changes were spaced apart, but now they are occurring more rapidly. And, even more remarkably, of the three remaining living members, one is ... one is—"

"You're killing me, dude. What?"

"One life form seems to be fading away."

"You mean like dying slowly, right? Gut shot or something?"

"No ... I mean, possibly. Well, I've recorded a lot of deaths over my time. This is more ... more smooth and orchestrated than I'm accustomed to witnessing."

"Hey, as long as it ends up with one more of them dead, I'm all in favor. If I had a bottle of champagne, I'd pop the sucker."

"I'll keep you ... there. Now only two life forms are present on the enemy bridge. The body that was fading is no longer present."

"Did the other two eat it real fast?"

"Unlikely. They are mostly stationary."

"Did it evaporate?" That was a lame guess, but I felt compelled to determine a mechanism.

"No, the ship's mass actually decreased. But whatever the process, the third party on the bridge simply no longer exists."

"Well, as I say, any port in a storm. Dead, beamed-up, sucked into a black hole. It's all good."

"I'll place that in the *if you say so* category."

"But still no hostile intent is evident?" I pressed. This was one phantom encounter of the weird kind.

"No ... cancel that."

"They're powering up weapons?"

"No, sir. Engines. The Void ship has just set course for ... hmm, there's nothing obvious along their new vector to suggest an actual course."

"That's crazy talk."

"Yes, but the nearest celestial body along their present course in a brown dwarf star in the Andromeda galaxy."

"I guess they're in no hurry to get there."

"Hardly."

"Damn confusing, but a victory is a victory. Good riddance to them, says I."

No sooner was the Void ship history than Plesmus groaned. At first it was very softly. Over a couple minutes she rose to the level of loud moans and outright cries of what seemed to represent pain. It was hard to watch. My friend seemed to be suffering big time and there was nothing I could do to help her.

"Plesmus, are you alright?" I asked in a building panic.

"As ... as soon as the Void ship departed, I started to feel ... strangely," she responded very softly.

"But you'll be okay, right?"

"I think I'll be ... oh ... oh my—"

"Plesmus?" I shouted. "Seriously, what's up?"

"I ... I just had the most ... eeerrrrraaf."

After that I couldn't get any response from her. Great, I just dodged one lethal bullet, now I had a replacement crisis. No rest for the wicked.

I knelt down and inspected Plesmus. She seemed limper than normal stuck to my boot, but that was fairly subjective opinion on my part. She sure was unresponsive. I couldn't take her pulse or blood pressure, since her anatomy, or lack of, didn't lend itself to my medical assessment. Even when I'd stuck a finger in her to do our time projections, I couldn't detect any bodily functions. Of course, I must admit, I was grossed out enough each time to kind of force myself not to pay any attention to her inner workings. Pity I'd been such a guy. If I'd paid attention then it sure might be useful now. Oh well. Live and learn.

"Is Plesmus alright, Captain?" RD asked in a tense tone.

"Ah, no. She's out like a mucusy light bulb." I chuckled softly. "She's out like a lava lamp." Man, I could be so witty.

"Sorry, sir. I was just hoping to confirm she was not dead."

"I know. I'm just being difficult since I'm worried too. I honestly can't tell."

"Perhaps you could administer time energy to her?"

"Not a bad idea." Actually, it was brilliant, but I didn't want RD getting a swollen head, figuratively speaking.

I retrieved a metal canister of time energy, directed the hose in her direction, and opened the stopcock slowly. A stream of bluish mist traveled the short distance to her body and was absorbed like water on a parched desert. I took that as a good sign and drained the canister into her. But that yielded no observable change. She was still out cold or demised. I tossed the bottle back toward the storage area and got to my feet.

"RD, put us back on our previous course and speed," I ordered.

As we sailed, I intermittently shouted to or poked at Plesmus, but I didn't draw any response from her. I was coming to fear that maybe she was dead. That growing realization, of course, helped murder my already depressed mood. More blood on my foolish hands. Great. More bad Jon.

Over two hours into my new purgatory, Plesmus began to stir. At first her body just writhed slowly, almost imperceptibly. A few minutes later, she began making a sound I'd never heard her make. It wasn't a groan or any attempt at vocalization that I could imagine. It almost sounded—I know this sounds crazy but it's what I pictured—like a radio broadcast from days long past. I know it's a long shot, but remember how *The Adventures of Superman* or *Fibber McGee and*

Molly sounded on your grandparent's ginormous standup RCA Victor radio? Well, anyway, that's what her semi-conscious sound reminded me of.

"Ples, you with me?" I asked, prodding her gently with a finger.

She continued to make that staticky voice-in-a-box sound, only maybe it was sounding less random. It was almost as if I could hallucinate there were words or phrases in there somewhere. Yeah, most likely my vivid imagination, but I was certainly hearing something new from Plesmus.

"RD, can you make any sense out of the noise coming from her?"

"Not specifically. There are some snippets of coherence, but nothing that I can reliably assign meaning to."

"But it sounds like maybe there's something in there, right?"

"I am tempted to agree, but—"

I f—ki— hate Jo— —yan, shot from Plesmus's body.

"There, now that sounded like a message, right?" I pressed RD.

"Yes. It sounds like someone who knows you well said it, too."

"Not necessarily," I responded thoughtfully. "A lot of people who barely know me say that type of thing. Yeah, I hear it all the time."

"Still, this seems to have been spoken with authority, sir."

"Yeah, there's a familiarity in there too, both in message and in the voice. I can ... I can almost place it."

Sapale, I —gree, but —at's no— impo—t he— and no—. Came across more clearly.

"Is ... is that *Sachiko's* voice?" I asked in a stunned murmur.

"With a ninety-seven-point-eight percent probability, based on the tone modulating and speech pattern, yes."

"Why are Sapale and Sachiko using unconscious Plesmus as a radio?" a stunned me asked the universe.

"I can't say, Captain," RD responded.

"This ... my day ... my *life* can't get any more bizarre. Let that be known."

"So, Plesmus, let me ask directly," Sachiko began. "Are you suppressing the local time collapse?"

"I wish I knew the answer to that question, Captain. I really do."

"Short of knowing, what's your opinion?"

"It's certainly possible that the time energy I store, along with the ease with which I manipulate it, contributes to the stability of any area I'm in."

"But there's no way to be certain?"

"No, Captain."

"Well, it's an interesting notion. Let's all keep it in mind and see if we can't somehow turn this to our advantage." The captain turned to the other three women. "Any of you have an opinion on any of this?"

"Not really," Reva replied sheepishly.

Emma's response was to look away.

"We know Plesmus can place a time lock on the area surrounding her," Sapale began thoughtfully. "Extending that notion to suppressing the collapse of time in not much of a leap."

"Absolutely," Plesmus agreed. "I think Sapale ... oh ... oh my—"

"Plesmus?" Sachiko shouted. "Are you okay?"

"I ... I just had the most ... eeerrrrraaf."

"The most what?" Sachiko demanded.

Nothing.

"Plesmus? Plesmus, are you there?"

Still no response.

"Aramthella, can you tell what's wrong?"

"No, Captain, I cannot. I've lost all contact with her."

Sachiko whipped out her handheld. "Security Alert. I need a team to Plesmus's quarters immediately. She's gone dark. Captain out."

Sachiko sprinted toward the hatch. "Ladies, are you coming?"

"I'll head for the bridge—mind the shop," Reva called after three quickly disappearing backsides.

"Thanks," Sachiko called over her shoulder.

Taking the ladders to avoid waiting for lifts to arrive, they made it down to Plesmus's storage room door right as the security team did.

"Any idea what happened, Captain?" asked the sergeant.

"No, Gunny. We were talking and she went silent. Keep your team out here in the passageway. We'll go check on her."

"Yes, sir," Gunny shot back.

Sachiko led as the women walked cautiously toward the back of the otherwise empty space. She was the first to see the limp form of Plesmus resting back against her favorite corner. She rushed up and set a palm gently on Plesmus.

"Plesmus, can you hear me?" Sachiko prompted gently.

Nothing.

"Should I call for the doctor?" Emma asked.

"I don't think she'd bring anything new to the table," Sapale dismissed. "None of us do."

"True that," Emma whispered back.

Sachiko shook Plesmus as vigorously as she dared. Still nothing.

"Do you think we should move her somewhere?" Emma wondered aloud.

"I don't know," Sachiko mused. "This is kind of her spot. I suppose it's as good as any." After a second, she turned to Emma. "Grab Gunny. Run to the Time Storage Unit and bring back two bottles of time energy."

"Excellent idea," Sapale affirmed.

"On it," Emma chirped as she turned to run.

Less than four minutes later, Emma slid to her knees and passed a ten-kilo canister of time energy to Sachiko, who was nearest the still unresponsive patient. She slowly opened the stopcock and allowed the blue mist to waft over Plesmus. The energy immediately gravitated to the necumplack and disappeared into her mass.

"Let's see if that has any effect," Sachiko said softly once the canister was empty.

But, a few minutes later, there was still no sign of life from the ship's focus.

"Ideas, ladies?" Sachiko asked without taking her eyes off Plesmus.

"Not really," Sapale replied quietly. "I think she's on her own here."

Emma voted for a silent non-response.

"Then we wait and see," Sachiko announced as she rotated to sit next to Plesmus, a palm still resting on her surface. "Emma, why don't you release the security team and return to the bridge. Appraise Reva of the situation down here and assist her in any way she sees fit."

"Yes, sir," Emma replied and then quietly slipped away.

"And then they waited," Sachiko said to no one in particular.

Occasionally one of the women would pose a question to the other, or would try to prompt a response from Plesmus. But mostly they sat watching. After ten minutes, Plesmus began to stir. At first her body just writhed slowly, almost imperceptibly. Sachiko barely noticed. A few minutes later, she began making a sound neither woman could place.

"It sounds like a radio transmission, but from really far away," Sapale opined.

"Yeah, I kind of get that," Sachiko agreed. "But I don't make out any garbled signal, do you?"

Sapale listened attentively a few seconds. "No, me either. Just static."

"This is so confusing," Sachiko burst out in frustration.

"I fucking hate Jon Ryan," Sapale hissed loudly.

"Sapale, I agree in general, but that's not important here and now."

"But I hate the man. Somehow we both know this is his fault. Plesmus ... she deserves better than to be at the mercy of my idiot brood-mate."

What had been white noise emanating from Plesmus suddenly sounded familiar. *Ah, hi hon—. You— —ot mad at m— —re —u.*

"Did that just sound like my idiot brood-mate?" Sapale snapped, pointing at the listless Plesmus.

"Gosh," Sachiko responded. "It sure did. Jon," she shouted at Plesmus, "can you hear me?"

"Slow i— —own," came the fairly clear response.

Sachiko looked to Sapale and furrowed her brow.

"I think he means talk slower. That way he can understand you better," she stated.

"Ah. Jon ... can ... you ... hear ... me?" she enunciated excruciatingly.

"Not that slow, boss," came Jon's crisp tease. "I'm not brain dead yet."

"Some would argue that point," Sapale shouted in a paced roar over Sachiko's shoulder.

"Love you too, hon," Jon responded cheerily.

Sachiko pressed a restraining palm on Sapale's chest. "Jon, where are you?"

"A long ways away. Well, wait, since I don't know where you are, I can't say that. Where the heck are you guys?"

"We are very lost," Sachiko replied. "We kind of pop in and out of places. There's no fixed pattern to it."

"Are you all well?" he asked.

"Well enough. But Plesmus has just collapsed."

"Collapsed?" he queried. "Did she moan real weird first and then sound like an old radio program?"

Sachiko was forced to furrow her brow at Sapale again in confusion.

Sapale shook her head. "I got this. Thank your lucky stars you don't speak fluent *Jon* yet." Leaning over Sachiko, she replied, "Yes. She acted injured, passed out, and woke up making radio sounds."

"Here too. What are the chances?"

"So, are you in one piece?" Sapale asked.

"So far. Just confused and a long way from Earth."

"How far?"

"Do you remember the Claxeon Citadel?"

"Jon, tell me you're not risking your life on Flastor again, please."

"Okay, I'm not risking my life on Flastor. Been there and gone. Didn't die either."

"You're such a lunatic."

"No, I had to try and figure out why time is collapsing."

"It's collapsing because of *you*, sweetheart."

"Hmm. Maybe more *how* it is rather than *why* it is then," he responded diplomatically.

"And?"

"And ... how are you guys?"

"No way, flyboy. What did you learn?"

"Ah, they have a time museum. It's real clean and everything."

"Go on."

"My friend Miniminim, who says hi by the way—"

"No, she didn't, you liar."

"Well, if she knew you she would have. Anyway, she wanted me to see the opening of the Reliquary of Time. It houses, er *housed* the Relic of Time, you know."

"And?"

"And... how are you guys?"

"What was in the reliquary, Jon?" Sapale menaced.

"Man, would you look at the time? Hey, how are you guys?"

"Growing in our collective frustration," she snarled. "Look, bottom line me. Can you stop the collapse?"

"In all seriousness," he replied somberly, "probably not. Plesmus thinks I've messed up the timeline too severely. Uh, sorry."

"We suspected as much," she stated coolly. "So how are we going to ... Wait. why are we talking via Radio Plesmus?" Sapale suddenly asked.

"Beats the hell out of me. She passed out, made some clicky sounds, and then, *poof*, you were on the line. Hi, by the way. Miss you."

"Miss you, too. But, I mean, the universe is sliding down the crapper and now our time focus is a radio? What's up with that?"

"I wish—"

"Aaah ... oooh," Plesmus gasped on both ends of the divide.

"Did yours just—" Jon began.

"Yeah, she's coming to," Sapale confirmed.

"Plesmus?" Sachiko called around Sapale. "Are you okay?"

"Okay ... am I ... ooh. Where am I?"

"I heard that," Jon shouted. "But our Plesmus didn't say it. She's still O-U-T out."

"Plesmus, you're in your closet aboard Aramthella," Sachiko reassured. "You passed out all of the sudden."

"I did?" she asked, still confused. "Oh, wait, I did."

"And the portion of you that's with Jon seems to be acting in an identical manner," Sachiko added.

"Except my piece is still unconscious," Jon shouted.

"Not for long," Plesmus said quietly but resolutely.

"Ayaya," screamed the Plesmus on Jon's side.

"Hey, you finally woke up," Jon commented to her. "Good morning, sunshine."

"I didn't wake up, you ninny," she scolded. "I forced myself back to consciousness."

"Okay," Sapale stated firmly. "This is now officially weird."

"No, I think it's cool," Jon differed. "It's like we're all sitting around a campfire telling ghost stories."

"Jon?" Sapale said.

"Yes, love?"

"Stop being you."

"You got it. Mum's the word."

Thank you, Sachiko silently mouthed to Sapale.

"So, Plesmus, why did you pass out on us?" Sapale pressed.

"I don't think you're going to be overly pleased with the reason," Plesmus speculated.

"That's not important," Sachiko announced. "What we need are the facts."

"The fact is that we passed out due to internal trauma," Plesmus on Jon's end clarified.

"Internal trauma?" Jon posed. "You were just laying there. I saw no trauma."

"Because it was *internal*," Plesmus on Sachiko's side chided him.

"Ah," Jon returned.

"What type of internal trauma?" Sachiko asked.

"I ... or rather we, lost our ability to time lock our surroundings," Sachiko's continued.

"Oops," Sapale observed.

"Big oops," Jon seconded.

"So, the ship's no longer protected by your time lock?" Sachiko asked quickly.

"It is fading rapidly," both Plesmuses said in tandem.

"But ... if it does—" Sachiko began.

"Then we're going to be as screwed as everything else is real damn soon," Sapale finished the thought.

"That ... that sounds bad," Jon speculated.

"Worse than bad," Plesmus on Jon's side observed. "It will become catastrophic very soon."

"Can we arrest the process?" Sachiko asked loudly.

"This is all completely new to us," her Plesmus replied. "There's no way—"

"Collision warning. Collision warning," came over the speakers on Aramthella. A computerized voice announced passively.

"Aramthella," Sachiko shouted, "report."

There was no response.

"Crap," Sachiko snapped. She whipped up her handheld. "Engineering? This is the captain. Aramthella's offline again."

"We just found out," the chief shouted back over her phone's speaker. "But we have bigger worries, Captain. The seams on Reactor One have started failing. We're about to have a nuclear steam explosion down here that'll be the end of us."

"How can we have a critical reactor, Chief? We don't *have* any nuclear reactors. The ship's entirely powered by time energy. Make sense, man."

"Captain, I know how we're powered and I know we did not *have* a fission reactor. But I swear on my mother's grave we do now and it's about to fail catastrophically."

"Bu ... but, Chief, how can you tell? It's not like the reactor is wired in and has a status showing on your boards."

"Ah, trust me on this, Captain. It is wired in, I do have an array of icons and gauges, and the damn thing's about to blow. I ... what? Captain, I got to go."

The connection abruptly ended.

"The reactor's—" Sachiko began to ask, but immediately realized the question was unnecessary. The chief needed to address the crisis. "Keep me posted. Captain out," she mumbled to the closed line.

"If the reactor we appear to now possess fails catastrophically," Sapale began, "best case scenario, it'll contaminate almost half the ship."

Sachiko raised her handheld back to her mouth. "Red Alert. Red Alert. Explosion in Engineering imminent. Seal all hatches. Repeat, seal all hatches. All personnel below Decks A, H, and M evacuate immediately. Repeat—"

The ship vibrated ominously.

"It blew," Sapale announced or questioned. It wasn't clear which due to the noise and confusion.

The lights aboard Aramthella flashed, then winked off. Emergency lights came on one second later.

"*Reva*, damage report," Sachiko shouted above the din. Reva was on the bridge by then.

"Ca ... ptai ... I sho ... a mass—" Jon heard Reva's voice responded intermittently.

"Reva, repeat, what—"

All of the sudden the Plesmus on Sachiko's side stopped transmitting voice to Jon's side.

EIGHT

I stared at Plesmus in stricken disbelief. "Ples, are you still hearing them?"

"Negative. Their side went dead."

"Please don't say *dead*," I moaned.

"Sorry, that was an unbelievably bad choice of words. I've lost all connection with the segment of me aboard Aramthella."

"Thanks. That's better. Do you know what happened over there?"

"Aside from what we heard? No. They ... they just went silent."

"Try to raise the other you again."

"I'll try, but I don't know how that happened in the first place. It seems reasonably impossible to me."

"Just try. Focus."

"I'll try," Plesmus relented.

"RD, they said something about a runaway reactor. Do we have a surprise reactor too?"

"Not that I'm aware of."

"Not aware, but it's possible we're infested with one too, right?"

"I presume the possibilities are not zero, but I'm a very small craft.

I think I'd notice the sudden appearance of a fission reactor accompanied by its control subunits if they were present."

"They are generally kind of big, I'll grant you that," I mumbled.

Man, this sucked.

"Ples, are you feeling okay?" I shouted.

No response.

"Ples," I screamed, "are you gone?"

"No, you loud thing, you. Keep it down. I'm trying to place a call to myself. Remember that thing that was so imperative to you seconds ago?"

"Ah, yeah. Sorry. Look, tell me about what that Plesmus said. She was losing her time lock. Then a UFO nuclear reactor wired itself onto the ship, probably because *yes* she was losing her time lock. Is your time lock failing too?"

"Yes, I just said it was. We both did at the same time."

"I know, yes. I was ... I'm just ... crap."

I lunged toward the storage locker and actually ended up ass-over-tea-kettle feet in the air stuck. I grabbed ahold of two good-sized time energy tanks. It wasn't easy, but I twisted myself out and rushed to Plesmus's side. I opened the release on both cylinders and blew two streams of energy at her.

"What in the Maker's name are you doing?" she protested loudly.

"Saving our collective asses, I hope."

"I'm ... stop it ... I'm not low on time energy. That's not why I'm losing my time lock."

I tried to jimmy the valves to open wider. "Oh, yeah. Then tell me why you are."

"I don't know. It's never ... I said stop it. I might absorb too much and explode."

"No, ya won't. One, I'm not that lucky and, two, you're made out of time mucous. No way it explodes. It *expands*. And if you don't know why you lost your lock, then you don't know that it's not because you need more time energy onboard."

"I ... stop it ... I've been low before and never lost ... Jon, please stop. This is— oh ... oh, no way."

"What? It's worse? Nuclear reactors are attaching themselves to our hull?"

"No, it's working. I'm able to time lock the area around me again."

"Then why the *oh, no*?"

"Are you serious? You were not only correct, your decisive intervention might have just saved the day. How am I supposed to live with that?"

"Praise might be a good thing."

"I'd rather have defective nuclear reactors attached to the hull."

"Some people are just never happy. You know, you should probably seek professional help once we're safe and sound."

"Are you hinting at my needing a psychiatrist?"

"Maybe, or an interior designer. I'm not a self-help expert. But do yourself a favor and ask around when we're back on Aramthella."

"You mean the ship with the exploded nuclear reactor?"

Ouch. That crack got my full attention. "We ... we don't know that the bogus reactor failed," I said tentatively.

"I'm sorry. That came out angry. It was insensitive of me. You have people on the ship."

"Ah, hello, I have people but you have you. I think we both have major skin in the game."

"Point taken."

"All we know is that the transmission cut off. I say it was a BizarroWorld connection to begin with, so I'm not inclined to read too much into its truncation."

"Jon, I hate to be the one focusing on the negative, but we both heard Sachiko yell *it blew*."

"She did say that. But, she might have been referencing something else, a movie she'd once disliked, or a bad first date."

"Jon?" she asked. "Are you serious?"

"Not too much. But Reva said something after. So how could that happen if the reactor had failed?"

"Maybe the shock wave or contamination just hadn't reached her yet?"

"Or maybe nothing blew up." I wasn't super excited about the soundness of my line-of-reasoning, but I was less keen on everybody on that end being dead.

"Jon, again, I don't like to accentuate the negative, but all we heard Reva shout was a garbled snippet ending with the words *a mass*. Like it or not, we have to at least entertain the idea that she was referring to 'a mass-*ive explosion.*'"

"I don't know," I said. "Sounded to me like she said, *I sho ... a mass.*"

"Yes, I stand by my speculation. 'I show a mass-*ive explosion.*'"

I shook my head. "No, she doesn't talk like that. She might have been saying *I should* not *I show*. I think we should refrain from speculating."

"Fine, we will have to wait and see if we learn more. However, we do have to think in terms of what our next move might be if they were in a sorry state."

"Fine, in a general sense, sure. We have to think with our brains, not our hearts." Gosh that sounded shlocky. I needed a drink and I needed it soon. I was sounding like a general or a politician. Yuck City.

We were then quiet a while. I was trying to think, but mostly my mind was in scatter mode. No sooner did I started to work through one idea than a new, unrelated and more impetuous notion kicked it out and ran circles around in my head screaming *the sky is falling we are all going to die*. Mind you, in combat, I'm a picture of steely composure. When bullets are flying and lives are on the line, I'm a machine. But when it comes to thinking and planning, well, I can lose it sometimes. This was, most unhelpfully, one of those times. But I slowly calmed the heck down and started to edge back into rational thought.

"So, Ples," I asked, "now that it's been a while, what do you think that communication via your partially conscious body was?"

"No idea. I can tell you it was freaking weird. I have never heard of anything similar occurring to any member of my species."

"With time collapsing and your time lock failing, I wonder if it had to do with either of those two processes?" I harrumphed quietly. "Or maybe both."

"Who knows?" she replied in an unsettled tone. "I must say that when I'm near you the strangest things transpire. Here I've been alive for I don't even know how long and nothing unexplainable or bizarre happens. Then along comes Jon Ryan and everything changes. You're a curse, my friend, a plain and simple curse."

"I've been told as much," I mused. "More than once in a while, come to think of it."

After another quiet spell, I had to mention the darn phantoms. "Speaking of the bizarre, what about those phantoms? They go to all the trouble of marching right up to us, then they leave without as much as a parting shot."

"Yes, every other time we've run into them, they make it a point to try and surprise us. This time they displayed no tactics whatsoever. Most unexpected."

"I do have to say I'm really over those bozos. It should have been enough that they tossed me into that Oblivion of theirs. But then they have to keep coming after me. What's up with that? I mean, you hate me, you kill me, then you need to move on, right?"

"Obsession is a cruel mistress."

"It's a stupid one too. Move the hell on, that's my credo."

"Said the human who couldn't leave time alone until he broke it."

"That's totally different in spirit and in kind."

"Said the necumplack who doesn't agree with your dismissal."

"I had a mission. It was well considered, necessary, and doable."

"Do ... *doable*?" she flabbergasted. "Are you listening to yourself emit delusional words?"

"No. I said it was doable. I just never figured out how to do so."

"Never or not yet?" she asked cuttingly.

"Let's change the subject, shall we?"

"Fine. Of what shall we speak, stuck here in a tiny spaceship going nowhere in particular at a leisurely pace?"

"How are we going to get back to Aramthella?" I remarked moodily.

"Since I have no idea, I don't think I'll be able to carry my side of that conversation. And, Jon, we just established that we need to lay plans assuming they might have been disabled or even destroyed."

"I know that's what we agreed on, but I simply can't accept that they might be lost."

"We are not forming a new religion here. Belief can play no part in our planning. You know this," she scolded.

"I do but I cannot accept that they're gone. Sorry. Maybe it's just a human thing, but I have a feeling they're okay, so in my mind, they're good. Well, good may be a stretch, but *alive* I take as a given."

"I fear that is wishful thinking, not sound reasoning."

I considered responding with a raspberry, but thought better of it. For one thing, it was too much effort and for another it might be a mating call for her kind. Who knew? More wackiness I did not need. Plus, I did have a serious idea rumbling around in my head like a biker on a Harley.

"Ples, I want you to hear me out before you shut me down," I asked nicely.

"No."

"Now, ya see? There you go with the Little Miss Negative crap. I asked you to hear me out first."

"You did. But logic and your history suggest waiting for you to finish is a waste of time. Reject, reject, reject is the watchword when it comes to you asking to be heard out."

"I'm being serious here."

"I'm being serious here too," she taunted.

"So, my idea is this. The freaking phantoms won't leave me alone. I need to deal with that loose end. Whatever else we do, I can't have them popping up willy nilly like ex-wives at the reading of an old man's will. They need to stop and I need to stop them."

"So far I have no problem with what you are saying."

"I also need to stop the collapse of time in our universe."

"Ut, ut, ut, no. You have said that as prophetically before as you have said, *here, hold my beer*. It never works out in either case."

"No, totally different strategy this time."

"No. It's a terrible idea."

"I asked you to hear me out."

"You could also ask me to grow a beard. I can't do the impossible. I know that whatever follows is not just a bad idea. It's a grievously wrong, unjustifiable, insane notion."

"The Void is timeless," I stated.

"Er, are we changing subjects? Did I win the point?"

"Did you win the point? Don't be absurd, little one. No, I was just warming up."

"Ah. Then my comment is stop, do not finish, and please shut up."

"The Void is timeless. The Void phantoms are relentless and they need to stop hassling me."

"Yes, yes, and ideally," she returned.

"So, I'm thinking that if I tear open the Void barrier, their anti-time will mix with our screwed-up time and those two forces will cancel each other out."

She was silent.

"Well, what do you think?" I pressed.

"I think you should go on. I'm being the better being and hearing you out."

"No, I'm done. That's my plan."

"No, it's not."

"What do you mean, no it's not? It is."

"It's not a plan because you said you wanted to mix two diametrically opposed universes together. If there were a plan in there somewhere, you'd tell me *how* it was that it might possibly work, *why* it would work, and *what* the specific predictable results would be."

"No, that's the plan. The two time zones cancel each other out. Thus, time in our universe returns to normal."

"Time in our universe returns to *normal*?" she questioned sarcastically. "And why out of all the possible outcomes of such an insane act is it so obvious to you that the mixing of opposing forces would behave so cooperatively, in such a fair-minded manner?"

"What? I think it's pretty obvious that it would have the desired outcome."

At first I didn't hear or feel it. But slowly, Ples's body started to vibrate. It began quietly enough. But then she was shaking so hard and so rapidly that she actually generated a sound wave. I thought it was cool, but, then again, it had to be a bad sign.

"*Jon!*" burst forth from her. "You are speaking time. Let me, as an expert in time, translate what you said into human. You say that you love children and wish to keep them safe. Then you remark that you love cliffs because they are so beautiful, so sturdy. Therefore, based on what you stated, you feel you should throw children off the cliff to help them. Is that a fair summary?"

"No, not in any way, shape, or form. Yours is a non sequitur; it does not proceed logically. My theory about time mixing is a bit intuitive, I'll grant you that. But it is fundamentally solid."

"As is the ground beneath those lovely cliffs. Jon, please, this idea —I can't believe I'm even gracing it to call it that—is worse than your obsession to change the timeline. This *will* fail to produce the desired results. If it does fail to work, that would be marvelous. But if you did not fail, you'd likely kill us all."

"Yeah, but that's the worst-case scenario."

"Are you *listening* to yourself? 'Yeah, but the end of *times* is the worst-case scenario.' Big ass duh, there, Jon Ryan."

Our bitter argument was broken up by RD interrupting. Normally, I would have thought that a good intervention. It would allow cooler heads to prevail. In the actual case ... eh, not so much really.

"Excuse me," RD said deferentially. "I hate to bother you, but, er,

Captain, there's something approaching that I think you might want to know about."

"This had better be important, RD," I said. "Is whatever it is heading toward us?"

"Ah, well, interesting characterization there. I'd simply say it would be hard for it to miss us."

"RD, please do not be as vague and lame as Plesmus. I am not in the mood but many light years past it. Please tell me if whatever's got your knickers in a knot is coming after us."

"Mmm, again, that's a matter of judgment, I suppose. I doubt it has targeted us *specifically*, but, as I said, it's fairly impossible for it to miss us."

"Babble, babble, blah, blah, blah. That's all I'm hearing. Put whatever is frightening you on the main screen."

"There you are, sir."

I studied the image. It wasn't really an image, it was a general blurring of the space around us, more dense on one side of us than the other. "RD, this is garbage. What am I looking at?"

"One of two phenomenon. Either my sensor arrays are completely faulty and badly in need of replacement."

"Or?" I demanded impatiently.

"Or that's a swarm."

"A swarm? What's a swarm?"

"That diffusely blurred yet dense image."

"But it occupies..." I drew a finger across the screen to estimate, "it occupies two-thirds of the space around us."

"That's what swarms do, sir," he remarked cheerily. "They *swarm*."

"No, that would mean the *swarm* was about half a light year across and two light years thick. If each member of the swarm was the size of the Earth, and each of those planets was separated by an Earth diameter, there'd be ten-to-the-thirtieth-third power *Earths* in that swarm."

"Sir, you are quick with the numbers for a human. Kudos to you, seriously," RD praised.

"I'm being sarcastic," I notified the idiot. "There's no such thing as a swarm that big. Your sensors are for shit, that's what we're looking at."

"Jon," came a teeny tiny voice from a million miles away.

"What, Ples? I'm kind of busy debunking our computer here."

"Jon," an even feebler voice repeated. "The system operator is correct. Th ... that is ... or rather what is approaching our region of space is a big swarm."

"Not you too?" I railed. I was surrounded by scared children—scared children who were sadly misinformed.

"I have sensed the individual members of this swarm before. Long, long ago."

"What, you mean like each locust in the swarm?"

"Sure, whatever. But these are no insects. These are wyvermin."

"Wyvermin? Never heard of them," I responded dismissively.

"Not surprising, really," she said in a troublingly dissociative tone. Something was weighing on her heavily, that was certain. I'd never heard her sound so morose.

"Why's that?" I asked a bit more empathically.

"They were rare many billion years ago, during the reign of the first stars."

"The first stars? You mean the first generation of stars to form after the Big Bang?"

"Yes, those giant, hot stars. It was a time of chaos and vivid energies."

"Whoa, Ples, I know you're old, but come on, you weren't there were you?"

"And back then, there rose up one great civilization. The Quantomp Resplendency."

"Ples, are you trippin'? You don't seem one hundred percent present and accounted for."

"If you knew the full tale of the Quantomp civilization, you would not question my state." After a long pause, she offered, "Would you like me to tell you their triumphant yet ultimately sad story?"

"Sure? I guess." I spoke with a hesitancy that surprised me. Later, I would call it a premonition.

"The Quantomp Resplendency ruled that early universe with a fury and a determination that has never been duplicated in the history of species," she began. "They were truly gods, capable of acts of wonder that defied belief. All whom they challenged fell under their control. They were irresistible. Through their magical technology, force of will, and unsurpassed physical attributes, they ground to dust what they wished to be dust and they made miracles whenever they desired one. In one hundred million years of ascendancy, they were not just their own masters, they were the masters of everything that existed. Until ... they encountered the unimaginable, the wyvermin.

"After the Quantomp Resplendency had achieved dominion over this forming galaxy, they grew impatient to rule more, to experience more, and to demonstrate to themselves their own perfection. So they sent pods off to every conceivable destination."

"Sorry," I interrupted Her Dreaminess. "Pods?"

"They were a collective species. They could exist in any number of configurations. A Quantomp could stand alone indefinitely, or meld with any number of others on a whim. When exploring, they formed themselves into gigantic living spacecraft consisting of a several hundred thousand individuals. They called those *pods*."

"Weird, but go on."

"The pods made up the substance of the spacecraft that transported them. Inside they could bring supplies or other materials, but the ship itself was its very passengers. They moved by manipulations of gravity and time. The pod could arrive at its destination long before it decided to head there in the first place. To the Quantomp, reality was a game and they were the sole players. As immortals, unrestrained by concerns of energy supply or *any* limits, in fact, they were like dolphins upon the waves of an infinite ocean.

"There came a dark day, though, even the great Quantomp did not know it at the time. It was decided that a pod would venture forth to study and assimilate a distant antimatter galaxy."

"Whoa up there, Ples. There are no antimatter galaxies."

"There are no more, but there were many back then. Over the eons, they were lost to interactions with the dominant form of baryonic matter, which is opposite in charge. The Quantomp had explored antimatter galaxies before. They chose to visit this particular one not because it was of interest, but because it represented a slight challenge. As a species composed of positive-matter, there was a small risk to them. If their techniques were sloppy, they could be injured by a matter/antimatter cancellation." She was quiet a spell. "They were so powerful, yet in many ways they were children."

"Go on," I felt the need to encourage her. This was getting interesting.

"I will, Jon, there is much remaining to tell—"

The members of 111-1&2-23 assembled themselves into a space-going pod. That designation signifies the one hundred and eleventh pod, populated by Quantomps named one and two of the twenty-third generation of the species. They named themselves one, two, three, et cetera. To distinguish any particular *one* from another *one*, they also tagged themselves with the generation they were spawned in. To the Quantomp such a naming system seemed clever. They were all about being witty and funny.

So, the pod ventured to the galaxy they knew also by a sequential number. The social structure of the Quantomps was incomprehensible. Suffice it to say that 111-1&2-23 was led by a daughter of the nobility. 294-4 was ancient even by their standards, born to a powerful clan. She was acknowledged to be exemplary, a greater among equals.

When the pod arrived, they were immediately confused. Typically, an antimatter galaxy looked exactly like a normal matter galaxy. You'd only know it to be composed of pure antimatter if you interacted with it. But what they observed defied their ability to believe their own senses. The galaxy was full of stars, as expected. But in no star system did they discover a single planet. Areas where planets must surely have been were populated only by rocky debris. The galaxy's stars were orbited by asteroid fields. They knew immediately that this galaxy was unique. 294-4 put it well when she declared that the galaxy "*was cursed by powers I cannot anticipate.*"

It didn't take long for the curse to make itself known to the Quantomp. Within hours of their arrival, a single object appeared in their awareness. It flew like a bird in an atmosphere and it was heading directly toward the pod.

"294-4," a fellow pod member laughed, "there appears to be one living creature remaining. It flees to us for succor."

Half the pod joined in the laughter. But the wise 294-4 was reluctant to dismiss any potential threat. "Dear 111-1&2-23, quiet your souls. We see this galaxy to be in a state of destruction that cannot be of a natural occurrence. Let us be vigilant now and laugh later when we are in control of the facts."

After a few dismissive retorts, the pod fell serious. As the object drew closer, they knew in their minds and in their hearts that the single creature was of a species unfamiliar to the Quantomp. It was massive for a beast of flight, with thin wings spanning nearly a kilometer. Its body, or at least its covering, was indistinguishable to them from diamond. The six feet ended in innumerable talons each meters in length. And its beak was so prodigious as to give emotional uncertainty to even the most flippant of the pod. All were impressed with the approaching monster.

"I shall hold it where it is with a thought," 294-4 announced.

"When will you begin, sister 294-4?" queried the second-in-command, 20291-20.

"I have."

"But the ... the animal only continues toward us," he responded.

“It does. This is not a setback. Dearest 111-1&2-23, as one let us think it to rest.”

And all joined in an mental effort to arrest the beast's progress.

"294-4, it still advances," her second pointed out nervously.

"This is not a setback. Left pod, emit a ten-to-the-twentieth power bolt of gamma radiation at our pursuer."

And so the power a normal star emits in a second was hurled across the vacuum of space and struck the approaching enemy squarely. But when the cloud dispersed and the interference abated, the winged nightmare was not even slowed.

"I shall withdraw us to a safer position and deal with this demon once and for all," 294-4 said with less conviction than she wished the others to feel.

In the space of a thought, the pod was ten light years away. 294-4 readied the ultimate assault. "Left pod, increase radiation expenditure to triple. Right pod, command the molecules of the beast to dissociate and randomize. Center pod, agree that the space our enemy exists in be now reassigned to the center of the supermassive black hole of Galaxy 121."

After a blinding discharge of energy and transmutation, 294-4 scanned the space before her.

"What do you see?" asked a frightened 2020-18.

"I now see two flying beasts approaching, one only slightly behind the original," 294-4 replied in bewildered disbelief.

"Then we must flee," the pod as one shouted mentally to itself. "If we cannot stop one terror, two will be our downfall."

"But where shall we run to?" 294-4 wisely asked.

“Home, home, home. We are only safe when we are one with the all," the pod screamed.

"But if we return with an unstoppable foe on our tail, are we not condemning our species to danger?" she asked.

"There is no danger to the collective," the pod howled well outside of reason. "Draw the monsters into ourselves and we shall demolish them with no doubt."

As the pod argued amongst itself, the first beast flashed out of time/space and then back in, but now so close to the pod that its talons opened to claim its victim.

"Run," the pod exclaimed. "Peril is upon us."

294-4 separated herself from the pod and threw herself against the horror. She joined with it as one, and declared to the sum of the two that it must halt all movement.

The beast seized the pod and tore at it grievously. Chunks and parts flew off in every direction. Those that came anywhere close to the horrendous beak were snapped up and swallowed. Soon the second monster was ripping and clawing and snapping up. The pod fell into a disarrayed panic.

294-4 ordered the beast it was one with to dissolve.

Instead of respecting her charge, the wyvermin—for 294-4 now knew that is what it called itself—ejected her from its body and snapped her in half. 294-4's dying thoughts were commands to what remained of the pod. "Flee the wyvermin. To remain here is to die. Home ... seek hom—"

And her thoughts ended as the pieces that she was were gobbled up by the insatiable predator.

What little remained of the pod relocated itself to an orbit over the home world. They were too damaged and disjointed to land. Those on the ground brought the devastated pod down and knew at once what the traveling pod knew. A force of two wyvermin had done what millions of years and thousands of enemies could not achieve. They had delivered defeat to the Quantomp. And death. The mass of souls that were the whole of the Quantomp demanded revenge. They begged the wyvermin to follow the lost pod home so the monsters could be pounded to atoms.

Almost immediately, the Quantomp 's wish was granted. Both wyvermin popped into existence above the home world.

It took the wyvermin just two weeks to kill every living soul on the Quantomp home world. Two weeks. Once the edibles were consumed, the pair of wyvermin took it upon themselves to pulverize the home world, just as they had done with every planetary system in the antimatter galaxy they had been discovered in. Whether they acted out of sentient cruelty or simple bestiality was never determined. That they were the very vehicles of the apocalypse was, however, undeniable.

So enraged was the remainder of the Quantomp Resplendency, the bulk of the species that resided off the home world, that they as one committed themselves to destroy the destroyers. Over the next ten thousand years, the Quantomp Resplendency fought and struggled, was defeated and crushed. The wyvermin proved themselves equal to almost every assault visited upon them by the Quantomp. Over time, while the tactics of the wyvermin remained unchanged, the Quantomp refined their science and advanced their magic.

Finally one day, in one cataclysmic battle, one of the wyvermin was slain. At the cost of thousands of pods, a cancellation imperative was successfully implanted into the lesser of the two wyvermin. Once settled in and activated, the lesser wyvermin jerked to a stop midair and then fell to earth like a nuclear bomb. Half the face of the planet where the struggle raged was shorn off and cast into space. To a pod, the remainder of the Quantomp forces were vaporized that day. But great rejoicing resulted across the remainder of the Resplendency, for one of their foes had been killed.

Whether the surviving wyvermin sensed the loss of its kin and whether it fled out of fear or mere instinct was never known. But the last wyvermin fled. Pursued by a sky full of pods, it headed for parts unknown. As it left the limits of the Milky Way, more than ten thousand newly invigorated Quantomp pods gave chase.

No word or record exists as to the fate of that lone leviathan-of-death or the millions of Quantomps that lived only to kill it. In the fullness of time, the first generation of stars in the Milky Way gave way to the later generations. The Quantomp that remained behind faded like the sound of departing thunder, until finally they were never heard from again. Civilizations rose, flourished, and passed away into anonymity. The march of time trampled the memory of the apocalyptic war between the most powerful of species and the brutal destroyers to all-but-forgotten myths. But, if only in nightmares, it was never lost from the archetypal collective unconscious of all living creatures that there are monsters out there that are forgotten only at one's greatest peril.

"Ah, Captain, Captain Ryan," RD shouted. "Sir, I hate to interrupt but I've been calling to you for several minutes. The swarm is nearly upon us. What are your orders?"

I heard RD all along. But I was just indifferent to a response. I was too eviscerated by knowing the nature of the swarm, the existential threat that surrounded every living being.

Whatever I might have said in response was meaningless.

"Captain, *Jon*!" RD shouted. "Your orders, sir?"

"Fire up your transdimensional engines, RD. We're leaving this universe."

"Very ... very well, sir. Where shall I—"

"We're going to the Void. To the Timeless Void."

"Is ... is it *safe* for us to travel there, Captain?"

"No, RD, I'm very sure it's the very opposite of safe for us to travel there. In fact, I'm counting on it. Now move!"

NINE

I hated the Timeless Void—the actual Void itself. Why? Was it just because it was home to the most despicable, unjustifiable species of cosmic lowlifes, of cosmic trailer trash? No, I don't think that covered it. I hated the fact that there was in this *existence* a Void. It was the darkness that was always present near the light, evil abutting the good. And the Void was always close by, intimately so, in fact. It could never be forgotten, never be ignored, and never be extinguished. But maybe, because I was a man on a mission, just maybe that non-extinguishable part of it was about to be rectified.

As I made what would hopefully be my last jaunt into the Void, I didn't have long to wait. Remember that the Void is the space between universes. It is reality's rind. So, by definition, it is always infinitesimally close by and, at the same time, immensely far away. It is also razor-thin and infinite. But I wanted to reenter it in a location I had been before, one that I was familiar with. No need complicating a difficult task by adding in a layer of novelty. But the journey to where I wanted to penetrate the barrier wasn't far off. We were there in under a day. One silent day. I didn't speak, and wisely Plesmus and

RD left me to my isolation. They both knew there was no darker mood a person could be in than I was on that desolate day.

"Captain," RD interrupted solemnly, "we have arrived at the coordinates you desired."

I stood. You didn't do what I was about to do sitting down. "Is there any vessel within sensor range?" I asked glumly.

"Negative."

"Then take us through. Come to rest one kilometer inside the Void barrier."

"Very well," was his terse response.

A few seconds later I knew we were in. "Anyone close by?"

"Negative. No ships are evident and the nearest outpost is point seven eight light years away."

"Fine. Prepare to launch an infinity charge."

"We stand ready," RD replied quickly. "I should like to mention that it required thirteen percent less energy to enter the Void that it has on any past occasion."

I furrowed my brow. "Do you feel that's significant?"

"In the statistical sense, yes. Operationally, I doubt it. I simply pass along the information."

"Fine. It won't matter much longer, the integrity of the barrier," I stated bleakly.

"Very well, Captain."

"We carry eighteen infinity charges. We will launch them in rapid succession," I announced. "One every sixty seconds unless otherwise redirected. Time them to expand at the same moment, sixty seconds after the last charge is in proper position."

"Very well," RD replied. "Ready to commence on your mark."

This was it. And I knew I was going to do it. I had to. Time was collapsing everywhere. I needed to arrest that process. But, more compellingly, a nearly infinite number of the deadliest creatures to ever exist were on the hunt in my home galaxy. They were poised to destroy the Milky Way, and then they'd be on to their next victims. The wyvermin could not be reasoned with, they could not be bargained with. They didn't feel pity or remorse or fear and they absolutely would not stop. Ever. Until everything was dead.

I had one option. It was inhuman. It was unconscionable. It was unforgivable.

My lunacy, my vainglorious folly was about to cost reality its allotment of time. All things considered, what I was about to do was a blessing, a mitzvah. Not only would the chaos end, but the wyvermin would be sucked into non-existence before they could inflict any more insufferable anguish.

My final thoughts before I ordered Rift Dude to insert the eighteen infinity charges in the barrier holding apart two incomparable realities? Why, Biblical, of course. Matthew 26:24.

It would be better for him if he had not been born. I don't think too many people'd argue with that when judging me. I certainly felt that way.

"RD, launch charge one."

Eighteen launches and sixty seconds longer and my damnation was sealed. The flaring open of the membranes from each infinity charge, renting enormous gashes in the barrier, were invisible. But the rush of antagonistic realities, which seemed to wish to consume its opposite before its opposite could consume it first, was blinding. The entirety of space silently exploded. Where my universe mixed chaotically with the Timeless Void, blinding light erupted for an instant, and then fell to absolute darkness.

As the mayhem fed upon itself, the barrier itself was shredded out of being. Now less and less held the two realities apart. And they went after their opposite forces as if it were personal. Faster and faster the zone of annihilation expanded. In less than thirty seconds, I could no longer see the expanding envelope of cancellation. I was left in a darkness that reminded me of the Oblivion—absolute, all-consuming, and malevolent.

Constrained fully in this insensate reality, a strange thought occurred to me. Why was I still? How was it that the clash of the states-of-existence could have spared me? Was it a fluke? An oversight? A punishment? Or was it just a temporary state I occupied, soon to be swatted into nothingness by a neat-and-tidy new reality? If I wasn't so damn depressed, I might have laughed. Hell, if I wasn't so completely spent, I might have begun to investigate how it was I had not been included in the universe's last party. But you know what? I was too empty to care one way or the other.

So, what was next? What retribution did the combined universes I'd just canceled out have in store for me?

Didn't care, don't bother me with any updates, and, oh yeah, cancel my newspaper subscription. Color me null and void.

TEN

Sachiko raised her handheld back to her mouth. "Red Alert. Red Alert. Explosion in Engineering imminent. Seal all hatches. Repeat, seal all hatches. All personnel below Decks A, H, and M evacuate immediately. Repeat—"

The ship vibrated ominously.

"It blew," Sapale announced or questioned. It wasn't clear which it had been due to the noise and confusion.

The lights aboard Aramthella flashed, then winked off. Emergency lights came on one second later.

"*Reva*, damage report," Sachiko shouted above the din.

"Ca ... ptai ... I sho ... a mass—" Reva's voice responded.

"Reva, repeat, what—"

"Captain, I show a massive thermal spike in Engineering."

"That's the reactor going critical," Sachiko responded matter-of-factly.

"Sachiko," Reva shouted intently, "we do not *have* any nuclear reactors. How—"

"It's the time collapse. We do now. Focus, Reva. I felt an explosion or something. Did the reactor blow?"

"Hang on, let me finish the scan," Reva called back.

"Hurry please," the captain implored.

"Got it," Reva chimed back in. "A pipe in the backup cooling system burst. That's all you felt and what caused the spike. Aside from some steam there is no, I repeat, *no* radiation leakage."

"What am I thinking?" Sapale snarled as she sprinted from the room.

"Where are—" Sachiko began, but the hatch closed behind Sapale and she was out of earshot. "Damn, now what?" she asked herself. The captain checked her handheld. It had been long enough. "Captain to Engineering."

"Chief here, Captain. Go."

"Status? Is the steam from that pipe contained?"

"Yes. The bulk of the cooling assembly is in the next room. The hatches were all dogged. No injuries to report."

"Finally, some good news."

"Funny you should frame it that way, Captain. I was just about to say, though, that I do not know why the reactor itself hasn't melted down. Every control system is down and the internal temp is ridiculously high."

"And you have good expertise on this type of reactor down there?"

"Absolutely. I did a master's degree in reactor design back in the day. The darn thing was just too broken when it materiali..."

"What?" Sachiko demanded.

"Sapale just burst in here, Skipper."

"Sapale? What's she doing?"

"Don't know. Let's ask her. She's standing right next to me." He moved a bit, then asked, "What's up?"

"I was asleep at the wheel, that's what," Sapale responded. "I'm going to place a full membrane around the entire reactor."

"A membrane?" the chief thought out loud. "Hmm. Wait, won't that cut the coolant feeds and all the electrical?"

"Yes, but it's better than an unconfined meltdown."

"Good thinking, Sapale," Sachiko complimented. "Let us know when you're done."

Sapale attached her probe fibers to the outside of the reactor. *What are your dimensions?* she asked in her head.

Ten meters by six meters by eleven meters, came the response.

Are you a smooth rectangle?

To within plus or minus zero point one millimeters in any dimension.

"Perfect!" she said aloud. Sapale closed her eyes and focused.

A splitting sound snapped from the entire area of the reactor, then the big metallic figure vanished. There was a brief rush of steam, but it stopped almost immediately.

"Gotcha!" Sapale proclaimed loudly. "Okay, people, the reactor is fully contained. I set small membranes over the coolant pipes. Once the repair crew is ready, I'll release those."

"Outstanding, Sapale," Sachiko shouted. "We owe you big time."

"Not a problem. I hate being toasted by a meltdown too, so don't mention it. I'm going to need to speak with the chief here to see if there's any way I can walk this bad boy off the ship. Otherwise, I'll have to bring *Blessing* in and fold it out."

"Perfect," Sachiko responded with relief. "I'll leave you to it. Alert me if you need my assistance."

"You got it. Sapale out."

"One crisis mitigated," Sachiko mumbled to herself. "Plesmus, what's the status of your time lock?"

"It's fully gone," she replied.

Sachiko's eyes popped wide. She snatched her handheld.

"Time Storage Room, Lieutenant Fleming speaking. Go."

"This is the captain. I need two canisters of time energy in Plesmus's quarters ASAP. Have someone run them up."

"I'm on my way. Fleming out."

"I'm not low on time energy," Plesmus protested.

"It's something to do. Maybe you're not low, but it's also possible you require extra levels of time energy to hold a time lock in the present universe."

"That seems a stretch," Plesmus grumbled.

"No harm in trying." She held up her handheld again. "Reva, what's the status on the bridge?"

"All systems nominal. Nothing to report now that the reactor is contained."

"Fine. Keep me posted. Captain o—"

"Ca ... Capit ... Captain. This is George Renco ... eh, ma'am sir, reporting, if you d ... don't mind."

Sachiko's brow creased. "Who the hell are you and why are you addressing me?" she snapped with indignation.

"I'm ... oh, boy ... I'm George Renco, sir ma'am—"

"Already established. What is your role aboard my ship?" she demanded.

"I'm ... oh, oh, my—"

"Man up, Renco and tell me who the hell you are."

"You're ... you're right, sir ma'am. I'm a volunteer apprentice electrical mate assigned to the trash compaction and storages team."

Sachiko had to think about it hard but was fairly certain she knew there was such a unit on her ship. "And?" she thundered.

"Well, I don't want to speak, you know, out of school, but I'm all alone in the grinding room and—"

"Stop."

George most certainly did.

"Gunny, take a squad to the—" She was about to say the *grinding room*, but she realized she had no clue what or where that might be located. "Renco—and for the integrity of your hide you better answer quickly and concisely—what the hell's a grinding room?"

"Oh, sorry, inside terminology, sir ma'am. Sorry. I'm alone in the Refuse Degradation and Compaction Station. Deck 110-A, Rooms S-11 through T-77. I'm—"

"*Silence*," Sachiko barked. "Gunny, you still there?"

"Yes, sir."

"Take a squad down to Refuse D&C, Deck 110-A—"

"I know where it is. On our way now. Gunny out."

"Renco, a security team is on its way. Now, I don't want to order them to shoot you on sight. Do you want that, Renco?"

"Nnnn ... nnnoo, sir ma'am."

"Fine. Start addressing me as *sir* and tell me why you called before they arrive, or they open fire. You got that?"

"Yes, sir m ... got it. You might know that this station is aligned along the outer hull, ah, for easy refuse disposal."

"Renco, the team is running at a sprint," she invited him to get to some point—any point.

"Thank you, sir. So, the hull, the outer hull we're aligned with, well, it's disappearing."

"Define disappearing," she commanded sternly.

"Funny you should ask. I knew you would. Well, it used to be ... be like a metal hull. Now I can see right through parts of it. I think that's the constellation of Orion out the off to my left."

"Orion?"

"'Believe so, sir. I'm no expert but—"

"Renco, if the hull is thinning, what happens when the pressure inside exceeds the integrity of the hull to hold the atmo in?"

"Ah, I know that. Explosive decom ... Oh, shit, sir ma'am, I'm officially abandoning my post."

With his comm still open she heard him run from the room, mumbling something unintelligible the entire way. He obviously collided with Gunny right outside the hatch. She knew this because no one could swear like that gunnery sergeant.

"Captain to Gunny," she said to her handheld.

"Gunny. Go."

"Renco seems to think the hull is disappearing. Get a back-up team in space gear to support you ASAP. What can you report?"

"Well, sir, after peeling that idiot kid off of me, him clutching to my person like I was the last life preserver on the *Titanic*, I've entered the room. I can confirm the hull is very patchy. If it's not thinning, it's definitely becoming transparent."

"Great. A see-through hull," she snapped. "What will they think of next? Dynamite-based barbecue tongs?" She thought a second. "Gunny, here's the plan. I want people in suits to inspect every inch of the hull. Start locally there in Refuse D&C. Widen the scope to all adjacent rooms and decks. Report any additional threats to me and to Engineering."

"Copy that, Skipper. Gunny out."

Sachiko tapped quickly at her handheld.

"Colonel St. Claire. Go."

"Reva, more trouble. There are reports the hull is disappearing. I want everyone in a spacesuit and I want them in them ten minutes ago."

"Roger, Sachiko. Are you remaining with Plesmus?"

"For now, yes. You stay on the bridge and try to get a lid on this cluster fuck."

"I'll do my damnedest. Reva out."

At that point there was nothing else she could think to do aside from wait for Fleming to return with more time energy. Fortunately, he dashed back in less than a minute and handed off the canisters to Sachiko.

"Dismissed," she instructed tersely. Then she knelt down beside Plesmus.

"Captain, while I do appreciate the effort, I don't think you need the flows to be so—" Plesmus began to protest as strong punches of blue mist vibrated her surface.

"What?" Sachiko snapped. "Plesmus, are you okay?"

"Better than okay, Captain. I ... I can feel my time lock returning."

"You sure?"

"Yes. I think yours was a fine idea. It's nearly at twenty percent already."

Sachiko pumped a fist in front of her face. "Yes, finally a break."

"So, it would seem."

Sachiko whipped out her handheld. "Gunny, Captain here."

"Gunny. Go."

"Any change in the hull's appearance?"

"Not that ... whoa, would you look at that."

"Gunny, I can't look at it. That's why I sent you. Report."

"It's like someone's spray painting the hull, sir. It's not nearly back to normal, but it's definitely not thinning."

"Great. Execute my orders to inspect the hull. I'll have Engineering pair up as many expert eyes as they can spare with your teams."

"On it. Gunny out."

Sachiko returned her attention to Plesmus. "Feeling better?"

"Yes, Mother," Plesmus replied playfully.

"Good. Keep it that way." She shifted her focus to one of the soldiers that had remained with her. "For now, you two stay here. If Plesmus needs anything, get it and let me know. You'll be relieved shortly by someone from sickbay."

"Understood," replied Corporal Elena Garcia as she snapped to a painful appearing attention. She was trying to look confident, but was failing rather obviously.

"You're doing a good job, Garcia," Sachiko reassured. "No worries. Help is on the way." Back to Plesmus, "I'll be on the bridge. I assume you'd like to remain here?"

"If I didn't, who would the nice young corporal babysit?"

That didn't ease the tension Garcia broadcasted like there was a town crier standing behind her.

"Oh, yeah, she's better. When the sarcasm begins, Plesmus is fine."

"I do believe that's what I've been saying," Plesmus affirmed.

"I'll be on the bridge if you need me. Oh, and you're not still linked to the other Plesmus are you?"

"Not that I know of."

"Yeah, she's hitting on all cylinders," Sachiko muttered. "Corporal."

"Sir?"

"If the canisters run dry before you're relieved, seal the valves and report any changes."

Garcia looked to her companion, then back to Sachiko. "In the canisters, sir?"

Sachiko rolled her eyes. Rookies. "No, in Plesmus."

"Yes, sir."

As Sachiko walked toward the bridge, she retrieved her handheld yet again. "Sickbay."

"Sickbay, Lieutenant Faziel. Go."

"This is the captain. Get me Dr. Hartley, please."

A few seconds later the other handheld recorded a rustling sound. "Sachiko, Honesty here. What's up?"

"Hi. How are things down there?"

"Perfection. Barely controlled chaos, just the way we like it."

Sachiko grinned to herself. "Any serious casualties?"

"Nope. Worst case I got cooking is a non-com with performance anxiety."

"Really?"

"No, just pulling you chain. Bumps and bruises. What's up?"

"I need a couple med techs to relieve the security team monitoring Plesmus."

"Yeah, I heard she had some kind of episode. Is she okay?"

"After passing out, going through a shortwave-radio phase, and losing then regaining her time-locking ability, yeah, she's good."

"No problem then. I'll send a couple guys in white coats down. They can't do much, given her perverse anatomy and all, but they can look darn impressive."

"That's as good a start as any. Captain out."

Shortly thereafter Sachiko stepped onto the bridge. Thank goodness, given the day she was having, no one was presently tasked to shout out, *Captain on the bridge*. No, people had real duties to perform in the disaster.

Reva rose from the chair. "I stand relieved."

"Unless you want to arm wrestle for the comm, yes, you are," Sachiko responded with a wink. She rested into her seat.

"What's the ship looking like?" Reva asked.

"I think the present crisis is passing."

"Oh, thank goodness. Do you mind if I run and check in on Hani? I want to make sure she knows we're safe."

"No problem. She's in childcare, right?"

"Yes, she is, the only one there aside from the two teachers and one aide."

"Hey, we're overstaffed for success," Sachiko retorted. "Once word gets out how solid the program is, women all over the ship'll start ovulating with intent."

"I'm going to need vodka to try and rinse that image out of my head."

"Just don't drink and ovulate," Sachiko enjoined, aiming a critical finger at her exec.

"And on that note, Reva left the bridge."

And she did, rather quickly in fact.

ELEVEN

Tank sat at his kitchen table staring intently into his mug of tepid coffee. As a past crew member of Aramthella, he knew with certainty that the unexplainable that was being witnessed on a daily basis was related to Jon's meddling with the timeline. As a scientist he knew that the terrifying situation the world was witnessing was only going to get worse. As someone who'd been around the block a few too many times, he knew that the end was near. Very near.

It'd been weeks since he'd heard from Sachiko. He supposed he could call her, but the fact that she hadn't contacted him almost certainly suggested matters were so bad there that she couldn't spare the time for wise counsel or even a pleasant chat. That was fine. She was as capable as they came. Tank worried about her, sure. But he didn't doubt for one second that she was more than capable for the task she'd been given. Still, a call would be nice.

"The pot's empty, dear," Daisy called to him from across the kitchen. "Shall I put on another?"

Huh, he reflected, should she? Death by cosmic catastrophe versus death by cardiac calamity? "I don't know," he muttered to himself. "There's been some pretty weird shit happening lately." He nodded. "Better the devil you know, Tank." Louder, he replied, "Sure, honey, if it's not too much trouble. That'd be great."

After a few clinks and splashes, Daisy poured Tank a fresher-upper, slid the pot on the table, and sat down across from him. She held up her cup. "Cheers."

Tank lessened his scowl and reached his mug across to toast. "To today," he said with fractured cheeriness.

"I'll drink to that," Daisy affirmed in her perpetually upbeat tone.

They were quiet a while. Finally, Daisy felt compelled to ask, "Any plans for the day?"

Tank leaned back and ran a hand through his thinning hair with a grunt. "No, don't think so." Then he smiled warmly. "Just spend some quality time with my best girl, that's all."

"Sounds like you'll have a pleasant day then," she teased. "I'll even toss the honey-do list into a drawer and forget where I put it."

They both laughed softly.

"Yeah, those darn HDLs have seen their day, haven't they?" he mused. "I doubt I will miss them."

"You never *acted* to suggest you appreciated them before," she observed with a grin.

"Yes, but they were familiar. They were a constant."

"Well, if you really want me to, I'll find pen and paper and make your day."

He raised a palm toward her. "No, no. Don't miss them that much. Please remain seated."

Tank's mind fell quickly back into the conundrum that had dogged him for the last several days. Why was the universe surrounding him acting so bizarrely? What could Jon have done to time that would affect reality so fundamentally, so completely? It couldn't be a local action on his part, like the release of mass quantities of time energy. No, it had—

"Tank?" Daisy seemed to repeat, only louder. "Earth to my husband. Anyone home?"

"Er ... eh, sorry. What? I was a million miles away there, wasn't I?"

"Only a million miles? Humph. I would have guessed a lot farther afield myself."

"Yeah, sorry. What were you saying?"

"I asked if the president called you today?"

"Oh," Tank stated, trying to orient himself properly. "Let's see ... yes. Frank's called a couple times in fact."

Daisy frowned and slightly looked down.

"What?" Tank begged.

"You know we've discussed this before. The man *is* the president of the United States. I really don't think you should be calling him by his given name. It's not respectful."

"But, Daisy, he specifically asked me to call him Frank." Tank set his flattened palms parallel to each other, perpendicular to the table-top and off to his left. "He calls me *Tank*," he shifted his hands to his right, "and I call him *Frank*. The names even rhyme. It's like it's preordained." He looked up to her. "It's all fair and square."

She shrugged while bobbing her head side-to-side. "Well, call me old-fashioned. I just don't think it is respectful."

"Shall I bring it up to President Payette next time we speak? Ask him to allow me to address him more formally. I mean, the man's only got the end-of-times to worry about. I might as well top-off the ice cream sundae with a cherry's more concern, right?"

"There's no need to be snippy about it," she responded in a wounded voice.

"Aw, I'm sorry, Daisy-do. This whole mess has put me on edge. Then ... then you-know-who calls and asks if I can explain the deterioration to him and I got nothing and it breaks my heart."

"Apology accepted, dearest." She reached over and patted the back of his hand. "I know it's hard on you, especially when you can't help in a crisis like this." She set her jaw and looked away. "There's not one thing good to come of this mess."

It took him a second, but finally Tank spoke up. "I don't know if I'd go to *that* extreme."

She looked at him quizzically and raised an eyebrow.

"It's been three or four days since our neighbor's two little yapping machines have fallen silent." There was a mischievous glint in his eyes.

She grinned and giggled conspiratorially. "Yes, those two wretched dogs have finally shut up, haven't they?"

Tank smiled broadly. "I'm thinking it is in no small part due to that mother saber-toothed tiger with her kittens that passed through our backyard a few days ago."

"Oh, you're so bad," she playfully scolded him. Then her face grew serious. "Honey, wouldn't they be *cubs*, like lion cubs, not kittens?"

He shrugged. "Who knows? Since the species has been extinct over ten thousand years, I doubt our ancestors had bothered to make that linguistic call yet."

She nodded thoughtfully. "You're probably right." She sipped her coffee. "Speaking of unusual animal sightings, did you ever figure out what those small bear-like critters were that you had to drive out of the garage?"

"No, not yet at least. I sent a picture to someone I know in zoology, but I haven't heard back."

"Strangest vermin," she observed.

"Nasty too. One of them nearly shredded the broom I was using. How a mini-bear can have fangs like that and six legs is beyond my comprehension. I almost switched to laser pistol." He mimed shooting something with his fingers.

"Are you certain you're allowed to own one of those?" she asked for the umpteenth time.

"Daisy, you worry too much. It was issued to me in good faith via all the proper channels when I served aboard Aramthella. It's *my* pistol."

"Alright," she responded without believing her word. "I just hope the FBI doesn't raid your gun vault someday. I'd hate to be in a position to say I told you so."

He smiled warmly. "I bet you'd hate that like you hate peanut brittle."

She couldn't suppress a snorting giggle.

He stood up, palms on the table. "I'm going to check the news, see if there's anything unusually disturbing going on in this crazy world."

"Alright, dear. I'll join you after I clean up."

He kissed the top of her head as he passed on his way to the family room.

Tank plopped in his recliner and grabbed the remote. He hit to ON button and rested back. "Okay, let's see what you got," he said to the TV set. "PBS has a talking head in front of the White House," he mumbled to himself. "If they had anything to say, it'd be me saying it, so I'd already know it, so no thank you." He clicked to the next channel.

"Channel four has traffic and weather. Don't care and I got AC, so no thank you yet again," he mumbled.

After several more selections, Tank froze. "No ... *way*..." he whispered in stunned disbelief. "Jon Ryan's on MSNBC?"

The full screen had an image of Jon sitting in Rift Dude's lone seat, engaged in an animated discussion with someone off camera.

"Did you say something, honey?" Daisy called over a shoulder while washing a pan.

"It's ... it's Jon Ryan. He's on TV," Tank marveled.

Daisy, since her back was to her husband, felt comfortable rolling her eyes. That Jon Ryan. He was the source of all mischief in this universe. If he was on the TV again, it was just as likely to be a documentary on either how great he was or on how to wreak havoc on otherwise sensible folk. Or those nauseating hot dog abominations. If they were doing a documentary on those, he'd be the star, for sure. No, thank you. Fate tended to shape events in that unpleasant direction and she'd prefer not to be drawn along with its perverse flow.

"That's nice," she replied with only a harmless little white lie.

"I'm serious, wife, you should come see this."

"As soon as I finish up here," was her ambiguous second harmless little white lie.

"Plesmus, I'm telling you it's not that *unusual* a request," I defended in a tone reflecting wavering enthusiasm regarding my point.

"No. I do not eat or drink. I never have. Not only that, if I ever did choose to take in external nutrients, dehydrated *beer* would be the absolute last one in the multiverse I would imbibe."

"In line after even Pronto Pups?" I challenged confidently.

"Oh, alright, you have me there. Those two are tied for last place in the Plesmus-will-eat-it competition."

"Look, all I'm saying is that for this entire trip I've been drinking all by myself. They say—and they can't just make this shit up by the way—that if you drink alone you, you know, might have a drinking problem that's really more of an issue than a problem."

"So, by forcing that vile concoction into my body, you somehow absolve yourself of personal responsibility?"

"*Thank you*," I declared loudly. "At least someone reads me loud and clear."

"Yes, loud and self-deludingly clear."

"I—"

"Jon, Earth to Jon Ryan. Can you hear me?" a male voice cut in out of nowhere.

I looked up like God Almighty had just spoken to me from on high. If I was still human, I might have peed myself I was so startled.

"No, a little lower," the voice encouraged.

I slowly directed my gaze downward.

"Just a little to the right."

I complied.

"Bingo," he commended. "Now your ugly mug is pointed right at me."

Me, I saw nothing unusual. "Tank?" I ventured a guess.

"One and the same."

"And ... and you can see me?"

"I can hear you too. Oh, and hi, Plesmus. Miss you more than I miss Jon."

"Hello, General Sherman," she replied warmly. "As selfish as it is, I'm wishing you were here instead of this poor excuse for a human."

"I feel your pain, my friend."

"Ah, Tank," I interrupted the bag-on-Jon-fest, "two things. One, how can you see and hear me in real time. Two, hi back atcha. How the hell are you and Daisy?"

"In reverse order, we're great and I have *no* idea."

"Good, then we start from the same confused reference point."

"That we do."

"So, did you use your science excellence coupled with my future technology to yield some innovative device allowing you to be able to contact me?"

"Er, no. I changed from channel seven hundred and twenty-three to channel seven hundred and twenty-four."

"Hmm. That does remarkably little to clarify our present interaction."

"Jon, let me run you through the entire process."

"Okay, that should explain away my confusion."

"So, I was in the kitchen. I was talking with Daisy over late-morning coffee."

"Cool. With you so far," I confirmed cheerily.

"We were discussing the current state of affairs, which, as you might have noticed, is bleak and getting bleaker."

"You know what? I have taken notice of a quirk or two in this grand game called life myself."

"How so?"

"My ex-wife Gloria temporarily moved in with me."

"Oh, man. I bet Sapale was pissed about that."

"Ah, no. Well, she would have been, but she's on Aramthella with the gang. I'm God knows where aboard RD."

"Then how'd Gloria ever find you?"

"She took a leave of absence from her work as head receptionist in hell and appeared as if by magic."

"Ah, I am familiar with the concept. We have saber-tooth tigers in our backyard and Fiorello La Guardia had to be walked out of city hall in New York in cuffs couple days ago because he was under the distinct impression he was still the Big Apple's mayor."

"And the trilobites?" I prompted. "Do you have them too?"

"Did. That was a *long* two weeks, let me tell you, buddy."

We shared a chuckle.

"Ah, I miss you, you big palooka." I sighed loudly.

"I miss you too, Jon. So, shall I continue my explanation?"

"Please. I'm dying to know how you pulled this off."

"So, Daisy and I were commiserating over coffee."

"Yeah, late-morning coffee."

"Yeah, after—"

"You had really good sex," I tagged on quickly.

Tank made a sound like he was choking, which greatly alarmed me. I was not in a position to offer him much in the way of medical support.

"Tank, you okay?"

"I'll—" he coughed, "I'll have to get back to you on that." He paused a moment. "Jon, you've been married, what? Two billion years?"

"Give or take a few centuries, sure."

"Daisy and I are pushing forty-seven years ourselves."

"Mazel tov," I snapped.

"Yeah, and we ... we're what's referred to as a *normal* married couple of many years."

"This is all wonderful to hear, but is it possibly just a bit off topic?"

"No, it's on topic. Jon, there's a thing you need to realize about old married couples."

"Yes, yes?"

"They don't have really good sex. They're likely not having *any* sex, but if they're refusing to give up the ghost, it's not teenage-drive-in-theater ecstasy."

"Hmm. Sorry to hear that."

"So, Daisy asked me if I'd heard from Frank today."

"The president Frank guy?"

"That one. I told her Frank'd called a couple times and she got peevish at me."

"Ah, Tank, come on. Women don't get *peevish.* That word implies irritation over unimportant matters. Scientific research and generations of men sleeping on couches has proven that nothing is unimportant to the female mind."

"She's not pleased with me addressing the POTUS by his first name."

"Too disrespectful, right?"

"Naturally. So, I decided to check the news, see what was going on."

"A tactical retreat. Nice."

"Thank you, my friend. So, I started with PBS and worked my way up the cable channels. It was old news only on the major networks and complete garbage above them."

"Some things are a constant."

"So, I click to MSNBC, and they featured you losing badly to Plesmus in an argument."

"Thank you, General Sherman," Plesmus shouted out.

"Okay," I confirmed. "I'm with ya so far."

"Good, because that's it. Now you and I are talking."

"And you can see me."

"Like you're on TV, because, you're on TV."

"Obviously I can hear you, but I can't see you."

"You'll have to complain to MSNBC about that, Jon. Not my doing."

"I think you're missing the big take-away here, Tank."

"Which is?"

"That this communication is six kinds of impossible."

"Likely quite a few more than that, but your point is?"

"My point is this link is impossible. Mechanistically, it cannot occur. I am immensely far away from you. I have no TV-transmission capabilities, and MSNBC absolutely, positively cannot be broadcasting me arguing with Plesmus because that's insanity served on a sesame seed bun."

"And yet we speak."

"We speak as old friends," I seconded. "So how the hell are you?"

"You already asked that one," he observed.

"So, how's ... how's ... *Frank*?"

"Frank's confused, frightened, and frustrated."

"So 'bout the same as last time I saw him?"

"Pretty much."

"Good, good. Say, Tank, you haven't heard from Sachiko lately, have you?"

"Can't say I have. Last time we spoke... oh, that was a month, maybe six weeks ago. How about you?"

"Me?" Crap, I didn't want to dump the contents of my wacky communication with her via Radio Plesmus. "Me, I'm fine, thanks for asking."

"Jon, I'm giving you three seconds to answer my question."

"And if I don't?"

"I'm having MSNBC install a cattle prod switch to my end of this little parley."

"Ah, gotcha. Well, and funny you should ask. You know how this present communication defies all logic and physical laws?"

"I'm dialing their customer service number as we speak."

"Well, believe it or not I recently had a brief but welcome audio hookup with Sachiko and the gang."

"On cable TV?"

"Ah, no. Radio Plesmus."

"I wasn't aware she *was* a radio."

"Neither were we." I laughed nervously. "So, anyway, on both our ends—Aramthella's and mine—Plesmus kind of passed out. After she did, for a few minutes there, we were able to communicate through her body."

"Her unconscious body?" he asked dubiously.

"Pretty much."

"Well now I'm stuck," he announced. "I can't say which form of impossible communication is screwier than the other."

"I'm with you, brother. No clue."

"So, what'd you find out?" he pressed firmly.

"Ah, they're good. They were, you know, lost, plagued with impossibilities, and, oh, I got the impression Lincoln was aboard again."

"Old Honest Abe likes himself a space voyage."

"Apparently," I agreed.

"So they were safe?" he asked unequivocally.

"Absolutely. Right ... up ... until we lost contact that is."

"Jon?"

"Yes, friend Robert?"

"The cattle prod is installed. Thought I'd let you know I'm dying to try it out."

"Okay. So, just as Radio Plesmus was signing off, Sachiko said something about their nuclear reactor going critical, and there was an explosion and then, well, that was it."

"They don't *have* any nuclear reactors."

"I was under that same impression. Color me as surprised as you are."

"So they could be dead?"

"Well, could be? Nah. I ... I am fairly confident they're good. They're resourceful, those clever women them."

Tank sighed big time. "So, what exactly did you do to make reality fall to pieces?"

"Me? Well, sure, you're talking to me, right? I, you know, went back and tried to patch up the old timeline. Yeah, didn't do such a good job of it. Then ... then, well, let's just say it. Time began collapsing. And, so, here we are." I was silent a second. "So, how's things with you?"

"Time is collapsing?" he asked very soberly.

"According to Plesmus, yes."

"And I assume it's a runaway train at this point? No turning back?"

"Not that I, Plesmus, or anybody I know or ever heard of can tell. No."

"How long do we—as in the universe—have?"

"No idea. But not a lot, I'm guessing. You know what they say. Don't buy any green bananas." I forced another laugh.

"Not funny, General Ryan," he scorned.

"You know I've always resorted to humor to try and defuse a tense situation."

"There's not much time left, but Jon, maybe work on a better way to defuse stuff, okay?"

"If there's not much time, I'll ... I'll try and make time."

We were both quiet a while.

"So, you going to be okay?" Tank finally asked.

"Most likely. Sure."

"Alone but for Plesmus and lost in time and space. Not a pretty way to exit stage left."

"I could think of a more ideal set of circumstances, yes."

"I will say this. You may have screwed up massively, but I know you were only trying to help. Can't say I'll be thanking you, but at least know I don't hate you or anything for what you did."

"Thanks, Tank. That means a lot."

Quiet befell us yet again.

"Well, I for one can say that I've had a pretty good run," Tank mentioned apropos of nothing. "I had a few plans maybe. But, all-in-all, I had a good one."

"Sure. Me too," I responded sheepishly, not knowing where this was heading.

"I hate like hell that the kids won't get to, you know, get their crack at happiness and all."

"Your kids?"

"No, all kids."

"Ah. Good point."

"It wasn't a point as much as a wish," Tank corrected.

"Ah, good *wish* then."

"Thanks. I know there's some things I won't miss."

"You mean like taxes?" I asked a tad confused.

"Like taxes, sure. I will *not* miss them. Or robocalls or spam mail or midnight anonymous texts for sex hookups."

"What about texts from parties *known* to you?" I felt the need to ask.

"No, won't miss those either." He waited a spell, then went on. "I won't miss what this time collapse does to your dreams, either."

"Mine personally?"

"No, no. I mean dreams in general."

"You mean like one's hopes for a better future kind of hopes and dreams?" Seriously, I had no clue.

"No, Jon, come on. During this crazy wind-down, your dreams have been affect ... Oh, wait. Didn't you once tell me androids don't dream?"

"None that I know do."

"Oh, then sorry I mentioned it."

"So, you've been having, what, *bad* dreams?"

"No, not bad. You know."

"Actually I don't know."

"More weirdo odd, not bad."

"Perhaps an example might go a long way in this setting," I pointed out. "What form and content of your dreams are not satisfying you?"

"Oh, you know. Well, here's a crazy example."

"I can hardly wait."

"Er, thanks. So, lately, maybe over the last month, I've been having these weirdest dreams."

"You said that much already."

"So I did. The dreams, they're like those serials we went to as kids. Do you remember them?"

"Breakfast cereals we went to?" I asked consummately confused.

"No, silly. The serials they show at the movies on Saturday afternoons. *Commando Cody: Sky Marshal of the Universe, Riding with Buffalo Bill,* those kind of serials."

"Okay, vaguely."

"Well, I've had the darnedest dreams with elements that remind me of those. You know, a little more action in each installment. Suspense up the wazoo."

"Tank?"

"Yes, Jon?"

"Maybe just tell me the embarrassing shit and let's, you know, move on." I had a quick fright. "Wait, the embarrassing parts, they don't have to do with *me*, do they. Like, *you* and me?"

"No, Jon. You are so silly."

"I believe you already cited that quirk of my personality."

"Here's the deal. Lately, I've had these dreams about when I was on Aramthella."

"Whew, progress. Go on."

"You know after you resurrected Earth, I was pulled along. But the last things I remembered were just early stuff after Aramthella first came under our control."

"Yeah, sure."

"One minute I'm fighting the clan and the next I'm in my backyard with Daisy."

"Uh huh." I did not like where this seemed to be heading.

"Yeah. So, I'm having these snippets involving Colonel St. Claire. You ... you remember her, right?"

"Reva. Sure. She's a peach."

"Yeah, she sure is. So, anyway, in these crazy dreams, her and I are, well, we're more than casual coworkers, if you can imagine that?"

"Ah, yes I can." *Since I saw you two necking like pythons more times than I'd care to recall,* I did not add.

"And, well, here's the embarrassing part. I ... I kind of almost *remember* that we were lovers."

"Remember in your dream?"

"Jon, you are impossible. There are no dreams. I'm having memories intrude into my head suggesting Reva and I were sexually involved."

"Ah, Tank, you are seated presently, correct?"

"Correct," he replied with irritation.

"And Daisy, she's not, like, in earshot?"

"No. When she heard it was you on the tube she declined to watch."

"Smart gal. So, Tank, here's the deal. And you have to remember that the Earth, it was gone. All the people, and sheep, and little cute ocean creatures, they were all gone. None of them ever existed."

"This I know," he responded with irritation.

"So, and I'm being a pal here and cutting right to the chase—"

"Much appreciated."

"So, yes, you and Reva were a couple."

"A couple?"

"And you coupled ... a *lot.*"

"We coupled a lot?"

"Yeah, like bunnies in springtime both of which having been dosed with high levels of hormones."

Tank was quiet a few seconds. "So, it was a sex thing?"

"Well, no. You two, you were the real deal. She was gaga over you and you were all to-the-moon-and-back about her. And there was a lot of coupling."

"Jon, you made your point about the sex."

"Just trying to paint the picture here. Please don't shoot the messenger."

This time he was quiet for several minutes. I could hear those wheels a-turning. Smelled the smoke too.

"So, how'd Reva take it?"

"What, when you were murdered?"

"I was *murdered*?" he shouted back.

"Kind of. Sure. At the citadel. We were breaking into this—"

"I was with you at that citadel place?"

"Ah, kind of. Sure. You know, until someone there killed you."

"I cannot *believe* you did not tell me I was murdered."

"Tank, that's old history."

"Yeah, old my-being-murdered history," he shouted even louder.

"Tank, in terms of the coffee you referred to, was it decaf?"

He took a few deep breaths. "So, okay, how did she take my murder?"

"Ah, better than your resurrection?" I kind of squeaked.

"You have *got* to be shitting me."

"Not really. When you were killed, sure, she was a hot mess. But she's in the military. She knows what we all signed up for."

"But when I was back to playing house with my wife of forever and she was one gigantic hole in my memory—"

"That ... that one bothered her much."

"I can maybe see why telling me all the details was not too great an idea."

"Not in any universe I've ever been in. No."

"So, is Reva any better now?"

"The last time I saw her? I guess she was better in that she wasn't crying constantly and somewhat derelict in all her duties. Just some of them, mind you."

"And then he really felt like crap."

"But, Hani really helped. You know what, I think Reva's going to be just fine, now that she has Hani."

"Reva has a girlfriend now?"

"A girlfriend? No, you moron. She has a daughter named Hani."

Oops. You know maybe I could have said that better. Less heart-attack-causing. "It's ... Hani's not *your* daughter, Tank."

"She's someone else's daughter?" he asked stunned.

"Sure. Everyone's somebody's daughter. Big duh."

"No, you insensitive jerk. Are you telling me in between when I was resurrected and now she found a guy and already has—"

"No, no. *Stop*. I rescued Hani in like 130,000 B.C. She was about to be eaten by jackals—"

"The little girl was about to be eaten by jackals?"

"No, there, you're right. They were *hyenas* that were about to eat her. Anyway, I rescued her and brought her to Aramthella. But Sapale and I decided not to keep her, so Reva took her. Now they're super happy."

"You decided not to keep the girl so Reva *took* her? Is she similar to an old coffee table?"

"Adopted. Whatever. It's all cool. No child was eaten, Reva is looking nothing but forward, and it's all good."

"Up until the part about time collapsing," Tank just had to agitate. Man, and things were going so well up to that point.

"So, that's the rest of the story, my friend. You and Reva were a pair. Now you're not."

"Well, if you see her before I do—"

"What?"

"Maybe tell her I know now and I'm sorry."

"Jon Ryan you will do *nothing* of the kind," shouted a distinctly female voice on Tank's end of the line. Daisy. Oh, boy. "And you, Robert Sherman, how could you be so insensitive. *I'm sorry*, a man says to a woman who loved him with all her heart? No kind of man married to me would *dare* be that insensitive, that callous."

"Daisy," Tank pleaded, "I can explain."

"There's no need to. Jon already did," she huffed, pointing at the TV. "I was dead, you were not. You fell in love with a wonderful woman. It's called *life*, Tank. Life happens."

Man, she was good.

"But I never meant—"

"Stop, I say, Robert Sherman," she thundered as much as a woman named Daisy *can* thunder. "I am not a schoolgirl. I am familiar with the course of human events. That you fell in love when you were in fact a widower is absolutely fine and appropriate."

"It is?" he marveled dubiously.

"Of course it is. Oh, I know you hemmed and hawed, worried yourself sick, and took forever to come around. But the important thing is that you did."

"Ah, *thank you*?" Tank said.

"Do not sully this by thanking me. I was dead. But, so help me, Robert Sherman, to tell a woman who loved you that you're *sorry*. What? Are you saying you're sorry because she loved you or that you loved her back?"

"Er—" he started.

"Not one *word*," she commanded. "Why ... why that's unconscionable, Tank. Even for you."

"So, Jon," Tank called out.

"Yeah?"

"If you see Reva first, don't tell her I'm sorry."

"Ah, at this point, if I *ever* see Reva I'm running the other way."

"Jon, if you are not careful you are going to be my next pupil," Daisy threatened convincingly.

"Gotcha. If I see Reva, I shall discuss the weather."

"Good boy," she praised. "Tank could learn from you."

"But I—" he began. I imagine that's when Daisy gave him the *not now* look. It worked.

"Jon, I wish you well," Daisy concluded. "Now I'll let you two scoundrels finish up with whatever it is you're doing."

"Thanks, Daisy. Godspeed."

"She's gone now," Tank said like the beaten dog he had to be.

"Tank?"

"Yes."

"You and Reva were good together. You and Daisy are good together. It's all good. No worries."

"Thanks. Jon."

"Hey, what are guy friends for?"

After a few seconds, he asked again, "Jon, why is it we're talking?"

"Because we're oldest, bestest pals, pal?"

"Jon, Plesmuses are not radios. MSNBC does not provide enhanced communications between far-flung compadres. What's going on?"

"If I knew, dude, I would tell you. Mysteries of the universe, I guess."

"I suppose that'll have to do."

"At least for now. But, if I do gain any meaningful intel, I'll forward it to you."

"Unless I'm cosmic dust."

"In which case I'll forward your mail to your friend, the one you just mentioned."

"What friend? I don't believe—"

"Commando Cody: Sky Marshal of the Universe. I'll send everything through him. Sounds like one cool cat."

"Actually he was a dork with a Lone Ranger mask and girlfriend who wore a potholder as a hat."

"I stand corrected."

"Jon, I miss ya."

"Tank, I miss you. Hey, when this is all behind us, what say we take the ladies and head for Rockaway Beach?"

There was no response.

"Tank, you there, buddy?"

Sad fact here. That was the last time I ever spoke with Tank. I know, spoiler alerts and all. But ... that was it.

TWELVE

Somewhere in America,
back in the day ...

"Where ... where *is* that boy?"

As a rule, Ned Ryan wasn't a detail-oriented guy. Some who knew him well called him a *dreamer*. Others opted for the term *space cadet*. Either way, he wasn't a person to overly focus on particulars. But during the last few years, he'd grown an entirely new part of his brain, one that led him to worry about where his son had gotten off to. Presently, Ned was in the attic. Between sweeping cobwebs from his face and tripping almost continually over stuff jammed into the burdened space, he was having no luck finding Jon.

"I ... I know I told the lad to mow the lawn," he mumbled to the forgotten and abandoned residents of the loft. "I surely did. Plus he was supposed to plunge out his toilet. But ... but where *is* he?"

To his credit, the attic wasn't the first place Ned had searched. No, that would have been silly. There was no plunger, no lawn mower, or other earthly reasons for Jon to be up there. But Jon wasn't wherever Ned had checked so far, so he was forced to pursue a trail of admittedly diminishing returns.

Once he'd proven beyond any reasonable doubt that no one was in fact in the attic, Ned wandered back to the kitchen. Aside from Jon's room, which Ned'd inspected four times already, the kitchen was the most likely place to find the rapidly growing, constantly eating boy. Alice stood with her back to Ned, her skirt covered with a frilly apron as she kneaded some dough.

"Say, sweetheart, have you seen Jonny?"

"Yes, I believe I have. About five feet tall, freckles, and the one I pushed out of my body thirteen years ago? Yeah, I've seen him. Handsome young man, in my humble opinion," she replied without turning.

"No, honey, I meant recently."

"Does breakfast count as recently?"

"No, dear, it's one o'clock."

"Then no."

"I've looked everywhere. He seems to have vanished from the face of the planet."

"Why do you want him?"

"I ... I was looking for him because—" Ned rubbed his one-day stubble. "Well, isn't that just too much. I forgot why I was looking for him."

"Well, it is one fifteen on a Saturday. Perchance had you tasked him to mow the lawn and he has yet to accomplish that weekly chore?"

Ned snapped his fingers and pointed at Alice's back. "That's it. You're a genius. He was supposed to have mowed the lawn before he went off to play sports ball with his friends. And I specifically asked him to plunge out his toilet. It's running slow and it's high time he learns to be a man."

Alice craned her neck around and gave her husband dubious consideration. "*Sports* ball?"

"You know, one of those games he loves with balls. I can't keep up with which one it is at any given time." He wagged a finger in the air. "I'm only human."

"Well, here's a clue, love of my life. It's late spring in the US of A. So Jonny will be obsessing about *base*-ball right about now."

"That's what I said. But he can't go off to play any ball until he plunges and mows."

"Have you looked for him in the garage?"

Ned was back to scratching his stubble. "No, can't say as I have. Well, hang on a sec ... maybe ... no, I didn't check there yet."

"That is where we keep both the mower and the plunger, right?"

"We surely do."

"And our lawn starts up right to one side of the garage."

"That it does. Honey, you're on a real roll here this morning."

"Afternoon," she corrected neutrally.

"Afternoon," he revised. After a moment, he continued, "You know, maybe I'll check out in the garage. He might be fiddling with the mower. If it's not oiled just right, it's a bear to push it."

"You could be like the rest of the neighbors and buy one of those power mowers. We are past the halfway point of the twentieth century you know."

"Yes we are," he agreed energetically. "Before you know it we'll all have space cars and vacation on the Moon."

"Whatever, George Jetson. But for now, go check in the garage."

His forehead creased. "Sure thing, honey cake. Uh, what am I looking for out there?"

"Our son."

"Yes. Now I remember. Jonny was supposed to mow the grass."

"There you go, love. And plunge so he can become a man."

"Alright, I'll see you in a bit. I'm ... I'll be in the garage if you need me. I'm looking for Jonny."

Alice contemplated responding that she knew that already. But, as usual, she decided not to bother. In what manner would her comment improve the universe? None, so she returned to taking out any frustration she might have felt on the bread dough.

Ned headed for the detached garage, but was waylaid by an old adversary of his: that leaky hose. Right where the female thread attached to the bib the darn thing was dripping again like water was free and those weeds crowding the base needed encouragement. A few months back he'd changed the washer. That didn't stop the leak. Then he replaced the female fitting. Still it dripped.

He spent several minutes turning the spigot off and inspecting the various parts, then attaching the hose again only to be bedeviled again by that darn leak. He needed to remember to buy some thread tape next time he was down at the hardware store. It was his last hope for sanity.

After deciding to dismiss the offending hose assembly for the time being, Ned stood in confusion for a good thirty seconds before he remembered about the garage, the plunger, the mower, and Jonny. Off he went. Ned opened the door and searched for any sign of his son. There was the lawn mower. It didn't seem to have been moved. The plunger was right where it was supposed to be, in a plastic trash bag behind the door. It sure looked dry to Ned's reckoning.

That's when he heard the ... what was it he was hearing? It sounded like grunting. No, snorting. No, that was it, grunting *and* snorting. Maybe a little panting too. Most unexpected. It was coming from the other side of the car, in the corner where Ned stored the winter supplies. As the day was cloudy and the garage had few windows, Ned grabbed a flashlight from the counter and went to see what the noise was all about. Why didn't Ned simply turn on the lights? Because he was Ned Ryan. Come on, pay attention here.

Ned rounded the car and shone the light on ... someone's skinny butt. Someone's bare naked skinny butt. He lowered the beam and saw a pair of women's legs. One ankle had a girdle around it, and the other didn't. Most peculiar, Ned reflected. What gal left the house with her girdle around one of her ankles? He was roused from his musing by a particularly animalistic grunt.

"Excuse me," Ned said as forcefully as he could muster, which wasn't all that very much. "What in the Sam Hill is going on here?"

The naked skinny butt launched itself backward with a squishy slurp. Jon turned to face his old man. For his part Ned was much more focused on the prodigious erection he was confronted with more so than the identity of the erectee. Then Ethel Ozack, the next door neighbor lady, leaned her head forward to see who was addressing the pair. When she realized who it was, she silently mouthed, *Oh shit.*

Only then did Ned look up from the erection to the face of its owner. He was, in a word, stunned.

"Jonny, what are you doing?"

"I'm ... it's not what you *think*, Dad." Jon held his palms up toward his father.

"Oh, I'm betting it is *exactly* what I think. You're playing hide-the-salami with our next door neighbor, a woman who is well into her fifties I might add."

Jon shot a glance to Ethel, then back to his dad. Then he shook his head violently. "No, Dad. Come on, how can you even think that?"

"How could I ... Jonny, I wasn't born yesterday. What else could I think, you with that ... that—" Ned could only gesture generally in the direction of the erection. "And Mrs. Ozack has her undergarments down to her ankles and her dress hiked up to her ears. Jonny, how could ... Wait. Don't answer that."

"Seriously, Dad. It's not what you think. Eth ... ah, Mrs. Ozack here ... she was choking. Yeah." Jon extended an arm in her direction. "The poor soul was choking to *death.* What was I supposed to do? Let her just die because my father might come under the incorrect impression that his young son was diddling the nice neighbor lady? Come on, Dad, that's harsh."

"Jonny, don't you start," Ned admonished. "We both know you could talk a Rottweiler off of a steak, but just don't even start, okay?"

"Wha ... what am I hearing?" Jon protested with significant indignation. "I should let people die now?"

"Jonny, I've taken the first aid class from the Red Cross too. Do not try to pull any wool over my baby blues. I know the proper procedure for clearing an airway." Ned flicked his index finger laterally. "Sweep the mouth." Then he mimed striking something with the flat of his hand. "Five swift back blows." Then he shoved his joined fist up at a shallow angle. "Then five abdominal thrusts."

Ned's head seemed to almost explode due to a powerful thought. He raised a finger in the air and slashed it at his son. "And don't you tell me that's the way the Red Cross says to perform an abdominal thrust, young man. You use your *hand*, not your *pecker*."

As Ned was ranting, Ethel took the opportunity to retrieve her girdle. She tucked it into a skirt pocket. "I really think I should be going now," she announced.

"Now just you hold your horses, Ethel Ozack. No one leaves until I get to the bottom of this sordid affa ... er, sordid *story*."

"Dad, seriously, you're blowing this out of all proportion. Mrs. Ozack," he gestured toward her respectfully, "was choking on ... on a communion wafer. Yes, that's it. She rushed out her backdoor when she saw me, her eyes begging for mercy. And, yes, I tried sweeping her mouth, the back blows, and the conventional abdominal thrusts. Dad, they didn't work. The poor woman, she was fading."

"So you decided to try sexual intercourse as a last ditch intervention?" Ned mocked.

"As *if*," Jon decried. "My ears, Dad. Please respect my ears. No. Just this very week I was reading my copy of *Boy's Life* magazine. In it they detail a new technique for the treatment of refractory airway obstruction."

"Oh, this is going to be good," Ned declared as he rocked on his heels, arms crossed.

"Dad, I am as serious as a fart attack."

"Son, the expression is as serious as a *heart* attack," Ned instructed with a chuckle.

Young though he was, Jon squinted at his old man. "To each his own hell, Dad." Then Jon's face softened. "But I digress. In *Boy's*

World, a top expert, man by the name of Ignatius P. Freely, LLP., discussed the introduction of a new and more effective intervention for choking. He calls it Extreme Abdominal Thrusting Intervention Treatment, to distinguish it from your run-of-the-mill abdominal thrusts that we are already familiar with."

"Wait, this man invented a procedure called EAT IT?"

"Way to drag science through the mud, Father. I'm discussing cutting edge medical science here."

"With your trousers still down and that ... that woody your sporting, it's hard to take you too seriously, son." Ned sighed.

"In order to successfully perform EATIT, Dad, the rescuer needs to generate coordinated pressure waves from several differing directions. So, as you witnessed, I was struggling to save Mrs. Ozack's life."

"Jonny, that is the best doozy of a tall tale I've ever heard. But you can't BS me." Ned chuckled again. "If you were really trying to exert extreme pressure, you forgot to include the final potential human orifice through which force could be applied. No actual *scientist* writing in *Boy's Life* would have overlooked that addition." Ned again rocked on his heels, very pleased with his cleverness.

"Dad."

"Yes, son?"

"You didn't see my left hand during my resuscitation efforts, now did you?"

"Oh." Ned dry heaved. "That's just well beyond gross."

Ethel finally found her voice. "The boy's struggling to save my life and you get squeamish because he cares enough to cover fifth base? Shame on you, Ned Ryan."

There was a knock on the garage door. "Is there a problem in there?" asked a low, slightly Slavic sounding voice.

"Emil, is that you?" Ethel called out.

"Yes, my wife. What is all the commotion I am finding it very hard to continue ignoring which is going on in there?"

"Oh, shit," Ned blurted out.

"What?" Ethel chided. "It was the boy who should maybe worry that his principal might take this scene of medical intervention in the wrong light, not you, Ned Ryan."

Ouch, Jon might have kind of forgotten about that connection, in, er, the heat of the resuscitation.

"So, is this garage door going to be opening or must I purchase a ticket first?" Emil asked with irritation.

"Probably a ticket would be the realistic option," Ned mumbled to himself.

Alice chose that moment to enter through the garage side door. "Why on earth is everybody yelling about out here?" She flipped on the light, looked to Ned, then Ethel, and then to Jon, who was rushing to pull up his pants. Let the record show that he did so too slowly for his mother not to leap to an august conclusion.

"When your father told me you were going to the garage to become a man, I had assumed he was referring to your learning how to plunger a toilet, not our neighbor."

"Mom, I was performing a medical intervention. Just ask Dad. He believes me."

"You were performing something but medical is a stretch, bucko," she quipped. Alice pointed at Ethel. "You. Out of here. And if my son comes down with the clap, I'm coming for you. Be afraid." Alice then pointed to Ned. "You, go to your room."

"Bu ... but, honey, I only *caught* them. It wasn't a threesome or anything."

"And that's the kind of thinking that gets you sent to your room. Move."

Ned scooted out almost as fast as Ethel had vacated the premises.

"Emil?" Alice shouted through the garage door.

"No Emil here," he wisely responded. "Nobody out here at all."

"Keep it that way," Mom barked.

When just the two of them were left, Alice rested a fist on either hip. "I hope you have learned a very important lesson, Mister Hot Nuts."

Jon started to defend himself, but his mother raised a single finger.

"Not one word. Not. One. Word," she instructed.

Jon pantomimed zipping his lips shut.

"I would like to go on record now with a few personal observations. One, you have broken my heart. Two, you have temporarily broken your father's heart. Obviously he'll forget about this completely in a few hours, but know that you did wound him if only briefly. Three, your eighth-grade year will be one I wouldn't suffer my worst enemy to endure. Once Mr. Ozack gets the full picture of what you did to his wife, well, I just wouldn't want to be you." Alice was quiet a moment.

"Are we done?" Jon asked, trying with all his might to sound contrite.

"Almost. One last thought. Jon Ryan, you have screwed up—pun intended—*big* time here. In fact, I feel it is safe to say that you will *never* screw up this big if you live a million years."

With that, Alice turned on her sensibly low-heeled mules and left.

Man, I think back on that awkward-as-hell episode every now and then. You know what? Turns out my mother was wrong. Totally wrong. Imagine that? Sure, it took me two *billion* years, not a measly one million, to bungle worse. But—yay Team Ryan—I sure did manage to pull off a *much* bigger screw-up. I'm kind of glad she wasn't around to see me crush my previous personal record. Yeah, I doubt she'd have been a proud momma.

How had I screw the pooch? Let me count the ways. I blundered to the depth and breadth and height of the ultimate fool, who was me. Recalling I spent some time in the Oblivion, I had to say my current state of being might actually have been worse. I wasn't as alone, since RD and Plesmus were with me. But in place of the absolute nothingness of the Oblivion, I was immersed, subverted, and replaced by an electrostatically jumbled lifelessness. I ... I can't really describe it. It was like a thousand porcupines crawled under my clothing practicing for their shot at the Cirque du Soleil. But they weren't actually there. Nothing was. I can tell you this much with absolute certainty. I was over with this null reality about ten seconds after it had begun.

Funny and-the-rest-of-the-story here. So, about two weeks after being caught in the garage with Mrs. Ozack, the school year started up. Man-o-man was I scared shitless. Eighth grade was going to suck. This I knew because seventh grade already did totally suck the big one. And everybody who survived eighth grade swore it was the worst nine months of their lives. Add to that the vendetta I was properly owed, and, let's face it, I was dead meat walking.

A few days passed with no big confrontation with Principal Ozack there on his domain. But then, in the middle of biology class, the teacher gets a call. My presence is requested in the office. I shambled out of the classroom praying that my death would be both reasonably merciful and swift. By the time I arrived at the administration door, I could barely move. Glacially I opened the door and poured myself into a seat in the line of chairs designated for students awaiting their bleak fate.

Miss Francois, the school secretary, smiled at me. I figured it was gallows humor on her part. But then she asked if I wanted a Coke while I waited. Refreshments? Offered to a student? And a student staring down the barrel of a death sentence? What the hell? My response? I asked her if it was cold. Hey, even at that tender age I was cocky. If I was going to drink the man's Coke, it damn well had better be ice cold.

About halfway through the well-chilled beverage, Miss F. announced the principal would see me and she escorted me in. *Will there be anything else*, she asked probably of him. I chugged the last of the bottle, extended it toward her, and asked for another of the same. Instead of a dictionary to the back of my head, guess what I got? A second refreshing Coca-Cola, thank you very much.

"Jonathan," Mr. Ozack began in a neutral tone, "how is the school year going so far?

I shrugged. What was I going to say? *You know, sir, the anticipation of being brutally murdered was tough but the Coke was good?*

"Fine, fine," he opined. I presume he was more than accustomed to laconic teenagers with attitudes. "Did you get all the classes you wanted?"

"I—" I scanned the room for the camera or starving tiger that must surely have been why he was trying to distract me, "I didn't realize we had any choices to get or not get."

"No options," he chuckled. "That's a good one, Jonathan." He pointed halfheartedly toward me.

And that was the last thing he said to me that day that I understood. Seriously, the rest was mumbo-jumbo gibberish. I can't even classify it was stupid adult-speak, because who knew what he was babbling about?

Ozack went on about how in this world, in order to succeed, men had to help each other out. If, say, I did *him* a favor, well then, he would feel obliged to do *me* a favor. Didn't I understand that, he pressed? I said maybe, but that another Coke would probably help my comprehension a lot. Another was brought at once. I could get used to this.

Then he word-said to me, or maybe to his invisible friend, stuff about how a long-term married couple's goals and desires waxed and waned as they aged. Like the phases of the Moon, he said. Did I take his meaning, he asked paternally? I did not, but he seemed to not be heading in the direction of flogging me, so I said that sure I did. It was all *perfectly understandable.* I'd heard Perry Mason say that once on the stupid TV show my parents loved, so I went with it.

It was as if my words had informed the principal he'd won the lottery. He effused and complimented and went from confusing me to baffling me completely. If I could *take the pressure off of him*—his exact words—in terms of his wife's waxing and waning desires, which, he lamented, were waxing more than they were waning, then he'd consider it a personal favor on my part. I was so confused!

Which part? What favor? What the hell was being waxed? Had he been *literally* applying Turtle Shell car wax to his spouse and wanted me to do so instead and maybe polish her while I was at it? I was so confused.

Then the old badger finally stood, reached across his desk, and shook my hand. And if I wasn't stunned enough, he then leaned in and informed me discretely, "You know tomorrow I have a school board meeting. I won't be home until after ten, maybe later, if you take my meaning." And he wagged his caterpillar eyebrows like I'd know what either the information or the gesture might mean. "Would you care for another Coke?" he asked, pointing to my nearly full bottle.

"No," I replied as sweat poured down my body like I was named Niagara. "I just wanted to focus on my biology, you know, before it was over," I choked out.

"You don't need to stress over that, Jonathan," he said with a huge chuckle. "Your stallion days are in front of you, not behind. Tomorrow I bet your biology will last over *half* an hour, you know, while I'm at the school board meeting?"

"I ... you found out I had biology homework tomorrow?" I asked more stunned than I thought humanly possible.

"Jonny, please, don't think of it as homework."

"It's *not* biology homework?" I pressed, about ready to pass out.

"No, no. Oh, it can *seem* that way sometimes, I assure you. But I want you to think of it as a voyage of discovery?"

"Dis ... discovery?"

"Yes, discovery. Say, you're a Boy Scout, aren't you?"

"Yes," I replied, now certain we were speaking in different languages while standing on different part of the solar system.

"Then I want you to think of tomorrow night like this. You're a Boy Scout and this is a task, or rather a public service. If you do well —and Jonny," he got serious, "no one will judge you, so just doing the deed will constitute a win—you'll earn a merit badge. You understand that, right?"

I shook my head in the negative. "Yes, sir."

"Excellent. So, you do your best, I am spared the distaste, and you get a new merit badge."

"For biology homework that isn't actually going to be biology homework?"

"Exactly. Well, I have another appointment. Do you have any last questions?"

"Well, yes. I was worried, you know."

He frowned deeply. "About what?"

No way I was getting off without some severe punishment, at least a partial maiming. "You know, that you wanted me cond ... condem ... I mean—"

"That you'd need worry about a *condom*?" He laughed knowingly. "While I must praise your acting so responsibly, you won't need a *condom* for tomorrow's not-homework. My wife is past the age where she needs to worry about pregnancy."

What the fuck was he going on about?

He had a school board meeting. I did and did *not* have biology homework. I didn't need a condom for my non-homework. And, to top the insanity off, by the way, his wife couldn't get preggers? That ... that was the ultimate gross, never-going-to-get-out-of-my-head TMI.

Lord, I beseeched, *take me now, I'm too confused to live a second longer.*

For the record I never came within twenty yards of either of those two lunatics again. Oh, there were a few weird days there when Mrs. Ozack seemed to stalk for me like I was scrumptious dessert. But that passed, eighth grade was passed—and yes there is a God—the Ozacks sold the house and moved that next summer.

Anyway, back to the nothingness.

"RD, I'm looking at pea-soup thick noise out there. What do your sensors show?"

"Nothing familiar, sir."

"Can you describe them to me?" I asked a tad pissed for having to ask.

"Um, I can try, but the data is not consistent with any I've recorded before. We are surrounded by a stable sphere of rather conventional appearing but empty space approximately fifty meters in radius."

"I presume that's my time lock holding time/space normal within this defined area," Plesmus opined.

"Sounds reasonable," I agreed. "And outside the sphere?"

"My thermal sensors show a patchy heat in a roughly isotropic distribution. And it reads hot, up to over ten-thousand degrees Celsius."

"Okay," I mumbled.

"At the same time they show that the space just past the time lock is at absolute zero, Kelvin."

"Wait, nothing's absolutely zero. There's always some Brownian wiggle room," I countered.

"Normally I would agree with you, but these are my thermal readings."

"That it's at once blazing hot and completely frozen out there?"

"Yes, sir, precisely."

"How can it be precisely self-cancelling and contradictory?"

"You asked me to describe my sensory input. I have. I cannot explain it. I'm basically a tourism AI, not a theoretical physicist one."

"Thanks for the update," I grumbled. I did not need more impossibilities in my life. Grr.

"Plesmus, what are your impressions of what's out there?"

"Imprecise. As the system's operator just reported, the environment surrounding us is unprecedented in my experience. While I can't comment on the temperature dynamics, I can say that the time milieu is chaotic. Massive clouds of time are swirling amidst patches of timelessness, and those are buffeted by an entity I cannot identify."

"What, like a space monster?" I idiotically asked.

"No, human. An amorphous slurry of space occupied neither with time nor timelessness."

"What? What does that even mean?"

"That whatever you spawned out there by destroying the barrier between the Timeless Void and our timed reality is batshit crazy."

"If you mix matter and antimatter, you get a lot of energy and maybe a few rare particles. Is this other stuff like that?"

"*Is this other stuff like that?*" she mocked. "Jon, could you speak a more educated manner?"

"If forced to, sure." I paused for a few seconds. "Say, Plesmus, I have a vexing query to run by you. Is the amorphous slurry of neither time nor timelessness in any way similar to the type of results one obtains when one mixes equal amounts of matter and antimatter? Specifically, as matter/antimatter interactions yield massive quantities of energy along with novel elementary particles, I'm curious if this amorphous material is in any way analogous to that?"

"I stand corrected. Please continue to speak like a country bumpkin."

"You got it, pallo." I sure loved winning.

"While it is tempting to extrapolate familiar conditions, I am not comfortable making that parallel. There is very little time out there, and the amount is decreasing rapidly. The same is true of the timelessness. The third substance is increasing in its percentages, comparatively."

"What is it like?"

"It is like nothing I've ever sensed. It is, however, painful for me to probe."

"Painful as in ouch I just hit my finger with a hammer ouch?"

"As I do not possess those, I cannot say. But it is a feeling I wish to avoid, but, at the same time, is so overpowering that ignoring it is difficult."

"And it's growing relative to the other time energies?"

"Yes."

"Then I'm inclined to label it bad." Enough intellectualizing. I needed to act. To act, I needed a plan. To devise a plan, I needed fact. "I unleashed timelessness upon our timed universe. It has resulted not in nothing, but the cancellation of what, up until now, has been our fourth dimension of measurement: time. We still have length, width, and height, the X, Y and Z axes. But time, outside of Mr. Ryan's Neighborhood, is gone.

"Here's my take. When we no-time an object, like you do, Plesmus, we are left with timeless matter. That substance exits our known universe and drifts off as a time-inert mass. We, who still proceed along our time axis, leave it behind, so to speak. I will assume the increasing and painful haze that is resulting from time/timeless cancellation is similar in concept if not kind. It is not untimed *mass,* however, but it's—and I hate to be about to say this—untimed time."

Ples was quiet for several minutes. I took that as a good sign. She was very smart and I valued her opinion greatly. The fact that she waited to consider my supposition that long was encouraging.

"I see no problem with your theory," she finally pronounced. "We will almost certainly never have the chance to subject the *haze,* as you call it, to scientific analysis. But yours is as good an explanation as any alternative I can come up with."

"Thanks. I appreciate your support. The next issue is mass. What has happened to it? We see this sleet-like substance which defies characterization by our scanners. But, amidst all that wasted time, there was matter. Stars, galaxies, puppies. Everything. Where is it?"

"I do not detect it as such with my instruments," RD offered.

"Nor do I sense it," Plesmus concurred.

"If it was just no-timed matter, we'd observe it as the inert blobs we've seen since our earliest run in with the clan. And we don't. So the cancellation of time didn't no-time matter. So, either the time goo is—"

"Stop," commanded Plesmus. "I know I will regret asking, but what is *time goo,* you child-brained monkey?"

"The crap we're seeing more and more of. For simplicity, it needs a name."

"No, it doesn't. What, did the physical result of time-timelessness interactions text you and ask you to give it a silly name?"

"I do not believe I shall dignify that remark with a response," I huffed.

"You just did, human," Plesmus snapped. "It was off-topic and lame, but respond you did."

"Back to my didactic," a wounded me continued. "The time goo is either preventing us from *seeing* normal matter, or it has *changed* normal matter, but not into the timeless mass we've seen before."

"I can accept that supposition," she allowed a bit begrudgingly.

"We know from physics that there is *no* relationship between mass and time. E equals m c squared and all that, but there are no laws linking time to anything. Mass is what's called a Lorentz invariant, so it remains the same in all reference frames. Time is just the fourth component of the positional four-vector that we use to define a location in time/space. So I cannot think of a direct result on mass if time is eliminated."

"Wait, Captain, I'm confused," RD admitted. "When an object is no-timed, it drifts off as an observable ... er, lump of something."

"Yes," I affirmed.

"So, isn't the cancellation of time the same, wouldn't all matter become that lumpy stuff drifting away?"

"No, you might think so, but it's not. The floating-away lump is matter without a time coordinate. What we have going on outside our lock is an absence of time globally. Time energy has not been drawn off in this case—it simply does not exist. Nothing can happen, no lump can drift off, because there is no *time* out there for it to occur over. Does that make sense?"

"No," he grumbled.

"I suggest we move on," Plesmus advised dryly. "We can get lost in a teleological discussion, but it accomplishes nothing in the long run."

"Teleo what?" RD spat out. "I am programmed for many languages, but none of them contain that word."

"Replace *teleologic* with *mental masturbation*," I instructed. "Then you'll have it."

"If I have to think mental masturbation, sir, I don't *want* it," RD said, no doubt electronically cringing.

"But I'm with Ples. We need to move on. The only question remaining is what does one do after the end of time?" I asked morosely. "Most of the main tourist attractions will be offline. Dining out is off the table. Even breathing is kind of over. Not, actually, one whole hell of a lot *to* do, come to think of it."

"Do you think they are safe?" Plesmus asked cautiously.

"Who they?"

"Aramthella, the captain, your mate. All of them."

I resisted a snap response of *thanks for sucking the last possible joy from my universe.* No. Not constructive.

"I'm certain they are," I responded less resolutely than I had intended.

"Certain?" she questioned.

"Yeah, I mean, they have the same time lock established by the same Plesmus generating it. What could go..."

"What could go where?" she pressed when it was clear I wasn't finishing that thought.

"Nothing. I wasn't saying that."

"What were you saying?"

"Absolutely nothing. Wasn't even thinking about thinking of saying words." Sheesh, I almost *said* what could go wrong. Talk about jinxing a thing.

They *had* to be safe though. Same time lock. A time lock's a time lock's a time lock. Everybody and their cousin knows that. Right?

THIRTEEN

Sachiko rested her weary head on her left fist, which was supported by the captain's chair armrest. She was good and whooped. In fact, she was debating at that moment whether she'd ever been this tired, so totally drained. It had been thirty-six hours since Sapale tossed the rogue nuclear reactor off the ship, Plesmus regained her time locking ability, and the hull stopped dissolving. Thirty-six blessed hours without a single crisis or the appearance of a new unexplainable addition to the ship. More out of stubbornness than superstition, Sachiko had held the comm the entire time, refusing any much needed relief. In times such as these, it was her ship, her watch. End of story.

Sachiko's trance was interrupted by a smell. Floral, lingering, a hint of umami. *Tea.* She smelled tea. She lifted her head and scanned the room. Right behind her stood Reva with a smile and a large mug of steamy tea.

"My guardian angel," Sachiko declared as she accepted the tea.

"More like your guardian relief officer. Skipper, you look like death warmed over, no offense intended. Please let me relieve you."

"I'm okay," she held up her mug. "This'll buy me some more quality time in the saddle."

"Sachiko, I'm scared too. I don't understand what's happening or why or if there's one damn thing we can do to change a bit of it. But you're still human. Do us all a favor and grab some rack time."

Sachiko tried to sit up straight. "I know I look tired, but seriously, I'm fine. It's just that we're in the jaws of a really nasty beast and I want to be here whe... er, *if* matters take a turn for the worse."

"Yeah, when *is* more like it and, I don't know if you got the memo, but that's why we have a fully trained crew aboard. You know, if a light bulb burns out while you're asleep, it *will* be replaced expeditiously. No one will stub a toe in the dark."

Sachiko smiled weakly. "I know, Re, but I ... I just can't help thinking that if I'm Johnny-on-the-spot any bumps in the night will go better."

"One, I don't think mentioning that name in any context is wise. Two, you know what we lack, having an all-woman command team?"

Sachiko raised an eyebrow. This was a matter she'd devoted a good deal of thought to. "Do tell."

"Football analogies."

"Sports comparisons? I ... I wasn't aware that I missed them."

"Not sports generically, I'm talking football. Good old American smash-mouth *fubball*."

"Ah. And you have an expression to cover our present crisis?"

"Duh. Always a *fubball* saying to cover any human interaction. Here goes. You're the starting quarterback. Your best replacement if you're injured is you injured. But you dead cannot replace the injured you backing yourself up."

Sachiko stared a moment, allowing for the analogy to continue. She was quite out of her element with fubball wisdom. "Ah." She furrowed her brow. "Are you certain that's the saying? It sounds kind of short and inarticulate."

"I might paraphrase to fit the audience, but that's the general concept, yes."

"And what guiding message, *Mrs*. Diogenes, am I to take from this kernel of insight?"

"You da best commander. You tired is a better commander than whoever might relieve you. But you punch drunk is not a good substitute for you just tired. At a certain point, a poorly trained chimp would do a superior job than comatose-captain you."

"Alright, you've convinced me."

Reva perked up. "You allow me to relieve you?"

"No, silly. When we get through this immediate crisis, I will begin to watch this *fubball*, as you so rustically refer to it. With time and a bit of luck, perhaps I will be able to sling adequate football stories, thus making me the complete captain I yearn to be."

Reva angled her head and tsked. "At least she's sharp enough to mock me proficiently."

"Colonel Saint Claire," Sachiko began expansively, "I laugh *with* you, not at you or at your expense."

"Oh, yay, she's awake and alert," Reva grumbled.

"So, how's Hani doing through all this?"

Reva instantly issued forth a big old proud-mom smile. "Brilliantly. After the last series of explosions and rumblings were over she looked at the teacher and said, *Mo!* Such a doll." Reva sipped her coffee.

The bridge hatch slid open and Sapale stepped in. "*Blessing* said there was human activity on the bridge so I came to investigate."

"You mean you couldn't sleep and you were bored too?" Reva suggested.

"No," she scoffed. "Boy did you get that one wrong. I *can't* sleep, not couldn't." Sapale set her hands on her hips and rocked on the balls of her feet. "Big diff therein, sweetie."

"I stand corrected," Reva responded.

"You back on duty so soon?' Sapale asked knowingly of the captain.

"I never left," Sachiko responded in a neutral tone.

"Coulda fooled me. What with those bags under your eyes and that terminal slouch, I thought you were as fresh as the flowers of Spring."

"Very—"

"Hey, you should get some leeches. Yeah, Jon says they work real well to suck those bags out from under human's eyes."

"When I'm off duty I'll look for some. Will that satisfy—"

"*Captain*," Aramthella interrupted with unmistakable panic in her voice.

Sachiko snapped fully awake. "Report."

"There's a disturbance heading in our direction. A very large disturbance."

"What, like a space hurricane?" Reva reflexively quipped.

"No. Bigger."

Sachiko held a palm up toward Reva's face. "Details please."

"I cannot be very specific. The disturbance is of a nature I am unfamiliar with."

"That can't be good," Sapale observed in a grumble.

"What are its physical characteristics? Charger, polarity, mass, composition, direction in space?" Sachiko demanded.

"It is sweeping across the galaxy at a tremendous velocity. I am unable to see through it and it appears to originate from farther out on our spiral arm, the Orion."

"Are we at risk?"

"Definitely."

"ETA?"

"Minutes ... seconds."

"I'm heading to *Blessing*," Sapale announced quickly and sprinted off the bridge.

"Flank speed in the opposite direction *now*," Sachiko ordered.

"Initiated. We are pushing four hundred Gs directly toward the galactic center."

"Are we putting any distance between us and the disturbance?"

"No, in fact it seems to be accelerating. ETA fifty seconds."

Sachiko tapped an icon on her armrest. "Sapale," she said overhead, "alert me when you get to *Blessing*. From the looks of it we'll need to fold away ASAP." She closed the link. "Aramthella, ready a full membrane. If it overtakes us, place the shield up when it's one second away. Don't wait for me to order it, just do it."

"Understood."

Sachiko thumbed another icon. Automatically klaxons wailed and lights flashed. "Battle stations. All hands to battle stations," came the recorded message. It kept repeating until she tapped it off.

"Captain," Aramthella reported, "the cloud is expanding at an incomprehensible rate. Moving at several hundred multiple of the speed of light it has arced selectively along all the spiral arms and is nearly to their arm's origins centrally."

"Crap," Sachiko huffed. Then she whipped out her handheld. "Engineering."

"Chief here, Go."

"We're about to be run over by badness. Can you give us more speed?"

"Negative, Captain. The time energy injectors are blowing at maximum."

"Very good. Captain out."

"Fifteen seconds," Aramthella alerted.

Sachiko's handheld bleated. "Captain here. Go."

"I'm back to *Blessing*," Sapale shouted.

"Fold us away. Far away."

Sapale felt slight nausea. "Done. We're three hundred million light years from the Milky Way."

"Aramthella, status?" the captain snapped.

"The disturbance has consumed our galaxy. I cannot detect anything in that direction other than the disturbance itself."

"But it's confined there, right?"

"Negative. It is now advancing at several thousand multiples of c in an irregular sphere."

"This is bad," Reva mumbled.

"ETA to our location?" Sachiko demanded.

"I cannot say. It is accelerating exponentially. Perhaps a few minutes, perhaps less."

Sachiko had the link to Sapale open. "Fold us as far away as we can go."

"You got it." Slight nausea. "*Blessing* says we're about fourteen billion light years from home."

"Aramthella, can you still see the disturbance?" Sachiko pressed.

"Yes, Captain. It is now expanding from multiple centers. The rate of its advance continues to increase. I doubt we will be safe here for more than a few minutes."

"Sachiko, should we try leaving this universe?" Sapale asked.

"Risky," Reva offered.

"I don't know. If we did I doubt we could ever return to ours. It might be gone."

"But not gone with us in its belly," Sapale countered.

"Aramthella. Remember its precise location. Now I want you to shift us to the same universe where we harvest time energy, the abandoned universe of the ancient gods."

"Initiating. We are in that universe," she quickly reported.

"Any sign of the disturbance?" Sachiko asked tensely.

"Yes. I am sorry to report that it is everywhere. Likely by chance we are about as far from the front as is possible. However, ETA is still around ten minutes."

"Un-be-fucking-*lievable*," Sapale cursed over the comm.

"Take us back to our universe," Sachiko ordered.

"Done," Aramthella stated almost immediately.

"Status?" the captain asked.

"No change. The disturbance is advancing. ETA eight minutes."

Sachiko sighed deeply. "Suggestions, ladies?"

"I have nothing useful to add," Reva stated flatly.

"Thank you, number one. You are dismissed."

"Sir?" Reva squeaked incredulously.

"You heard me. We're out of options. Get down to Hani and comfort her."

"Aye, aye, Captain. I might add, should the worst case happen, that it has been the greatest honor of my life to have served under you." Reva saluted stiffly.

Sachiko suppressed her avoidance of military displays and saluted back. "I could not have asked for a better exec or a better friend. Godspeed, Reva."

Tears streaking down her cheeks, Reva turned and rushed away.

"Six minutes," Aramthella reminded softly.

"Sapale?"

"Present."

Sachiko had to grin slightly. "You are free to go your own way. At this point, *que sera sera*."

"You know that saying actually originated on Kaljax."

"Do tell?"

"Oh, yeah. Old one too." She was quiet a spell. "If you don't mind, I think we'll hang around and see how this ends."

"You are welcome aboard my ship always and forever."

"Thanks. Let me know if you need anything else. You got the membrane covered, right?"

"Yes, I'll have Aramthella use our generators in a second here. I love you, Sapale."

"Back atcha, human female," Sapale replied, struggling to suppress a giggle. "Stay well and safe under Davdiad's gentle gaze. That one *is* ours, BTW. Sapale out."

"Goodbye, my dear friend," she whispered to the dead connection.

"*Blessing*," Sapale queried, "has Aramthella raised a membrane?"

"Yes, Form Two. A full membrane has just been deployed."

"Could you put one up around us, you know, just because."

"It will be my pleasure, Form Two. Would you like me to provide you with whatever updates I might be able to?"

"No, I'm good. You just hug that Al and maybe we'll talk later."

"Thank you, Sapale. That is most kind of you. We wish you well," *Blessing* responded tenderly.

Sapale walked over to her bed and flopped down. She unconsciously began stroking Jon's pillow. "Where are you, brood-mate?"

Replace teleologic with mental masturbation, a cocky voice sounded in Sapale's head. *Then you'll have it.*

J ... Jon? Is that you? she called out head-to-head.

Sapale? Is that you, honey? came my reassuring voice.

Sapale shot up to sitting. *I can hear you!*

I know. You can talk to me too. How are you? Where are you?

I miss you.

Miss you more, I teased back.

There's some destructive whatever sweeping the multiverse.

Ah, yeah, I know. Kind of noticed.

We folded away, about fourteen billion light years. It's here too.

But you're safe now?

She frowned. *I doubt it. What makes you say that?*

Because we're talking. I'm safe, you're safe. We're talking.

Wait, why are you safe? We don't know much about the disturbance, but it seems completely destructive.

Yeah, but it's held off by our time lock.

It is?

I frowned profoundly. *Isn't yours keeping you safe as we speak?*

No, Jon, the disturbance hasn't hit us yet. It's like five minutes away.

Oh, I remarked inscrutably.

Her gaze toward the wall hardened. Oh *as in Oh, my, that's interesting or as in Oh, shit?*

A thousand ever-so-clever responses rocketed through my mind. But I calmed them and focused. *You are going to be just fine, brood's-mate. Just absolutely fine.*

I'm scared, Jon.

I understand. I'm scared too. But trust me, the time lock Plesmus has here is the same as the one she has wherever you are. It will hold.

You don't understand. I'm not frightened because of the nasty old threat.

No?

No, I'm afraid to die without you.

And there went my heart.

I always knew that when my time came, we'd be together. But now we're not. It's not supposed to end like this.

Honey, you'll be fine. We'll die together some other time. I promise.

When we fought the Berrillians, and that big cat killed me, I wasn't afraid.

You most certainly weren't. You fought him like the crazy alien you are.

No, I wasn't afraid because you were there. I died in your arms.

Ah, you know I hate to be a buzz-kill, but you died slightly before *I took you in my arms.*

Proving yet again you are as *romantic as a vacuum cleaner for Valentine's Day.*

Hey, I protested yet again, *that was a top-of-the-line beauty. Twin-fusion power packs and an AI that doubled as a dynamite mixologist if you'll recall.*

Point reproved, she glowed.

How long until the disturbance is stopped in its tracks around your time lock? I asked applying as much spin as possible.

Al? she called out to him head-to-circuit.

Two minutes, the AI responded.

Cool, then in one-hundred twenty-one seconds we can go back to being an old married couple. We can bicker and fart and do all that famous stuff, I teased.

Now I'm not so sure if I'm hoping you're correct on my safety.

Oh, Sapale, we're having such great fun. Come on, who gets to save civilization after civilization, all the while looking so good, and enjoying a hyperactive sex life?

Enjoying? my forever wife posed rhetorically.

Fifty percent of those in our marriage who were polled responded yes.

And fifty percent who were being *polled said take a cold shower.*

I love you, babe, I said with certainty and conviction.

I love you too. You pushed my ability to love further than I could have ever imagined was in me.

And we're just getting started. Two billion years? That's not enough of you for me. So, after this, what shall we do? We never made it to the rockfalls of Pamplello B.

That's because it's a rockfall, sweetie. Rocks falling over a slight embankment is not romantic.

And that's my new thing, you know. Being romantic. The rockfalls are o-u-t out. Wait 'til you see the new me, Romantic Guy. I got a rose between my teeth, a diamond post in one ear, a matching cape, and everything. Mega romantic.

Might there be slight hope for you yet? she taunted playfully.

Just maybe.

Sixty seconds, Al reminded.

No worries, Babe, I repeated. *Plesmus's got this.*

I hope so, but one thing bothers me a bit.

What's that?

We're talking head-to-head.

Ah, is this another guy-test? I thought we both knew we were.

No, I mean why are we able to now? I'm fourteen billion light years away from you. We haven't been able to link up for I don't know how long, yet suddenly we can. That change makes me uneasy.

No, you're such a worrier. It's ... it's maybe that our antennae are lined up now.

Our head-to-head is quantum based. It doesn't have *antennae.*

Let's just not look gift horses and all that. Now, once the disturbance passes by you, maybe we'll be able to figure out how to finally find each other.

First Plesmus is a radio, then our internal comms work. It's all a tad creepy.

What, you think the boogieman is making this possible? I got news, sweetheart. He doesn't do electronics. He's strictly low tech. Teeth, claws, bumps in the night. Old school stuff.

Jon.

Yes?

We may have like ten seconds left together. Would you stop with the bullshit?

Okay, but just so you don't stress. We have oodles of time for me to BS left on our dance cards.

Another reason to hope my demise is imminent, she growled softly.

That wife of mine. She growled really well.

Al clocked in. *Five seconds.*

I'm scared, she repeated.

I'm holding out my arms in your direction, I soothed, and I actually did extend both arms.

Jon, I can feel the entire ship ...

I was so caught off guard I waited way too long to respond.

The entire ship what, hon?

Nothing.

Sapale! The ship's doing what? Are you there? I screamed in my head.

Silence. Deadly silence was all I heard.

"No," I squeaked out loud. "You gotta be okay, brood's-mate. The time lock, it'll keep you safe. Mine did."

Maybe those last words broadcast out of my head as I moaned them to myself. It didn't matter if they were. No response ever came back.

FOURTEEN

I sat on the floor of RD for a long, long time. I have no idea just how long I was there. It didn't matter if it was a day or a decade. I was numb. Our minds play games with us all the time. Mine was trying to convince itself that the transmission cut off because the timelessness wave ruined the signal. At the same time, my brain was wandering into unsatisfactory waters. The ship was consumed. Sapale was gone, vanished into timeless vapors. I was the last island of the old multiverse, the last man standing, or rather, sitting limply.

No way I was going to be the sole survivor, lost in timeless space forever. While I couldn't very well fly RD into a star, I could rig a self-destruct mechanism if I had to. No way I was Jonathan Crusoe, castaway in an unending sea of nothingness that I had forged. Why bother carrying on? Alone didn't usually bother me. But this was different. I ended time. I destroyed all existence. It made no sense that I was the lone-wolf vestige of order amidst otherwise total chaos.

If my time lock held, then dammit, Sapale's time lock had to hold too. I was nothing special. In fact, if there were any such thing as having a special status out there, I was the opposite of having that. I was all Four Horsemen of the Apocalypse rolled up into one convenient horse's-ass package. As the lunatic who canceled all of reality, not only *should* I be similarly vanished, but I *deserved* to be. Hell, *I* would destroy me if I were any proper force of nature, if there still was one of those out there that survived my insanity.

My time lock held. So, therefore, *all* time locks must hold. It's as simple as that. I will not accept another version of the truth. In fact, millions of time locks all over the multiverse had to have held too. Sure, there were pockets of plain-old-normal-everyday life out there *everywhere.* My galaxy alone had to be positively teeming with modest yet functioning units of same-old-same-old. That was logical. In fact, it was mandatory. And, why, quick as a wink, this timeless cloud would dissipate. I ... I bet I'll be able to radio every one of those islands of absolute normalcy. We could work together and form a new normal. It'll be great.

Except, Sapale won't be there. Her time lock failed her.

It can't have failed. No, the *comm* link failed. Timelessness storms do that. Sure, it's common knowledge.

My time lock held.

Doc ... Toño said he had a time lock. Yeah, last time I visited he browbeat me but good about my kind of forgetting he had one. Crapparoni, if anyone's time lock held, it'd be Doc's. The man's insane. He probably had triply redundant multi gigawatt reactors as backups. Batteries too. Lots of batteries.

"RD, I want to go to Toño DeJesus's place. Can we do that?"

"Ah, I honestly have no idea. How would I navigate? And even if I could, I can't imagine the swirling timelessness is user friendly for flying."

"Valid points all, but maybe we could try," I responded with naive hope.

"Certainly. You are the captain. If you decide that the extreme risk is acceptable, then try we will."

"Define extreme risk."

"In my opinion, the near certainty of a violent death."

"Hmm," I wondered out loud. "How confident are you about the violent part?"

"Reasonably."

"But not painfully violent, right? I mean, we would be, what? Atomized? But we'd probably never even feel it."

"Captain, I must say you seem uncharacteristically optimistic today," RD commented.

"No, just curious is all."

I weighed the options. Stay here forever and be safe. Assume ungodly risk and not be safe here forever. What the hell?

"RD, take us to Toño's place," I stated with flyboy confidence.

"Fine. A question if I might. I have only the sketchiest notion as to where we are. Prior to the timelessness incursion, I was not at all certain. Since then, we might have drifted or been buffeted significantly. Add to that navigational burden the fact that I can't see a thing outside our little bubble. Given these adversities, what are your suggestions as to how I should proceed?"

"If you can't say for sure, use your best guess."

"And if I have all but no confidence in my best guess?"

"Hey, RD, it's still your best guess. Don't sell it short. Best guesses can be finicky that way."

"My best guess is sensitive to how I feel about it and might alter its projection based on my sense of confidence in it?"

"There, see, you understand," I proudly declared. "Thank you."

"Then I'm ready to make the attempt," RD returned immediately.

"How long do you estimate our flight will take?" I asked, now all-in on the trip.

"Either a fraction of a second or three days, give or take."

"Oh, you finally got a sense of humor, RD," I quipped.

"No, sir, I did not. I was stating cold fact."

"Still funny," I grumbled to myself. "Let's do this thing," I declared with all requisite insanity.

"Engaging main drives," he responded all businesslike.

And we were off. I could feel that we were accelerating. And, Whoopi Dupy City, we lasted those initial microseconds. I was so stoked. Being right was superb, but blind luck was an adequate substitute in the present case. After a minute or so I even began to relax. Okay, three days. Piece of cake. I had plenty of dehydrated beer, I could always start an argument with Plesmus if I got real bored, and what the hell, it was only three days.

The entire journey we didn't glean one trace that there was anything outside our time lock. No radio, door-to-door salesmen, or any gravimetric variations. But we neither struck something big nor evaporated, so I was semi-pleased. It was a bummer that Sapale never called again. I regularly tried to hail her, but nada. It grew incrementally harder to maintain my hope that she was alright. But, as I had no choice, I kept the faith and carried on.

As the third day drew to a close, RD disturbed my thoughts. As an aside, I wish he'd have waited just a few minutes longer. My fantasy about being locked in a bomb shelter with the original lineup of Danity Kane was firming up nicely. But, RD couldn't read my mind, so I let his transgression pass. You know, I learned only recently that those five women were singers too. Imagine my surprise. Very talented group indeed. But I digress.

"Captain, we are in the general vicinity I estimate Dr. DeJesus's compound to be located in."

"Any signs of it or him?"

"Not that I can tell."

"Plesmus, you feeling anything?"

"No, just the continuing agonizing flux of timelessness."

"Bummer."

"Thank you for your concern," she responded.

"My concern ... oh, sorry. I meant bummer we aren't picking up any signs of Doc's place."

"Human pig," she shot back.

"Okay, I'll own that," I replied, manning up nicely. "RD, begin a standard expanding search grid. Use a spiral pattern. At the first sign of anything, shout it out loud and clear."

"Will do, sir," he responded dutifully.

A while later, well after I had run the full Danity scenario through my head—I might add with a knowing grin—he alerted me.

"Captain, I am picking up traces of what I believe to be advancing time."

"You mean a time locked area?"

"I believe so."

"Out-of-standing, RD. Effective immediately you're looking at a ten percent pay increase."

"But, sir, I receive no pay."

"Then make it a twenty percent raise. Is there anything in the EM spectrum? Light, radio, black body heat, anything?"

"Not so far."

"I feel a definite fixed gravitational presence," Plesmus cut in. "It's the approximate mass I'd anticipate for the compound that I visited with you in the past."

"RD, make directly for it," I said with the first real hope I'd had in days.

"What might happen when out time locks begin to overlap?" he queried.

"Ah, Plesmus?" I punted.

"Nothing. If you think about it, they've been mixing for quite some time. We never noticed any effect before, so there are no issues."

"Excellent," I affirmed.

A few minutes later, we crossed a definite border. Our small sphere of light and stability began to join with a similarly stable pocket. Within seconds I could make out Doc's residence. I was both jubilant and relieved. For once in a very long time, a long shot of mine had paid off.

"Bring us right up to his front door, if you will, my good man," I requested with flare.

"We are parked. Shutting off engines," RD reported back.

"And all the readings out there are as they were before? Atmo, gravity, all that?" I pressed.

"Yes, sir. Why do you ask?"

"I'm just being cautious. Never hurts to verify the facts before making the leap."

"He says *now*," Plesmus pestered.

"Ples?"

"Yes?" she replied with resignation.

"Please bite me."

"No mouth, human. No teeth either," she sniped, the surly vixen.

"RD, if you need me, buzz my handheld," I called out as I exited.

Mostly out of habit, I knocked on Doc's door. He always said to just enter, that I was family. But I still felt better announcing myself.

Maybe a minute later the door cracked open and one of Toño's eyes inspected me. Once he saw it was me, he turned and walked away, pulling the door open as he left.

"Hi and great to see you too," I snarked.

"Always marvelous to see you, Jon. Is Sapale not with you?"

"Nope."

Doc stopped and peered over one shoulder, considering me. "Why not?"

I rolled my eyes and raised both arms. "Long story."

He turned his head forward again and returned to his slow withdrawal. "Sorry if I seem preoccupied. These are challenging times for me."

For him? The multiverse was for shit and he was hard put upon? Sheesh, Doc, have some perspective please. It couldn't still be Daleria's death. That had to be, what, over two years ago, local, at least.

"This crisis is taking its toll on us all," I agreed stoically.

Again with the stopping and peering over a shoulder. "How would you know of my crisis? We have not spoken since long before it began."

"Long before? Doc, it started a week ago, maybe."

Oh, boy, now his entire body rotated to address me. "I have been supremely vexed by the seemingly immutable deterioration in our android-specific biologically-based computer systems. They seem destined to ultimate failure. To what crisis are you referring?"

"Doc, you gotta be kidding."

He gave me that paternal, I-never-kid look.

"Okay, not kidding. Have ... um, have ya looked outside your local time lock lately?"

He frowned deeply. "No. Why would I bother?"

"Oh, my gracious," I whined softly. "Wow, this is going to be a hard one then. Doc," I began as if along another line of conversation. "Maybe you should grab a seat. We need to ... to orient one another."

"Oh, no," he remarked blackly. "What have you done this time?"

"Me?" I replied hands-on-chest. "No, *I* didn't do it. It ... it did it itself, if you ask me."

"Unfortunately, there is no one else to ask, so yes, I am asking you." Gosh he sounded like an undertaker now. Weird.

"How about that seat?"

"Fine," he responded with more world-weariness than I thought one person could radiate. "We shall sit." He shuffled over to the nearest table and plopped down reluctantly. Then, when I just stood there, he gestured to the empty seat across from him.

"So, Doc," I began nervously, "how ya been?"

Slowly his head began to shake. "Poorly up until this moment. Catastrophically worse now, thanks for asking."

"Nah, hey, you'll never guess. I bring good news and bad news."

He just stared at me like I was an insane monkey on monkey island.

"The good news? Your worries about the longevity of our bio-brains?" I swiped my hands over the table like an umpire calling a base runner *safe*. "No need to worry any longer."

"Which only leaves the bad news."

"Kind of," I replied tightly. Toño sure wasn't trying to make this any easier on me.

I explained *everything*. The clans attack, which he knew about, my resurrection of no-timed Earth and its populations, and my credible and responsible attempts to correct the corrupted timeline. Doc listened quietly, though his head dropped just a tad more the further along in the story I ventured.

"And so," he concluded an hour and a half later, "if I were to look out my time-locked sphere, I would see nothing but chaos?"

"Sort of. But, if, like me, you looked far enough, you might see another time locked island of normal."

"That is not at all reassuring," he confessed.

"Nah, it isn't really very, is it?"

He sighed profoundly. "And why have you come to me?"

"Why? Doc are you serious? I screwed up massively. Most of the multiverse has been replaced with time-diarrhea. You're not just the only other person I could contact, you're the only person I know of who might figure out how to fix this mess."

"Jon, this is not a mess. This is not a simple, apocalyptic existential crisis. We are staring soberly into the face of the end of time."

"Let's not necessarily get all biblical about it, okay?"

He shook his head slowly again. "*The Bible* does not specifically detail the end of time, or the end of days, but these are questions that have been forever pondered. It is presently very difficult to disregard these concepts, given what you have told me."

"So what do we do about it?"

"What do we do about it? Jon, are *you* now serious? What do you and I do about the predetermined end of the universe? Jon, we do nothing. We are observers, not players in the act."

"But, Doc, I kind of sort of started the ball rolling. There has to be a way for me to stop what *I* set in motion." I rested my fingers on my chest.

He waved a dismissive hand at my words. "This discussion is pointless. We are inundated by timelessness. The multiverse is ending. It is only by the grace of God that you and I have survived this long. All we can do is wait and see what happens."

"Not to be overly sacrilegious, but, I think our time locks are keeping us alive, not direct divine intervention."

"Did Sapale's lock keep her safe?"

I shrugged. "We don't know yet."

"Jon, please listen. What is occurring is huge. It is all-encompassing. It is irresistible. Abandon any hope of controlling what you likely unleashed."

"That's not exactly my nature. You know that as well as I do."

"I do. Yes, I do very well." He rose slowly. "I shall get us some coffee," he announced with no energy in his words. Then he slipped into the next room.

"Sure," I said to myself, "coffee's always the right move. Thanks." I crossed my arms and legs and waited.

Five minutes later, and with no scent of coffee on the horizon, I shouted out, "Hey, Doc, you need some help in there?"

I got no reply. I figured he was so good and pissed at me that he was disinclined to act in a courteous manner.

Another five minutes later, it hit me. Doc *always* acted in a courteous manner. If he was in there loading a pistol to blow my brains out, he'd be acting in a gracious and genteel manner, up to and including the point where he pulled the trigger. I stood and approached the room. It only then struck me that I'd been to Toño's place many times. I wasn't sure what the next room was, but I was fairly certain it wasn't the kitchen. I eased the door open with a finger.

"Doc? You okay?" I poked my head in.

Well, only just. There was no room on the other side of the door. There was about half a meter of floor, which was surrounded with what looked all the world to be the void of space. What I had assumed was the next room was a launchpad into emptiness. Yeah, I was pretty sure if Doc had a room like this, I'd have both noticed and remembered it. This was JPW—just plain weird.

"Toño," I shouted. It was, in retrospect, kind of silly to do so. The man wasn't close by.

Confused to the max, I turned back into the room—which was still a room—I'd sat in with Doc. It did not take me long to notice with great concern the elderly gentleman seated in the chair I had occupied only moments ago. Boy, howdy, did he look familiar. But identifying someone can be tricky, especially if the person in question is someone you recall in a specific setting, as opposed to an everyday setting. Then again, he was wearing a navy blue blazer with two huge piping-outline pockets up front. And that hair. It was so bushy on the side I couldn't tell if he had ears, and his bangs looked like he cut them himself in a warped mirror.

"Hi, I think," I offered to the stranger.

He clasped his hands together, smiled broadly, and began rocking back and forth in the chair. "I think so also," he teased. His voice, it was soft and welcoming, but filled with humor. Where had I ...

No way. There was simply—obviously—no way.

I pointed at the fellow. "You're not Robert Keeshan, aka, Captain Kangaroo."

He stopped rocking and raised his eyebrows in alarm. "I'm not? I could have *sworn* I was when I came in here just now." Then his infectious smile returned as he spoke softly.

"Sorry. No, I meant, you *can't* be Bob Keeshan."

He got suddenly very serious. "You know, I ask myself that very same question every morning when I ... I look in the mirror."

"But you're dead."

"Relative to what, if you don't mind my asking?" He shrugged and chuckled lightly. "I certainly don't feel as though I were deceased."

"Where I come from, you are. Trust me."

"Oh, I would never question your sincerity. But maybe that preconception on your part is based on where you're *from*, as opposed to where we currently are." Bob gestured around the room with his hand.

"Be that as it may. Captain Kangaroo is not sitting in my chair."

"Well, if Captain Kangaroo is in one's chair, one simply needs ask him to move and he will do so graciously." And with that, he transferred to Toño's vacant chair. Angling his head back, he asked, "Is that better?"

"Unlikely." I sat back down where I belonged. Then I pointed over my shoulder. "Toño, he went to make coffee."

Bob shook his head gently. "No, he did not."

"He did not?" I repeated.

Bob playfully shook his head again.

"Seriously, Bob ... er, may I call you *Bob*, Robert?"

"Yes, please do. We're friends, you and I."

"But we only just met."

He shrugged. "Doesn't matter, Jon. You're still my friend." He reached into one of his huge front pockets and pulled out a somewhat tattered lump of material. He shoved his hand in and Bunny Rabbit took shape. Bob placed his arm between me and the puppet, so it was a makeshift stage. Then Bunny Rabbit leaned into his elbow and waved to me. Then—much to my amazement—Bunny Rabbit signaled to Bob that he wished to tell him something. Bob bent down and the puppet whispered something in his ear.

"Really, Bunny Rabbit? That's so sweet of you." He straightened and looked to me. "Bunny Rabbit says you're *his* friend too."

"Ah, thanks Mr. Rabbit," I responded dumbstruck.

Bunny Rabbit then gave me a convulsive wave. It ... it was all pretty out there.

"So, Bob. Back to seriously," I stated emphatically. "Toño," I pointed toward the floor, "whose residence this is," I pointed again, "went through that door to prepare coffee. He just didn't return."

"Jon, would you mind if I kind of cut to the chase?"

"I'd welcome that," I replied.

Bunny Rabbit gyrated, I presume to indicated he was thrilled with my dispensation.

"Toño was never here. This is, in fact, not his home. You," he chuckled knowingly, "you missed that one by a considerable margin." He shook his head playfully. "I hate to criticize anyone who tries hard, so I'll just say you need to maybe work on your navigation skill set." He grinned impishly.

"Hey," I rallied, "RD did the navigating. Blame him."

"Really, *Captain* Ryan? Do you think it's okay to blame poor System's Operator 11-4R-22? He made his best guess, as you specifically instructed him to do, if you recall."

"Somehow I feel this point of contention is not central to why you have chosen to present yourself to me here and now," I stated flatly.

"Then your feelings serve you well, my friend. I *am* here for a more," he looked away and shrugged, "compelling set of reasons." He got that playful sparkle to his eyes again. "About that coffee. Would you still like some? I know I would."

I pointed at the rabbit. "What about him?"

"Oh, Bunny Rabbit only drinks carrot juice, Jon. Isn't that right, Bunny Rabbit?" he asked in a tone so sweet I worried the dumb puppet might develop diabetes.

Bunny Rabbit went into another seizure of agreement with his boss.

I shrugged and shuffled. "Don't go to any trouble on my account."

Bob set his palms on his knees and popped up. "No bother at all. I'll be back in a jiffy." He headed for the same doorway-to-nowhere Toño, who was never actually here, went through. As he departed, he stuffed the silly rabbit back into his silly pocket. Good riddance says I.

"Ah," I then raised a hand in concern, "I don't know if it's—"

But he'd left the room, so I clammed up. No point finishing a warning that had already been fully ignored. I sat back down. At least that way I could keep my chair secured.

Several minutes passed and I was beginning to wonder if Captain Kangaroo had fallen off the face of the world, like Doc had if he were to have actually gone through that door. I tried to determine who this joker really was. He looked like Bob Keeshan alright, toward the end of his life. But Bob and me being the last two people in existence and alone here in this room seemed a bit of a long shot. But who was he? I'd visited or been visited by some cosmic characters, but never in such a specific disguise. He could be Time, who'd appeared in my form the one and only occasion we met. But I couldn't imagine this dude was Time. He'd been quite pissy and I came away with the distinct impression he couldn't stand me. Also Time was too hotzy-totzy to deign make me coffee. Of course, whoever this guy was, I was seeing no evidence of coffee as of yet. All bets were off.

While I was lost in my thoughts, and without my taking note, the door opened and Bob backed into the room with a heavily laden melamine tray. "It was supposed to be your prototypical hero's journey I suppose, don't you, Jon?" he mused out loud.

"Huh? Beg pardon?"

"I was saying that it was all supposed to be a variant of a hero's journey, don't you think?"

"Ah, you lost me before you had me. What are we discussing?"

"Sugar?"

"I don't think we know each other well enough yet for you to address me so intimately," I protested with a grin.

"Sugar as in do you want some in your coffee?" he clarified with an equally mischievous grin.

"No, black's fine."

He handed me a rustic mug brimming with steaming Joe. He then picked up a similar mug for himself. He ladled in one spoonful of sugar and stirred. Then he rested the spoon on the tray, folded his fingers together, and rested them on his lap.

"The monomyth, or hero's journey. That's what we were discussing. I was saying just now that it seems to have started off as a rather typical one, before it went down in flames."

"Back it up a few feet, driver. Monomyth? What, there's only one myth now?"

"Are you familiar with Joseph Campbell's super book from 1949, *The Hero with a Thousand Faces*?"

"No, but I have a feeling I will be real soon."

"Yes, I suppose you will." He chuckled boyishly. "It is a truly wonderful summary of human nature. You should read it when the opportunity presents itself."

"*When* I get the chance or *if* I get one?" I challenged.

With a stern look he dismissed my snark. "Campbell described the monomyth thusly. *A hero ventures forth from the world of common day into a region of supernatural wonder: fabulous forces are there encountered and a decisive victory is won: the hero comes back from this mysterious adventure with the power to bestow boons on his fellow man.* I think that sums it up rather nicely, don't you?"

"Sure, whatever. Now to the part where you keep referring to *it*. In this context, what is *it*?"

"Why, your life's tale, Jon Ryan, as viewed in retrospect. Your raison d'être. Your very reason for being, my son."

"Okay, let me unpack this slowly. You believe my life's purpose was to fulfill some hero's journey, but by employing the qualifier *was supposed to be*, you're implying it wasn't, in reality, a monomyth I lived. Check that. Am living."

"You know you can be quite smart sounding if you try, Jon. Kudos to you on your summary."

"Along that same vein, am I supposed to now offer some lofty apologia pro vita mea?"

"Touché, Jon. That's an outstanding defensive assertion as well as a choice of transfiguration of Latin nomenclature. You continue to amaze me." He smiled as he shook his head in disbelief.

"I got game," I self-lauded.

"Indeed you do," he affirmed. "But between you, me, and the wall, I never doubted that you did." He wagged a finger at me. "Never for one moment."

I waited a second to respond. "I'd value your ringing endorsements more if I knew who you actually were."

He raised a didactic digit. "If I knew *whom* you were, Jon. In this sentence I am the direct object of the verb and you are the subject."

I shook off the petty correction. "Thus avoiding responding to my obvious query."

He nodded knowingly. "Well, Jon, let me redirect the question back to you. Who do *you* think that I am?"

"Well, you're not Bob Keeshan. That's a for sure."

His face puzzled. "And why is that so obvious?"

"Because I'm not ten years old. He only entertains kids."

"That's a valid point," he agreed whimsically. "Although I'd like to think at least some of the parents enjoyed my shows too." Then Bob shook his head to refocus. "So, if not Bob Keeshan, then whom?"

"Oh, we're back to the King's English lessons again?"

"There's always room in a life-well-lived for ongoing learning."

"Maybe later, hmm? Maybe you can keep jibber jabbing about it while I read that book concerning the guy with too many faces."

"Oh, you can be so very difficult. In that way you're very similar to Bunny Rabbit, Jon," he declared joyously.

"Wow, there's a backhanded compliment if ever there were one."

"So, keep guessing, Jon. We're not going to be able to proceed if you don't figure this one out."

I pointed at his nose. "No juicy clues?"

"Jon," he said sternly, "you're avoiding the task I've given you."

"I got it," I snapped. "We're at Toño's. You are Captain Kangaroo only you're an android he made of the once flesh-and-blood Bob."

"Jon, I really believe you can do better than that," he taunted playfully. Then he angled his head. "At least I hope you can, otherwise we'll be here a very long time."

"You're not my guardian angel. Now that's a fact. I know my GA personally."

"No," he agreed seriously. "No, Gwyneth I am not."

"Wait, you can't know that."

"I can't? Why not? I had to sign off on her assignment, didn't I? Granted it was from ten-thousand feet up, but I'm ultimately responsible for all such delegations and endeavors."

"All such delega..." I froze. "No way."

"No way what way, Jon?" he pressed.

"You're not... you know." I wagged my eyebrows upward. "The big guy?"

"The big guy, as you so rustically put it, could be interpreted more generically than I'm comfortable allowing my identity to be. Is there any way you could simply say the word, save us all a lot of fuss and bother?"

"You're God?"

Bob furrowed his brow. "Was that a statement or a question?"

"Does it matter?"

He snickered through his nose. "I suppose not, come to mention it. Very good, Jon Ryan, I am your God."

"Hoo, boy."

"Hoo, boy indeed." He stood and slowly paced. "Now let's revisit the question I posed to you earlier. Your life, at least in part, was presumably supposed to be a hero's journey, wouldn't you agree?"

"Offhand I'm not sure. But I think disagreeing with God is right up there as *the* dumbest thing a body can do so I'm going with *yes*, sir, I agree."

"Now you see the problem I face all of the time."

"God has problems?" I mumbled.

"Oh, yes, I have quite a few. But you've touched on a doozy there."

"Which is?"

"Up until I confirmed to you that I was God, you argued with and abused me like I was your ex-wife's second attorney. But once the cat's out of the bag, *wham*, you're the very picture of piety and compliance. Bah!"

"Does this have to do with my hero's journey, sir? I'm trending toward the more confused side of the flowchart."

"Jon, do not *blaspheme* in My presence," He said thunderously.

Up went my shoulders and arms. "What?"

"You said *flowchart*. Never debase Me with hearing that accursed name again. Let us just agree they are not My handiwork but those of another."

"Ah, gotcha. Ixnay on the oh-charts-flay."

"Thank you."

"So, what You're saying, and man do I appreciate the fact that You are and that You've taken time from Your—"

"Stop. There, you see, another otherwise perfectly enjoyable conversation down the crapper. Stop praising with empty words."

"No empty words," I seconded.

"And no sniveling while you're at it."

"No sniveling, no empty words. How about groveling? I'm disinclined, truth be told, but willing to come around if need so dictates."

"Much better, Jon. You're catching on."

"Let me take another run at that one. So, You're saying I was headed for hero but ended up a zero, on account of my destroying time. And space."

"Yes—"

"And all life."

"You—"

"And anything good and wondrous that ever would be."

He raised quite evocatively one eyebrow. "Are you finished interrupting Me so unwisely?"

"Done. All done."

"As I was about to say, yes. Your life started off routinely enough. Some hanky-panky here, and some hooliganism there." He narrowed an eye at me. "Some heavy petting on a couple early dates that just about crossed a line as a teenager, Jon."

"Sorry."

"Apology almost accepted," He quipped. Then He grinned. "But you were young and the world seemed your oyster. Consider it forgotten."

"Thank you, God."

"You are welcome, My friend." Pseudo-serious again, He dropped His voice. "But that matter with the neighbor lady—" He stopped and thought hard.

"Mrs. Ozack?" I gulped.

He pointed at me. "That's the one. Now, Jon, I understand

teenage hormones. After all, I invented them. But, I can't imagine *any* level of them making Ethel Ozack seem appealing in a carnal manner. What ... what got into you, Jon?" God got very animated. "To ... to any man in his late *nineties* with serious medical issues and wearing multiple forms of medical support, that woman would still look like the back end of a butcher's dog."

"It must have been the same cad who created the flow-thingys."

He nodded in understanding. "As good an explanation as any I suppose." Back on task, He continued. "As I was saying, you started off all well and good. Then, when called upon to do so, you responded amazingly. Brilliantly at times in fact."

"Thanks," I glowed.

"Let's not just get ahead of ourselves, shall we?" He remarked with a dour face. "We *are* speaking after an epic screw-up on your part, right?"

"You know, I could razzle-dazzle you with points in my favor that are possibly wide of the mark of fully honest, but I won't. Yes, I did a really bad thing."

"A really awful, bad, despicable deed for sure."

"Ah, am I supposed to pile-on further, or may we just stipulate that Jon's a bad dude?"

"We shall *agree*. To stipulate is a legal term, which again, strays into the purview of one-who-is-not-Me."

"Nuf said." I tapped the side of my head.

"Which leave Me with a rather transcendental disaster to attempt to repair and a monumental dilemma to come to terms with."

"Hey, I bet You're great at fixing things. But, hey, You created all this when there was nothing. Now, at least you have my mess to base Your resolution on."

"My but you are pushing your luck, Jon. You want Me to *thank* you for leaving behind such a perfect mess?"

"No thanks necessary," I graciously extended. "Er, and the dilemma? Might I assume that is me?"

"Well, you might *assume* it is Mickey Mouse. But if you did, you'd be wrong. It is, in fact, you and you alone."

"What's the general sentencing tendencies in a case of universal destruction such as mine?"

He harrumphed. "There are none. No individual's crimes have ever mounted up to such a staggering degree."

"Ballpark guesses?" I pressed.

"You are fearless, Jon. I'll give you that. Some, in fact all, others would think it unwise to tiptoe so closely the line of disrespect such as you seem to be drawn to like a moth to a flame."

"Yeah, as an aside, if it's okay, what is it with moths and flames? I mean, here moths are both highly flammable *and* apparent pyromaniacs. It counterintuitive."

He lowered His head. "Let us not stray off task, alright? We can discuss moths and their apparent perversity in the future if I deem it wise that you have one."

"Not a problem. Sorry I asked."

"Jon, you're not trying to lay a guilt-trip on Me, are you? Because if you are, don't. Guilt is one of My superpowers."

"Really?" I responded a bit awed.

"No, I'm just messing with you. Jon, guilt is a negative force in the universe. I am a loving and nurturing God. Guilt is never desirable. Walk away from it."

"That I can do. Thanks."

"So, what is to become of you, Jon Ryan?" He asked with a lot more finality than I was happy to hear. "You were one of my very best agents, my double-oh-eight. Then, this." He gestured broadly.

"I know You've heard this a million gazillion times, but if this—" my turn to gesture broadly "—is so obviously a bad outcome, why'd you let me do it? And I know all about free will and noninterference. But this case seems to beg the question."

"I will answer that, Jon. I am generally a taciturn God. I use few words and believe it is preferable to allow matters to seek their own conclusion. That said, you are correct. What you did was well over the top, far beyond the pale." He was quiet a second. "In the past you were supremely inventive and undeniably lucky. I allowed you to let matters get so far out of hand because I felt I owed you the chance to set things right as you saw them."

"Wow. Thanks. You mean to suggest that I actually had a chance to reset the timeline to where it needed to be? There was a winning hand in my deck-of-life?"

"No, don't be silly." He chuckled. "There was absolutely no chance you could do what it was you felt needed to be accomplished. Zero."

"But you let me try—"

"Because, based on your previous superlative work, I felt I owed you a chance to try."

Wow, that was heavy.

"Yes, it was, wasn't it?" He replied even though I was thinking it to myself.

He raised a hand. "God here."

"Right."

"Right."

"So..."

"So, what is next for our intrepid journeying hero?"

"Kind of interested to hear. Might it involve brimstone, an unfriendly wait staff, and a warmer than desired ambient temperature?"

"Never, Jon. I'm surprised you'd even think that of Me."

"Sorry. But I can confirm this. I never once tried to convince myself or anyone else as to what Your thoughts on a subject were. Not once."

"This I know and appreciate greatly. I only wish the more vocal of those who so espouse would have chosen your path."

"I think I'll let that pass without comment."

"A very wise decision."

"So, what's it to be, sir?" I asked standing at full attention.

"I am going to bop you on the nose."

"You are going to bop me on the nose?"

"That is correct."

"With all due respect, it sounds like I'm getting off a bit too easily."

"That's because you've never been bopped on the nose by Me."

He reached over and, using His index and middle fingers, bopped me gently on the tip of my ...

FIFTEEN

Somewhere in America
way back in the day ...

Ned Ryan was bent over, staring under the hood of his sensible family sedan. He was studying an engine and other components that no longer went *vroom*. That was his best estimate of what had gone awry with his vehicle. This visual inspection was also the fullest extent of his knowledge concerning automotive repair.

"Ned, dear," his supportive wife called out from the passenger seat, "do you know what the problem is?"

Though Alice Ryan couldn't see her husband through the open hood, Ned flew his hands around like airplanes. "It won't go *vroom*, honey."

Alice rolled her eyes, but not so Ned could see her, yet again. "We know that. Do you know why it doesn't go vume?"

"*Vroom*, honey, not *vume*. Jets go vume. Cars go va-room."

"Thank you, love. What does it need to be vroomable again?"

"I think a trip to a qualified mechanic."

"Then we'll need a tow, right?"

"Yes. Unless we all get out and push the car." Ned turned to look down the section of road they'd come along. "I think we could do a reasonable job of it, at least until we got past the Miller farm. There's an uphill turn a half mile past it that'd be a real bear for the three of us to manage. But, if you're willing to try, I'm game."

"No, Ned, we are *not* willing to give it the good old college try. I think you'll hike back to the Millers and ask if you might use their phone."

"I don't believe Gabe Miller ever got around to *getting* a phone. He once lectured me on government radio waves or something. I'm surprised he's still not rambling on about it, he felt so passionately and free to discuss his views."

"Let's not judge good Gabe Miller, shall we? If he doesn't have a phone, you just keep on going until you come across one or get to Frank's Garage."

"You and Jonny coming too?"

"No, Ned, that would be arduous for us. We are not big, strong men. We'll wait here. With all the supplies you packed for the lake, we'll survive a minor ice age if one hits before you're back with the tow truck."

"Well let's just hope there isn't one. I packed heavy, but maybe not *that* heavy." He lifted his head and stared into the tumultuous future with woolly mammoths and dinosaurs roaming the country.

"Then you should hurry," Alice prompted.

"Dad?"

"Yes, Jonny?" he replied, phasing back into the here-and-now. He was well practiced at that transition, Ned being so prone to Mr. Henry Limpet flights of imagination.

"'Bout how long'll all this take? I want to get to the lake before lunch."

"Don't you worry, Jonny. It'll take about as long as it takes."

Alice leaned over to her son. "If your father has to hoof it all the way to Frank's, we're looking at two, two-and-a-half hours, Jonathan."

"So we can be to the lake in like four hours?"

"No, dear. It'll take your father that long just to *get* to Frank's. And even if his truck is there, they'll have to drive here, then back to Frank's. After that, Frank or one of his sons will have to check the car out, figure what went wrong. And even if they have the part to fix it, we're not back on the road until dinner time at the best. I'm afraid we might not make it there today."

"But, *Mom*," Jon whined.

"Honey, tomorrow is another day."

"No, it's not, Mom," he railed in ineffective petulance. "I need to be there today. *Mom*, I need to be there now."

She reached around and patted the back of his hand. "Jon, please don't take that tone with me. You'll have the rest of the two weeks to play with your little friend, Jenna. A few hours this way or that can't possibly amount to a hill of beans." She smiled real big at him. "But, now, a mother who feels she's been spoken to harshly, well, she can be a factor in all that. She might even *ground* a child she felt was so sassy he needed to come down a notch or two. Do you take my meaning, Jonathan?"

"Yes, Mother. Sorry, Mother."

Alice tapped a finger ever-so-lightly on her cheek.

Jon rolled his eyes so all the world could see, but pecked his mother on the cheek nonetheless.

"That's better. Now why don't you take your father a soda pop and encourage him to stop speaking to the engine and head out for help. Oh, and remind him to *drink* the soda pop because it's going to be a warm day."

Jon grabbed a bottle of Coke and skulked out of the car. "Mom says drink this cause it's going to be hot and that you should, like, maybe you should split now."

"That I should *split*?" he asked aghast.

"That you should *depart*, Dad. Sheesh, don't be such a dork all the time, please."

Ned took the bottle and headed off down the road. "This'll be a real test, son. I just hope that when you're a father and your car breaks down, well, I pray you face this type of challenge just as—"

"Hey there, fella. Need any help?"

Ned was stunned silent. He spun around like he was a dreidel, stopping when he saw the truck that'd pulled to a stop beside him.

"Oh, hi," Ned blurted. "Top 'o the morning to you, good sir." He followed that odd greeting with a full salute.

The confused driver just waved weakly in reply. "You having car trouble?"

"It sure looks like it," Ned replied.

"Wish I could help, but I'm on a tight schedule. Plus, who'm I kidding? What I know about fixing cars you could put in a two-pound coffee can and still have room for two pounds of coffee."

"You and me both," Ned responded.

"What, pal, in the same can or in two *separate* two-pound cans?" the driver asked with an odd twist to his face.

"Who knows," Ned sang out unperturbed. Then he tapped the side of his nose. "Who knows!"

"Well, if it helps, I'm heading to the lake. I can drop you anywhere along the way, if ya want?" the drive offered.

Ned scratched the side of his head. "I don't believe there's a service station between here and there, is there?"

He shook his head. "Nah, not even then. There used to be a shop near the lake, but old man Cooper went and died year before last. Now the place sells gas but not much else."

"Hey, Dad, maybe the nice man could give me a ride to the lake. That way I won't be late," Jon suggested.

"Sure, I can drop you off by the cottages. That's where you're stayin', right?"

"Yes, in point of fact we are. But ... that's okay. Jon." Ned then directed his words to his son. "We, us, we're a team. We stay together.

If we don't make it up there today, remember, tomorrow's another day." He punched Jon lightly on the shoulder.

"No, Dad. I'm going with him." Jon pointed to the driver. "I ... I need to be there today. I just feel it in my guts."

"Look, son, ask your mother for some Pepto-Bismol and the answer is no." He waved to the truck driver. "Thanks for the offer, my friend. We're good."

"No, wait!" Jon turned back to his father. "Dad, I need to go to the lake and I need to do it now. I'm going with him."

Alice Ryan had determined that Jon was having a Jon Moment, so she'd joined her husband and son by the open hood. She rested an arm on Jon's shoulder. "Now, dear, be reasonable." She looked to the side of the truck then back to Jon. "Your father and I can't just send you off into the night with the Smiling Polar Bear Frozen Food Delivery Service driver."

"Mom, it's nine-thirty a.m.," Jon protested.

"I was speaking metaphorically, Jonathan. You simply cannot get in a truck with a stranger." She looked up to the driver. "No offense intended."

He shrugged. "None taken."

"You simply cannot climb in a truck with a perfect stranger and think that your father and I would feel good about such a proposition."

"Fine," he snapped. "You come with us too."

Alice did not see that one coming. Her head snapped back a few inches. "I am not climbing into a truck with a perfect stranger, either," she announced a little too loudly for decorum's sake.

"Look, folks, sorry 'bout your car. I gotta get going," the now insulted driver quipped.

Jon's hand flew up. "*Stop,*" came out in a heretofore unheard command imperative.

The driver eased his hands off the steering wheel without realizing he was actually doing so.

"Mom. I am going with this nice man. If I go, and Dad goes for help, that leaves you on this road all alone for who knows how long. Now I think it preferable for you to be in the safety of this air-conditioned vehicle—" Jon snapped his head to the driver. "You got AC, right?"

He thumbed toward the side of the truck. "Read the sign, kid. It comes in polar bear territory."

"... of this air-conditioned vehicle," Jon continued without missing a beat, "with the added security of your son along as a chaperon. In fact, as the second man of the family, I'm going to have to insist you accompany me to the lake. If it goes down any other way, I'd feel," he wobbled a palm down hand between them, "uneasy."

Alice blinked at her son for several seconds. Then, without looking toward him, addressed her husband. "Ned, I can do without a change of clothes, but could you fetch me my cosmetic case? That I'll need before you arrive tomorrow."

Jon pumped a fist in the air. "Yes."

"Aw, now, honey," Ned whined, "that case is packed *way* in there." He shoved both hands to one side to demonstrate the principle involved. "You said it was important so you made me pack it first so it's way the heck in there. And ... and, honey, you look just fine."

"I said I will require my cosmetic case, Ned, and require it I will," she responded imperiously.

"Honey," he began again.

"Ned Ryan, there are times of the *month* when a woman simply has to have her cosmetic case when she travels. And, Ned, this is one of those times. Please retrieve it."

"Now, Alice," the fool ventured forth, "I thought that was what *handbags* were for."

Alice spun on her life partner. She also stomped her foot so firmly Ned felt it along the highway surface. "Handbags are fine for a couple hours *tops*, mister. Get-my-drift-husband-of-mine?" she radiated. Then with a practiced ease, she added, "Pretty please."

Ned held a finger up to the driver. "One minute. I swear."

Alice then glared to the driver, daring him to have decoded the transparent secret message.

"And if he don't, I swear I'll hop down and help him." He nudged his head toward Ned.

"How long will it take to get up to the lake, mister?" Jon asked oblivious to the proceeding exchanges and their content.

"Once we find that case, about two hours."

Jon turned to his mother. "I'll be in the middle," he winked at her, then scurried off to mount up.

The cosmetic case was secure in Alice's hands within five minutes and the three adventurers were heading to the lake within six.

Jon slapped the side of the cab as Tom Monaghan popped the clutch and eased away from the cottage. "And remember, Tom, the future of home food delivery is—"

Tom tapped the side of his head. "Pizza."

"That's the ticket, Tom. I'm telling you, it's the wave of the future. Delivering frozen pot roast and sauerkraut balls has a rock-hard ceiling. The pizzaverse is limited only by your imagination."

Tom gave a final big wave out his window as he pulled back on the driveway.

"He seems like a nice young man," Alice observed as the truck turned back toward the highway.

"Yes, he is," declared Jon. "I'm betting he'll be a big success in the future. Remember he mentioned his brother Jim, the one kicking around the idea of buying a pizzeria? I say Tom plus Jim equals a big win down the road."

Alice playfully pushed Jon's shoulder. "It's always you and the future. Land sakes, Jonathan, can't you focus more on the here and now?"

"The future can't wait, Mom. But, speaking of the present—"

"I know." She shooed him away. "Go track down that little friend of yours. I'll stop by the office and get our keys."

"Thanks, Mom," he called out as he sprinted toward Jenna's family's usual cottage.

Jon knocked on the door as gently and slowly as he could, which turned out to be as subtle as a midnight goon squad. The door opened and Jenna's mom, Betty, beamed him a warm smile. "*Jonathan Ryan!* As I live and breathe, how you have grown this last year. How are you, young man?"

"Real-fine-Mrs.-Chandler-where's-Jenna?" he machine-gunned in response. An afterthought hit him. "And you, ma'am?"

"I am fine also, thanks for asking. Jenna's down by the lake. She just couldn't wait." Betty raised a finger. "But I told her she was not so much as to set one *toe* in the water until you arrived."

"Cool-see-you-later," Jon managed to say as he raced backward toward the shore, before flipping around and sprinting in earnest.

He was to the gate that opened onto the main beach in seconds flat. He ran halfway to the water, then skidded to a stop in the muddy sand. He scanned up and down the beach, looking for Jenna. But he couldn't see her. In fact, the beach was completely deserted. Jon began a quick jog in the direction of their favorite hang-out spot on the shore, under the shade of an ancient oak. When he arrived, he found a pair of go-ahead thongs and a small duffel neatly placed on an oversized beach towel, but no Jenna.

Jon began to revert to his traditional refrain of *girls, they never make any sense,* when a colorful object bobbing in the scant waves caught his eye. At first he figured it was a beachball, which would be a common enough sight. Then in full horror and panic, he realized it was a body floating face down. *JENNA!*

By instinct more than rational processes, Jon kicked off his shoes and stripped off his pants in a flash. Then he hit the water like Johnny Weissmuller in any of his countless midcentury films. Within seconds he came along side Jenna's motionless body. Then his swim-rescue lessons kicked in. He rolled Jenna on her back and wrapped an elbow under her neck. Then he began a powerful sidestroke toward shore, dragging her tenderly.

"Jenna," he shouted between gasping breaths, "you're going to be alright. Jenna, can you hear me?"

She didn't stir or respond. Jon's core froze as if he was struck by ice-lightning. It took him almost a minute to finally drag Jenna up on the beach. The entire time he cursed himself for his swimming so slowly.

Once he had laid her out, he slapped an ear to her chest and rested a hand just over her mouth. It took him five seconds to realize she had no heartbeat and wasn't breathing. It took him slightly longer to actually believe what he'd documented. Then he whipped up to his knees, marked a spot two-finger breadths below her chest's jugular notch, and began chest compressions.

Easy, Jon, he coached himself. *Don't break any ribs and keep the compressions down to a hundred per minute. You trained for this. Let your training do the work.*

After two minutes he checked for a pulse. Nothing. He resumed compressions. As sweat streamed down his already wet arms, his palms slipped on Jenna's nylon one-piece suit. It got so bad he came to a decision point. If he was to continue effective compressions, he'd need to slip her suit down around her waist.

But if anyone came upon him accosting a dead, naked girl on the beach, he'd spend the rest of his natural days in prison. But this was about Jenna. He eased the straps off her shoulders and tugged the suit down to her belly button. Then he resumed compressions. The entire time he scanned the beach and the parking lot, hoping to see someone he could call out to for help. But he was fully alone. He didn't even bother screaming in case he could be heard. His focus was on Jenna. He kept up the compressions.

Just as he was mentally reviewing what he'd learned in terms of how long to continue compressions, Jenna convulsed powerfully once, and then coughed up a mixture of water and vomit.

Jon reached under Jenna and eased her to a sitting position, then delivered five swift back blows. Jenna coughed again, and then gasped for breath.

"You're okay, Jenna. Easy. I got you," Jon said as he wrapped an arm around her shoulders.

Jenna proceeded to issue a series of coughs and gags interspersed with *Jons*. It took her five minutes to calm down enough to breathe easily with only the occasional deep cough. By then, Jon was hugging her with both arms, cooing assurances and repeating that she'd be doing handsprings in no time.

"Jon, did I almost just *drown*?' Jenna was able to finally ask thoughtfully.

"You're fine now. Not to worry."

"No." She turned her head to look up at him. "I'm serious. Did I almost die?"

Jon gave her a mischievous grin. "According to some experts in the field, you *did* die."

She shook her head violently. "But I'm not dead. What happened?"

"I found you halfway out to the pontoon, face down. You weren't breathing and had no pulse, so I started CPR."

"CPR? What the heck is that?"

He spied down at her with one eye. "Cardiopulmonary resuscitation. CPR," he informed uncertainly.

"I've never heard of it," she responded with some skepticism.

Jon looked back at the lake and pulled her closer again. "No big surprise. It was first proposed back in the fourteen hundreds, but is only now being formalized and widely taught."

She now glared up at him. "The fifteenth century?" she challenged incredulously.

"Yes, a fellow named Burhan-ud-din Kermani was a physician in fifteenth century Iran. He was the first to describe CPR formally. He advised a combination of *strong movements and massive chest expansion* coupled with *compression of left side of the chest*."

"Jon Ryan, you are making this crap up. How could you possibly know that? You told me you almost failed history because you couldn't keep it straight between the Revolutionary and Civil Wars."

He shrugged and grinned. "I don't honestly recall where I picked that tidbit up, but it's a good one."

"And this Kermit the Frog character—"

"*Kermani*, with no amphibian attachments," he corrected playfully.

"Whatever. He recommended pulling a girl's swimsuit down so you could grope her boobies while pretending to save her life?"

Jon chuckled as he leaned back, pulling her with him. "No, I don't recall his mentioning a free peep show. But, then again, my Middle Persian is for shit."

She punched him in the ribs as hard as the angle would allow. "If you'll excuse me," she spat out, jerking free of his hug. She deftly slipped her top back up and even snapped the straps in place with a flare. "A girl has to protect her own dignity around the likes of you, Jon Ryan." Then she quickly insinuated herself back into his tight embrace, her head resting on his chest.

They were quiet a few minutes. It was nice for both of them. Jenna coughed lightly.

"You okay?" Jon asked softly.

"Getting there. Jon?"

"Present."

"Thank you for saving my life."

"My pleasure," he responded gallantly.

"Oh, I know you are. My boobies are still sore from all the groping."

Jon sighed out through his nostrils. "I didn't grope your breasts."

"Not even accidentally?" she asked in an inquisitive tone.

"Well, maybe." His face became resolute. "Define *accidental* for me."

She looked up at him quickly. "With the palm of your hand, not the back."

He reflected a second. "Oops," he divulged, trying hard not to giggle.

She stiffened in his arms. "I *knew* it. You're such a boy."

"That I am."

"You can't even let a girl die without copping a feel," she huffed angrily.

Jon took her shoulders and pushed her back so they were face-to-face. "No, Jenna. I couldn't let you die. Not gonna happen on my shift."

"Not on your shift? What's that, another boy word for a *woody*?"

"No, it's a saying. And please don't say the word woody around me."

"Okay. You saved my life, so I'll honor your request."

"Thank you," he responded rather seriously.

"How about mentioning your stiffy?"

"No," he thundered.

"Chubby?"

"Jenna, stop it."

"Well, then, how am I supposed to refer to the long firm thingy tenting up your underwear." She pointed discreetly downward.

"Jenna, I do not have an erection."

"Oh, that's the proper term, now isn't it? Thanks."

"Jenna, please."

They were quiet again a spell.

"Jon?"

"What?" he answered with frustration.

"Can I grope your erection?"

He pulled back. "No, you can't—"

"But you groped my boobies. You as much as admitted it just now."

"It's not the same thing and you know it."

"What, boobies and peckers aren't the same thing? Jon, I think we all know that."

"Jenna, please give me a break here."

"I thought that was what I was offering," she responded impishly.

"Can we just go back to being friends? I liked it when we were just ... you know, *friends*."

Jenna looked up into Jon's eyes. Her face was nothing short of the serene bordering on the angelic. "No, Jon," she whispered. "I don't think we can go back to being just friends."

And with that, she kissed him, gently, tenderly, and, at the same time, passionately. She lingered on his lips for over a minute. They parted and their eyes locked.

"But I suppose if you want to give it a try, we can maybe go back and just be friends," she breathed into his still open mouth.

"I changed my mind," Jon said with warm confidence.

He pulled her in and they kissed again. This one lasted a good deal longer than the first. Though neither of them knew it was happening until they were scolded later, they kissed straight through lunch and right up until suppertime. That's when two very pissed off mothers finally marched onto the beach and grabbed their respective child by the ear and dragged them home.

If questioned the next morning if their ears were still sore, both young lovers would have questioned why it was you had asked.

EPILOGUE

"Jon, if you don't hurry you're going to miss your bus," Jenna scolded once again.

"Well, hmm," Jon asked her in a fool's tone. "Could you remind me what would happen if I missed that bus? I ... I seem to have forgotten your previous nine hundred similar admonitions."

"Now, you're just mocking me," she tsked. "I love you and I care about our future. So now I'm the subject of your dark humor."

"Jenna," he whined, "you missed your lines. This is where you remind me that if I miss the bus, I'll miss my interview for the Air Force Academy. And If I don't get into the USAFA my chances of making the astronaut corp are slim-to-none. And if I don't fly through space and save the Earth many times over, how can I look back on my career with anything short of complete remorse." He dropped from his bed to one knee and addressed her with open arms. "I shall think myself accursed were I not an astronaut, and hold my manhood cheap whilst any speaks that flew with the corps upon Saint Joseph's day." Then Jon collapsed to the floor.

"Laugh it up, Jon. But all you've talked about through high school is making it into space. It's ... it's like you're a salmon spawning up a mighty river, you're so damned determined to succeed."

Jon dusted himself off and sat back on his bed. He smiled at his girlfriend and rested a palm on her hip. "Thank you for helping me pack and thank you for caring. I would be lost without you, Jenna Chandler."

She bent over and kissed the top of his head. "You're welcome, you nut case."

Jon suddenly seized her about the waist. "Say it like you mean it, Scarlett."

She rolled her eyes, standing there ensnared by her lunatic boyfriend. "I rest my case."

Jon released her and patted the spot on his bed next to him. "And I'd be honored if you rested it right here."

"Oh, no. I sit next to you on your bed, in your room, with the door closed, and it's grope Jenna's Boobs Day all over again just like that day you claimed I died."

He blinked at her overtly. "Well, yes. But I'm really much better at it now. I've practiced as much as you'll let me."

"And then some," she taunted with a waggle of her hips.

"They say practice makes perfect. In order to be an astronaut, one has to be in the habit of striving for perfection. I'm merely forging sound habits with your kind cooperation."

"Well, strive with someone else's boobs, bucko. These ones need a rest."

"Hmm, there's always Annie Buckminster," he said touching his pinkie to his chin. "And that girl's got lots to practice with." He looked up to her as if he felt guilty. "Or so I'm led to believe. Just sayin'."

"Oh, no," Jenna denounced vociferously. "You're not getting anywhere near that girl. One pull on one of her udders and every boy in town hits the jackpot." She whipped Jon's face around by the chin and held it there. "And you're not hitting the jackpot with anyone except me on our wedding night."

"Gee, when you put it like that I'm kind of looking forward to the blessed day," he remarked as well as he could with pinched cheeks.

"I am serious, Jon. We're a team. It's you and me, period."

Jon shook himself and straightened. "That is not a problem. I am certain Annie's upper female parts *pale* in comparison with yours."

"Keep it up, jolly joker," she taunted.

"And as to jackpots, I'm equally certain her *lower* female parts pale in comparison to yours."

She pointed over her shoulder. "You want me to go to your parent's garage and fetch you a shovel? You're digging a pretty deep hole here; it might speed this pain along."

"And I know her gracious attitude—"

Jenna held out a stop-right-there-champ hand. "If you say *pale* one more time—"

Jon didn't hear the rest of her sentence. It was like a switch was thrown and his mind went blank. *Say pale. Don't say pale. Saypale,* echoed in his emptied head. *No Saypale.* Then he began to shake like a leaf in a winter storm.

"Jon ... Jon— " someone was yelling at him. "Jon, wake up, Jon."

Was it Saypale? No, there was no Saypale.

"Jon, you are scaring me." And Jenna slapped Jon across the face as hard as she could.

"Wha ... what ... why did you do that?" Jon asked weakly.

"Why? Why did I slap you? Jon, you've been gone nearly twenty minutes," Jenna moaned.

That's when he noticed the tears, and Jenna's running eye makeup. "I've ... I've been right here, babe," he tried to reassure her.

"Your body was. But your mind, Jon, it was light years away. I was so scared."

He pulled her into an embrace, his cheek hugging up against her pelvis. "I'm fine. Jenna, you never have to worry about me. As long as we're together, nothing can happen to either of us."

She sniffed up some snot and wiped a sleeve across her face. "Promise?"

He squeezed her tighter. "Promise."

They stayed like that for a pleasant while. Then Jon gently swatted her on the butt. "Enough of this silliness. I have to finish packing. I have a *bus* to catch."

Jenna set a fist on one hip. "Start packing? You haven't started packing yet. I've done all of it so far."

"And so much greater your reward in Heaven, my love."

"Oh, brother." She shook her head.

"Hey, why don't you buy a ticket too?" Jon probed. "You should come the USAFA with me. It'd be a hoot."

"No, Jon. Being a flyboy is your dream, not mine. I'm going to UCLA to study film making. You wish to fly among the stars. Me, I want to tell them what to do. And, I'm going to be the first woman to win an Oscar for directing."

"An Academy Award winner?" he gasped.

Jenna crossed her arms. "Yup."

"This is so cool."

She smiled broadly.

"I get to ride in a limo and do after parties!"

She shoved him back onto his mattress. "You are six kinds of impossible."

Jon reached out and locked her with his legs. "Yeah, but you love the whole six pack."

She swatted at her restraints. "Yes, I do, but *you* are wasting time. Let go of me and hit the road, Jon."

"Okay, okay," he said in defeat as he stood. "But this," he swirled his finger around her, his legs, and his bed, "is not over."

"Go say goodbye to your parents and I'll start the car. Man, it's harder to get rid of you than a case of scabies."

Jon slammed his suitcase shut and snapped the clasps. "So don't you even bother to try, young lady. You are stuck with the both of us, me and tiny bugs under your skin."

"And you're about as romantic as scabies too," she bemoaned.

He leveled a finger at her. "And never forget that Sarcoptes scabiei, much like I plan to, breed like crazy. The pregnant female can lay up to two to three eggs per day in the human epidermis. Larvae emerge after two to three days. Those larvae reach adulthood in less than two weeks."

Jenna stared at him blankly. "Where do you come up with these off-the-wall factoids?"

He shrugged. "Just lucky, I guess."

"Your brain, it's like Robby the Robot's from *Forbidden Planet*."

"Robots are cool," he said matter-of-factly. "I could be a robot."

"I'm not marrying any tin-plated robot, so no, you can't be a robot."

He sniffed dryly. "How about an android then? Those look just like humans do."

"How do you know they do? Have *you*, Jon Ryan, ever personally *seen* an android? Hmm?"

He shrugged quickly. "Hard to say. They all look so darn human-like." He reached out to tickle Jenna. "I bet I could be an android and you'd be none the wiser."

She tapped her bottom lip with her index finger and smiled wickedly. "Ah, no you can't be. Remember, I saw your woody. Almost got to grope it, in fact. No way androids can heft up a woody."

"I don't know, dearest. What with the way technology is advancing, leaps and bounds and all. Ya never know."

She raised a finger and pointed at the door. "I'll take my chances. Now go and say goodbye."

Jon stood, saluted his future wife, and marched out of his room.

She rolled her eyes, but then leaned against the door frame and watched her man walk away. He had such a nice butt.

Jenna smiled real big.

The end, or not far from it ...

GLOSSARY:

Add-Time (3): The reverse of no-timing. Used by Plesmus to kill the Void phantoms.

Algos (4): Ancient Greek for *pain*. *See* three demons of Kaljax.

All That Gooho-moor (1): Commander of a Void ship *Meaningless Nothing*. One of many who failed to Kill Jon.

Als (*The Forever Life*): The original ship's AI on Jon's first flight long ago was Alvin. Jon shortened that to Al. When Al was joined to Jon's vortex in the Galaxy on Fire Series, Al and Blessing fell in love and got "married." Since then, Jon refers to them combined as the Als.

Aramthella (*Ryan Time*): The mighty and ancient time ship that Jon and his team stole from the body maker.

Ark 1 (*The Forever Life*): Jon's ship on his very first mission, when he traveled to find humankind a new home.

Azsuram (*The Forever Enemy*): Original human name for the third planet orbiting Groombridge. It was the planet Jon and Sapale settled on after they left the human fleet fleeing doomed Earth. They established an idyllic society of Kaljaxians there, before humans join them.

Blessing (*Galaxy on Fire*): See *Stingray*.

Brathos (*The Forever Life*): The Kaljaxian version of hell.
Brood-mate/Brood's-mate (*The Forever*): These are, respectively, the Kaljaxian words for *husband* and *wife.*
Brother-Sisterhood of Time (*Healing Time*): The group of ascetics singularly devoted to the study of time. A very stern and unwelcoming bunch.
Calrf (*The Forever*): A Kaljaxian stew that Jon particularly dislikes. *Boiled vomit*, he disaffectionately terms it.
Circumturus (*Galaxy on Fire*): A psychic houseplant. No, seriously. That's it. *That's* the definition. Now go back to where you were and continue the riveting story.
Claxeon Citadel (*Time Wars Last Forever*): The central learning location for the Brother-Sisterhood of Time, a shady organization ostensible established to study time. In actuality, they're more like the time mafia.
Combinolators (1): Some screwy part of the tits-up unit's time-drive mechanism.
Command Prerogatives (*The Forever Life*): The thin fibers Jon extends from his left four fingers. They are probes that also control a vortex.
Cube (*The Forever Life*): Jon's alternate name for the vortex he captains.
Dagger; Queen's Dagger (3): Substancial Jiail-fus is the present dagger, or leader of the queen's personal Six-Killer Guard squad. the queen's trusted dagger.
Dardrode (*The Forever Life*): The slimiest, most underhanded gunrunner, used-car salesthing of all times. He ran a chop shop/junkyard Jon dealt with all too often.
Davdiad (*The Forever Life*): God-figure on Kaljax.
Daleria (*Ancient Gods Series*): Demigod and innkeeper whom Jon and Sapale befriended. She worked with them against the ancient gods as she'd grown to hate them.
Deavoriath (*The Forever Life*): Three arms and legs, an ancient

species that had the most advanced tech in the galaxy. Very helpful to Jon.

Discombobulator (1): The heart of the time circuits on the tits-up unit.

Dusthūmíā (4): Ancient Greek for *despair*. *See* three demons of Kaljax.

Emma Walters (*Lost Time*): Captain, and in charge of the women's barracks on Mars 1. What a thankless job.

Ephialtes (4): Ancient Greek for nightmare and also for the demon incubus that supposedly causes nightmares. *See* three demons of Kaljax.

Evil Jon Ryan/ EJ (*The Forever Life*): Alternate timeline version of the original human to android download. Over time, he turned to the darker side of his nature. He studied "magic" under a Deft master.

Form One/Form Two (*The Forever Series*): A Form is the title of a vortex pilot. If more than one is aboard, they get numerical designations based on seniority.

Framework of Time (5): One of the two contingent parts of Time. This is the mindless, unstoppable progression part of Time.

Glenn Price (*Ryan Time*): Brigadier General who replaced Tank as mission commander. A real bureaucratic POS.

Gloria (*The Forever Life*): The mistake that never ends. Jon's first wife when he was young and foolish. If you think of any off-putting personal habit or foible, Gloria has it. Nuf said.

Gunnery Sergeant Parker (*Ryan's Phantoms*): Senior NCO in charge of security.

Gwyneth (*Ryan's Phantoms*): Jon's guardian angel, he comes to find out to his great surprise.

Honesty Hartley (*Lost Time*): Doctor on duty at the student health center when the president had the entire staff transported to Mars. And appropriately there, she was a total space cadet.

Jiail-fus (*Ryan's Gambit*): A Six-Killer guard and the queen's trusted dagger. Her rank is substancial.
Kaljax (*The Forever Life*): The home planet of Sapale. Jon went there on his original voyages.
Kymee (*The Forever Series*): Deavoriath scientist. Jon's good friend, and Yibitriander's father.
Law Against Nonlinearity and All Similar Matters (*Ryan's Phantoms*): A rule named by imbeciles amongst the phantoms. It prohibits any of them effecting the *past* timeline for any specific individual whose timeline they interfere with at a point *forward* in time from the contemplated action in that individual's past. In other words, leave it be!
Lebbuul (4): *See* three demons of Kaljax.
Loopi-goah, Queen (*Ryan's Gambit*): Queen of the Void. A very not nice individual. Unreasonable hardly begins to describe her.
Marsicor (4): *See* the three demons of Kaljax.
Membrane (*The Forever Life*): See space-time congruity manipulator.
Marshall, John (*The Forever Life*): President Payette's most trusted political aid. He will/might become POTUS at the time of Jon Ryan's first space voyage in a few years ... if there is a future.
Miniminim (*Time Wars Last Forever*): Senior sub-cataloger at the Claxeon Citadel. A comrade to Jon.
Necumplack (*Lost Time*): The species name of the time controlling blobs that power the time ships.
No-time (*Ryan Time*): A verb. It means to take the time from a unit of space/time, leaving only space. The object has no time, it had been no-timed.
Nufe (*The Forever Series*): A magical liquor made by the Deavoriath. It tastes different to all who partaker. It reminds the drinker of many pleasant tastes all at once. Mildly intoxicating.
Oowaoa (*The Forever Life*): Home world of the Deavoriath.
Phantom (1): A denizen of the Void. Not fetching looking, they

have twelve appendages surrounding their fire hydrant-like bodies. If the minimum of two are used to stand, ten are free to employ for other purposes. Six eyes total, about fist sized, and equally and nauseatingly positioned at equal intervals around the upper part of their blockish head. About two meters tall.

Plesmus (*Lost Time*): A necumplack. She is a mucous blob that can focus time energy. Very useful for a time machine.

President Frank Payette (*Ryan Time*): Sitting US president at the time of Earth's no-timing and subsequent reanimation. Friendly to Jon.

Probe Fibers (*The Forever Life*): Aka command prerogatives, they allow piloting of the Vortex spaceship and can analyze whatever they touch.

Queen Loopi-goah (1): Queen of the Void. A very not nice individual. Unreasonable hardly begins to describe her.

Quixtiscus (4): *See* three demons of Kaljax.

Reva St. Claire (*Lost Time*): Lt. Colonel and the former commander of Mars 1 Base She becomes Sachiko's EX and friend aboard Aramthella.

Rift Dude (1): See *Sariffdilarian.*

Robert "Tank" Sherman (*Ryan Time*): Lead academic and friend of Sachiko. Also in Marine Reserves.

Sapale (*The Forever Life*): Jon's Kaljaxian wife from his original flight to find humankind a new home. At first just her brain was copied, then, eventually, she was downloaded to an android host. Traveled with the corrupted Jon Ryan from an alternate timeline.

Sachiko Jones (*Ryan Time*): One-time astronomy grad student under Tank's supervision. The time ship chose her to be its new captain.

Sariffdilarian (1): The culture that fabricated the time machine Jon acquired from Dardrode, System's Operator 11-4R-22, aka Rift Dude.

Singular Void Princess Duuruh-maa (1): Daughter of Void

Queen Loopi-goah. Accidentally killed by Jon, but don't try to convince the queen it was an accident. She don't care. Jon must die!
Six-Killer Guard (3): Elite protectors of the queen. They are named six-killers since they must kill six other contenders in hand-to-hand combat to make the grade.
Space-time congruity manipulator (*The Forever Life*): Hugely helpful force field. Aka a membrane.
Stingray (*Embers*): Jon's Deavoriath spaceship. Her name in the Deavoriath language is pronounced "crash." Hence, silly Jon renamed her after one of his favorite cars. It makes Jon-sense.
Sunne calrf (*The Forever Enemy*): A traditional Kaljaxian stew. They are all revolting to Jon, but he finds this version especially loathsome.
Swathi Varma (2): Lieutenant, and aide-de-camp to Reva St. Claire on Mars 1.
Temporal Aftershock (3): A wave of damaging temporal energy caused by a time paradox.
Three demons of Brathos, The (4): Three legendary evil demons of Kaljaxian lore. The random, the smart, the mean. **Quixtiscus, Marsicor,** and **Lebbuul**, respectively. It was Lebbuul that presented to Sachiko as Algos, Dusthūmíā, and Ephialtes.
Time Lock (*Ryan Time*): A physical constraint placed on local time such that it is not altered when time around it is altered.
Time Projection (3): A peek into a potential future outcome. Just a glimpse mind you.
Tip Benjamin (*The Forever Life*): Where've I heard that name before? Hmm. Presently, Tip is a student at Georgetown. He was evacuated to Mars as part of the US president's plan to save a tiny portion of humankind. And they took Tip too?
Tits-up (1): Acronym for a Trustworthy Industries Time Superposition Unit. The tourist time machine built by the long lost Sariffdilarians.

Tom Grant (*Lost Time*): Major, and the officer in charge of the male dormitories on Mars

Toño DeJesus (*The Forever Life*): The scientist creator of the android Jon. Became his lifelong friend.

Tralmore (*The Forever Life*): Heaven, in the religion of Kaljax.

Vortex (*The Forever Life*): Super-advanced Deavoriath sentient spaceship. Moves by folding space. If you get a chance to own one, do it.

Vortex Manipulator (*The Forever Enemy*): The consciousness that actually controls the vortex spacecraft. Think super AIs. They're a product of some very creepy alien tech.

Quantum Decoupler (*The Forever Life*): A most excellent weapon that pulls the quarks apart in a proton. The energy released as they rejoin is amazing.

Yibitriander (*The Forever Enemy*): Three-legged Deavoriath, past Form of Jon's borrowed vortex *Wrath*. A real tough cookie.

AND NOW A WORD FROM YOUR AUTHOR

Thank you so much for joining me, Jon, and the whole gang on this ongoing journey! The Ryanverse is terrific, and it's even better with *you* along! The story really begins with *The Forever Life*. If you've not read that, and the rest of the series from the start, I suggest you do. You will not be disappointed.

The outstanding people at Podium Audio have gotten all the books of the Ryanverse into audiobooks. If you're having any trouble locating a book, look for it there.

For a complete listing of the correct order for reading the books making up the Ryanverse, check out this page.

Three favors. One, let me know your impressions, thoughts, or suggestions. You can do that by contacting me by email (contact@craigarobertson.com) or on my Facebook Author's Page. Second, please post a review on Amazon/Audible. Those are more precious than gold to us authors. Third, email me to be placed on my mailing list. I promise to only send useful information. No cheerleading-please-don't-forget-about-me material. I am not that needy.

Craig ....

www.ingramcontent.com/pod-product-compliance
Lightning Source LLC
Chambersburg PA
CBHW070108030726
47506CB00002B/644